Out of the Dark

Short Stories

Peter Malin

Quaint
Device

Published by Quaint Device Books
99 Vanner Road
Witney
Oxfordshire
OX28 1LL

email: petermalin24@gmail.com

ISBN 978-0-9956593-0-8

Printed and bound by Print Design Focus Ltd, Witney, OX28 6EY

To the reader

Some of my favourite stories feature among the greatest ever written, from the exquisitely subtle character studies of Katherine Mansfield to the deceptively detached tales of entrapment and longing that make up James Joyce's *Dubliners*. The stories in this collection, however, draw their inspiration from the writers who have fired my imagination since childhood with their alternative worlds of time and space, of crime, passion and supernatural terror. Their names alone are sufficient to evoke visions of ghosts and vampires, of futuristic dystopias and alien invasions, of human cruelty and detective ingenuity. Edgar Allan Poe, H. G. Wells, Charlotte Perkins Gilman, Arthur Conan Doyle, M. R. James, Daphne du Maurier, Ray Bradbury, John Wyndham: these are the imaginative source material for the tales that follow. I hope you enjoy reading them.

Peter Malin

An earlier version of "In the Machine" was published in *All Hallows: The Journal of the Ghost Story Society*, 12, June 1996.

Errata

- On page 27, the third paragraph should begin "Ruby noticed..." not "Ingrid noticed..."
- On page206 line 8, for "palette" read "palate".

Also by Peter Malin in Quaint Device Books:

Fragments: Poems 1968-2010
Love and Other Business: Poems and Stories

CONTENTS

Jonathan's Dragon

Of course, no one believed most of the stuff that came out at Alice's trial. It was obvious she'd been stitched up, and the prison sentence was widely regarded as a cruel joke, but most people just shrugged and moved on – after all, that's how it is these days. Too busy. I managed to talk to her a couple of times, after she was moved to the secure unit, but by then she was largely incoherent. I'd met her once or twice previously, before it all happened – whatever "it" was – but I can't claim to have known either her or Jonathan particularly well. Well enough not to be surprised, though, when the details of their relationship emerged at the trial. It's only in the past few weeks, however, since I formally took over responsibility for the Fairbourne Forest development, that I've been able to piece together a story for Jonathan. I say "a story": it's not definitive; frankly, it's incredible, a fantasy I'd say, if...

It reached me in a variety of ways: anonymous texts, email attachments with elaborate and astonishing pictures, mysterious pop-ups appearing at random on my laptop. I've talked to people too, those who survive; but they're wary, evasive: it's a dead issue, the media lost interest long ago, and what good would it do to dig it all up to be raked over yet again?

What clinched it for me, though, was a chance remark by one of Jonathan's oldest friends that led me to the attic of his childhood home – the same house where he met his spectacular demise. Here, neatly stashed away in a random assortment of damp cardboard boxes among the ancient Christmas decorations, the broken toys, the picture-books of myths and legends, of knights in shining armour wielding their bright weapons against damsel-clutching monsters, was a batch of small exercise books crammed with neat, schoolboy script. In these irregular diaries of childhood triumphs and disasters, of grudges and gripes and sulky recrimination, of revelations and epiphanies and everyday trivia, lay the final, dazzling pieces of Jonathan's narrative jigsaw.

I could have just let it lie, shut it out of my mind and got on with my life, got on with the endless meetings, the time-devouring machinations and manipulations of creating the biggest residential development of the 21st century in the south of England, the transformation of this redundant tract of ancient woodland into a network of roads and houses and shops and schools and hospitals and leisure facilities and everything else that makes life worth living. Suddenly, though, I've begun to feel afraid. So perhaps it's better if I try to set the whole thing down, to shape it into some kind of narrative coherence and commit it to cyberspace so that it's available for anyone to access, to download at the click of a – dragon? Just in case...

*

Jonathan – or Jonty as his parents called him when he was a little boy – could never remember exactly when the dragon had first come to him. On and off it seemed always to have been there, perched on the corner of his playpen when his parents were out of the room, or curled up asleep at the foot of his bed through the long nights of winter with smoke drifting wispily from its gently pulsating nostrils. It was a very small dragon, the size of a puppy or a large kitten, and its most striking feature, apart from the fact that it sometimes flew round the room breathing out fire, was its glittering, scaly hide that shimmered in an ever-changing, billion-coloured kaleidoscope, like a chameleon on fast-forward.

The dragon never spoke, as dragons sometimes did in books, but it didn't need to. Its eyes said everything. When it looked directly at Jonty, which it did only sometimes, moving its head in his direction with purposeful intent, he was shifted in spirit to another world, a world that actually understood him, that forgave him his misdemeanours even before he had thought of committing them. It was a soft, green world of velvety twilight that held him in a comfort deeper than the warmth of his bed and more loving than the enfolding of his mother's arms when he woke screaming from a nightmare.

Jonty told no one about the dragon, except for one close friend, whose reaction was painful enough to silence him on the subject thereafter. After all, he was not so childish as to believe that other people regularly saw dragons, even though they often featured in stories and pictures and therefore must be real. He would do better to keep quiet about it in future.

As Jonathan grew up, the dragon appeared less and less frequently, and indeed he had almost completely forgotten about it – until one dismal evening in late September, just before his twelfth birthday. It had been one of those wet Saturdays when plans are disrupted and tempers tested by disappointment and frustration. Jonny, as he now liked to call himself, had been looking forward to a day's hiking with his father in Fairbourne Forest, feasting on tinned stew heated over an open fire under the ancient tree canopy poised at the threshold of its miraculous transformation from brilliant green to the yellows and crimsons of autumn. Despite the impenetrable curtain of wet, they were still willing to give it a go, sparked by a spirit of reckless adventure inspired by countless cowboy movies and tales of fantastic quests in strange lands. Jonny's mother, however, put her foot down, and his father had to acknowledge the depressing common sense of her arguments. "It's not as if you can't go some other time," she concluded with maternal finality.

Jonny had never quite grasped the appeal of common sense, and its invocation now drove him to an unprecedented outburst of crying and screaming. His parents were shocked; they'd had no idea how much the day's outing meant to Jonny, and didn't really know how to handle his frankly terrifying behaviour. His father, emollient as ever, proposed a trip to the cinema to see the latest *Star Wars* movie as a means of assuaging the boy's immoderate disappointment. His mother, sensing a crisis in their son's emotional development that needed firm handling, insisted that Jonny had been far too naughty to deserve such a compensatory treat. Instead, she sent him to his room, threatening to lock him in there all day if he didn't say he was sorry. His father essayed a half-hearted protest, but knew there was no stopping the juggernaut of his wife's determination. She won, of course.

It was late in the afternoon, while Jonny was alternately crying and sulking in his room as dusk fell prematurely and the dark, forbidding shapes of the trees that brushed against his window dripped relentlessly on to the steamy panes, that the dragon came. There, suddenly, it was, stretched languidly

4

across his desk, its tail curled into a wavering spiral and smoke rising gently from its nostrils. It was three times as big as Jonny remembered it, just as he was himself, and the glittering kaleidoscope of its scales steamed mistily as if it had just come in from the rain.

For the first time ever, Jonny was startled by its sudden appearance, but he was not frightened. Slowly the dragon's long, leathery head turned in his direction, its eyes not so much boring into him as swallowing him up. The eyes were neither angry nor accusing, but Jonny nevertheless felt a surge of guilt at his bad behaviour. He realised he had been stubborn and selfish, but these faults were cleansed away as he bathed in the cool, fresh pools of the dragon's eyes. He felt himself to be deep in a forest glade, where the sun scattered itself through the leaves and the spray from the waterfall showered its glistening drops over moss-covered rocks. He was surrounded by a glistering curtain of light and moisture as he swam and splashed in the deep, clear water of the pool, sunk in a world of green and gold and the clearest of clear blues, now smooth and swirling and mysterious as he snaked below the surface; now broken into sparkling fragments as he splashed upwards into the sunlight and the deep green shade. High above the waterfall, on a jutting crag, perched the dragon, still watching him with its infinite understanding and its indisputable authority.

When Jonny woke up, it was completely dark in his room. Outside it had stopped raining, and the windows were steamed up from top to bottom. He peered into the darkness, searching every corner of the room, but the dragon was gone. He lay there for a while, feeling he had had an experience far superior to any that could have been offered by Fairbourne Forest, but aware, too, that he had been warned: he had let down his parents and himself with his childish tantrums, and in future he must be sensible and well-behaved. He sensed that on this occasion he had been spared, but that the wisdom and understanding of the dragon's eyes could quite easily be replaced by the blazing inferno of its breath. When his mother came up, he would say he was sorry.

Jonny grew up into a fine young man and the dragon became merely a distant childhood memory. If he thought about it at all, which was rarely, it was as a far-off dream, something which had seemed real at the time but was nothing more than a fantasy spun by the brain of an over-imaginative child. School made way for university, and his parents became increasingly proud of their son's academic success. Coming themselves from what they called a "humble" background, they could scarcely believe the dazzling career that was opening up before their Jonny – or Jonathan, as he now preferred to be called. To them, a career as a teacher or small-town solicitor would have represented the highest they could ever imagine their son aspiring to, but now here he was, well up the ladder of political achievement: a newly-elected Member of Parliament for the Fairbourne constituency; well-acquainted with public figures who were household names throughout the land; and with the Prime Minister, no less, taking a close personal interest in his career. His parents were only sorry that they were able to see so little of him, and they regretted that he had sacrificed the potential happiness of marrying and raising a family to his political ambitions. Nevertheless, he was serving his country with honour and distinction and they were happy, in their small, increasingly shabby home, to bask in the reflected glory of his success.

When his parents died, within a few days of each other, Jonathan, at the age of thirty-nine, had just been made a junior minister at the Department of the Environment. He had also, for the past two years, been having an affair with the Minister's wife.

Jonathan attended to his parents' funeral himself. It was a quiet occasion. Neither of his parents had any living relatives, so there were few mourners at the service – just the vicar and one or two villagers. For the first time in many years, he slept in his old room that night. Like the whole house, it seemed dingy and cramped, with a musty odour that contrasted sharply with the bright smell of wax polish and air freshener that had given it its pervasive atmosphere when he was young. His mother's meticulous housekeeping had finally succumbed to arthritis and failing eyesight, while his father had long since given up tending the garden, which had deteriorated into a tangled wilderness.

As Jonathan lay in his old bed, the emptiness of the house began to oppress him. It was far from silent, though. It creaked and cracked, whispered and rustled as if alive. He fell into a restless sleep, troubled by intense fragments of dreams featuring not only his parents but also his job – and Alice, his lover. And behind all these figures, half hidden from his comprehension, were two huge eyes, staring relentlessly at him: calm, unblinking, knowing everything.

Jonathan's original intention had been to sell the house, but as he didn't need the money it occurred to him that it would make a perfect retreat for him and Alice – somewhere they could spend their precious moments together with less risk of being seen. It would make sense, in any case, to have a house in his constituency. He had never bothered before, his London flat being only an hour's drive away, but it would certainly go down well with his local party. This was an especially opportune moment to be on the spot as Jonathan was currently at the centre of a controversy over proposals to develop a large chunk of Fairbourne Forest into a massive new town. The Minister was due to make a decision in a few weeks' time, and Jonathan's advice would be crucial. Local opinion was strongly against the proposed development, and Jonathan was presently engaged in preparing his final report, recommending that the application be rejected. Fairbourne was one of the few surviving areas of ancient woodland in the country and Jonathan, along with most other people, favoured the idea of focusing much-needed new housing and its associated infrastructure into the enormous amount of derelict land still available within every major city.

So it was that Alice and Jonathan – or Jon, as she called him – began to spend more time together during the week at the Fairbourne house in its semi-rural seclusion. Meanwhile, the Minister, his workload gradually increasing, had taken to staying mostly in London, only returning to his and Alice's loveless home at weekends. It would have been the perfect set-up; but Alice, finding herself running two households, began to feel exploited. On a Monday morning, she would wave goodbye to her husband from their own house before driving the sixty miles to Jon's place, stopping off at an out-of-town superstore just off the M4 to do their shopping for the week. When she arrived, Jon would already have left for London, leaving her to her own devices until he returned at six in the evening or later. From Monday to Thursday they spent the evenings and the nights together, except when Jon had constituency meetings to attend, and on Friday morning she left shortly after him to drive back home, stopping at the same store to pick up the weekend provisions for her and the Minister, as she now tended to think of her deceived husband. For Jonathan, the arrangement was ideal. He never really paused to think how Alice occupied her time during the four long days a week at his parents' house. After all, he told himself, it was no different for her than if she were at home; and after all, he hadn't forced her into this. He was the one in the awkward situation, having to work five days a week in close proximity to the boss he was cuckolding. At least he phoned her once a day for a twenty-minute chat, and he texted her whenever he could steal a private moment. The Minister didn't call Alice at all during the week, spontaneity and romance long having vanished from their marriage; this was what made the arrangement possible without arousing his suspicions.

Alice, though, began to feel increasingly ill-at-ease in Jon's family home. She felt like an intruder, putting the shopping away in cupboards, tidying and dusting and hoovering. It was almost as if Jon's parents were watching her disapprovingly. The feeling was worst in Jon's room, the room where they slept together – and, increasingly, sleeping was about all they did. She couldn't understand why they didn't use his parents' room, which was bigger and had a double bed, but Jon was funny about it. So they had to make love – or not – cramped in Jon's old single bed in his small, dark room – a room where Alice felt there were always eyes watching her: enormous, unblinking, invisible eyes of reproach that noted her every movement.

They had been living like this for two weeks when the threatening emails started to arrive, soon followed by letters – one in every postal delivery for five days running. Put bluntly, they demanded that Jonathan should withdraw his opposition to the Fairbourne Forest Development Project, or details of his affair with Alice would be leaked to the media. For the first four days, Jon said nothing to Alice about the anonymous communications, but the fifth letter, which arrived just before she left for home on the Friday morning, was addressed to her. It threatened not only revelations, but physical violence. It pointed out to her that she was alone all day in an isolated and secluded house, and suggested she should use her influence on Jonathan to persuade him to extol the virtues of the development in his report to her husband. Jon and Alice spent all weekend furtively texting each other, trying to decide what to do. Alice was all for ending their relationship; for her it was a good excuse to escape from an affair that had turned sour. Jon, with his puffed-up dignity and childish bravado, talked about principles and insisted no blackmailer was going to dictate to him. They agreed that Alice would come as usual on Monday, that Jon would have the day at home, and that they would decide exactly what they were going to do.

By the time Alice arrived on Monday, though, Jon had already made his decision and acted on it. His principles hadn't held out for long against the prospect of a shattered political career, and he had worked solidly all weekend on finishing his Fairbourne Forest report, producing an eloquent and closely-argued defence of the proposed development. As Alice arrived, he had just emailed it to her husband.

She was furious. It was typical of a man to take the decisions that affected them both. She had already reached her own conclusion in any case: Jon could do what he wanted about the blackmail; she didn't much care whether their affair were made public or not, but whatever happened she was going to leave him – and she would probably leave her husband too. As far as she was concerned, Jon's submission of a positive report was an act of craven weak-mindedness that merely clinched her resolution. She felt as strongly as most other people about the environmental vandalism that was steadily destroying the country, and she had been going to suggest to Jon that they go to the police, regardless of the consequences. But he was not big enough to put such altruism before his reputation and his career. Well, she was right to leave him to his own sordid little world...

It was strange, then, that despite her anger and her determination to walk out on him, she agreed to spend one last night with him. He spun her some story about his sleepless nights over the weekend, wrestling with his conscience as he worked on his report; of lying in bed alone, equally frightened of going to sleep or of staying awake, fearful of some threatening presence in the darkness of his room; of half-waking, restless dream-fragments in which reproachful eyes glared at him, flames glittered on metallic scales in a kaleidoscope of shifting colours; snatches of nightmare in which he ran frantically through forest and desert from the scorching advance of a nuclear firestorm.

Her presence in bed with him that night, though, seemed to make no difference to his restless state. After their perfunctory lovemaking she was aware of him lying awake, breathing heavily, turning backwards and forwards in the bed, until finally she herself fell into a fitful sleep. Her dreams, too, were troubled by disturbing sensations, just beyond the edge of comprehension: half-conceived glimpses of claws and leathery wings; of smoke and fire; of leaves burdened with drops of moisture; of multi-faceted crystals of light flicking through a glittering array of colour-changes; and of two huge eyes, watching, penetrating, probing, waiting.

She was awakened by Jon suddenly sitting up rigid in bed. The room was unnaturally light, with the moon casting its sickly, pale glow through the flimsy curtains. Sweat trickled glistening down Jon's face and back, and his hair trailed in moist, tangled ropes across his forehead and down his neck. Instinctively, Alice reached out to take hold of him, but at her touch he let out a piercing cry and pulled himself away from her. His skin was so icy that contact with it made her gasp. Frantically, he threw the bedclothes aside, staring towards the window, his face contorted in terror. He leaped out of bed, made a rush for the door and stumbled out on to the landing. By the time she got out of the room herself, he was standing at the bottom of the stairs, looking back up towards her, staring not at her but past her, the same look of terror at first twisting his features but gradually relaxing into an expression of relieved recognition and, apparently, calm acceptance of whatever he saw there. Alice stood for a moment uncertain what to do, but before she could come to any decision, Jon's body erupted in an incandescent flash of spontaneous combustion, the flames apparently ignited from within. She could only stare, her mouth open and her throat gripped by some kind of seizure, unable to make a sound as the flames licked round him in a billion-hued kaleidoscope, the eyeballs popped out of his disintegrating face and exploded in star-fragments, and the remainder of his body crumbled into white-hot flakes that floated gently to the floor. Within minutes, all that remained of him was a pile of ashes with a few flickers of blue flame still playing around them before these, too, died away into the shifting greys of dawn.

Nothing else appeared to have been touched by the flames, not even the carpet where Jonathan's remains lay cooling.

As Alice continued to stand there, still rigid at the top of the stairs, the house was filled with a whispering exhalation of relief, and satisfaction, and unutterable sadness.

Conrad's Party

Ruby could feel the blood rushing into her cheeks. She imagined it streaming through every tiny vein, stretching its thin red fingers under the surface of her hot skin, infusing her whole face with threads and blotches of crimson. Her hand tensed round the handle of the small, sharp knife with which she was chopping vegetables for the evening's casserole. The uneven wooden chopping-board bumped and shifted under the pressure of her heavy strokes. She concentrated all her fierce attention on the task in hand, refusing to turn and look him in the eye.

"It's only a bloody party," he said, trying to push back his own rising anger. "I don't see why it should be such a big deal."

That was the problem; nor did she. Except that it was Conrad's party.

She had nothing against Conrad – not really. He and Fred were colleagues, occupying back-to-back work stations at a small, North London publishing firm specialising in books on European travel. They were also drinking partners, spending extended lunch hours at a variety of local bars and shooting off every Friday for an after-work drink in the centre of town. Ruby wasn't jealous, exactly; in fact, she appreciated the extra few hours it gave her to herself before the weekend kicked in. Despite this, when Fred got home, never drunk but invariably flushed and excitable, he always felt the need to justify his lateness on the grounds that the rush-hour exit from London began much earlier on a Friday and he might as well spend the time pleasantly with a friend as sitting fuming in a traffic jam, exposing his precious 1960s MG to the reckless driving of desperately escaping commuters.

Ruby threw the chopped vegetables roughly into a pan. She always browned them in oil and butter before adding them to the meat and stock that was already simmering away in a slow oven.

"It's not a big deal," she said slowly, picking up his annoying phrase and emphasising each word as if this somehow made her seem more reasonable. "I just don't want to go."

"I don't know why; we never go anywhere these days," Fred replied, his voice falling into that hard-done-by whine that made Ruby wince.

Ruby had only met Conrad a couple of times, but as far as she was concerned, that was quite enough. She had no strong feelings about him. He just seemed utterly bland; "colourless" was the word that came to mind whenever he was mentioned. Perhaps that was the problem: the idea that Fred found this insipid man more fascinating than her.

"Why don't you go by yourself?" she suggested.

"He's invited us both," Fred answered pedantically. "It's his flat-warming. He's my mate. I can't understand why you're being so awkward."

Ruby knew she'd have to come out with it sooner or later and risk arousing his suppressed fury. She was aware that all the muscles in her face and jaw were tight and tense.

"It's too far to drive just for a party," she blurted out. "And I won't know anyone else there," she added, as if this would somehow conceal or cancel what she had just said.

"For Christ's sake, not that again," Fred muttered, half to himself. "I've had enough."

He turned and stalked self-importantly out of the kitchen, and Ruby heard him clumping angrily up the stairs. As she transferred the vegetables to the bubbling casserole dish, tears began to well up in her eyes. She slammed the oven door and grabbed a tissue, obliterating the moistness that was blurring her vision before it had even begun to pool out from under her itching eyelids.

Conrad's new flat was in town, not far from the office. Fred and Ruby lived in Beaconsfield, twenty miles out west along the M40. Maybe to most people it wouldn't seem far, but Ruby hated travelling any distance by car; it stirred memories she would rather leave undisturbed. She knew that by the time they arrived at the party she'd be in what Fred contemptuously referred to as "one of her states".

She thought again about Conrad. He was younger than her and Fred, in his mid-thirties, she supposed. He wasn't married but, according to Fred, had recently shacked up with a German girl he'd picked up on a business jaunt to Hamburg. Ruby objected to Fred's misogynistic colloquialisms: "picked up" made the girl sound like a virus. Suddenly, it all became clear. Ruby laughed involuntarily, wondering why she hadn't seen it before: Fred was actually jealous of this girl; that's why he was so anxious to turn up to the party with his wife in tow. In his adolescent mind, that would be one in the eye for his so-called friend and the new attachment that was putting distance between them. She should be flattered, she supposed. Perhaps he still found her attractive after all; enough, at any rate, to be displayed in public whenever he needed to make an impression. Her face tightened with anger as she turned the oven down by ten degrees and went off to get a bottle of red wine.

Later that evening, after their meal and a few glasses of rich burgundy, Ruby capitulated, as she invariably did. Fred promised to buy her a new outfit for the party: a figure-hugging, creamy satin dress she'd had her eye on for a while, with matching bag. A couple of drinks before they left would ease the journey, and help her to face the trials of socialising with strangers. Even the thought of Conrad's pale, flabby dullness couldn't put her off now; perhaps it wouldn't be so bad after all.

The evening began inauspiciously. The late September dusk had started to encroach on the day's piercing blue much earlier than usual, thanks to a bank of leaden cloud piling in from the west, squeezing the falling sunlight into deep crimson bars and casting an unearthly radiance ahead of them across the eastbound M40. Ruby had forgotten to have her anaesthetising drink before they left, and Fred's driving, in the reddish-grey haze of sunset, was even worse than usual, so that she spent the entire journey rigid with apprehension. She made a conscious effort to focus on whatever disconnected reflections flickered through her mind. She imagined the rich scent of the still-blooming roses in their fading garden. She tried to visualise the spectacular view of Naples from the terrace bar of the hotel where they'd spent their honeymoon. She struggled to avoid fragmented glimpses of mist-wreathed mountains, of light glinting on arched windows, but her thoughts veered only as far as the creepy old Hammer films Fred used to take her to in what she still called their "courting days". She'd always had to

17

pretend to be scared, so that he had an excuse to push his physical attentions on her, but she wasn't pretending now. It was real life that was genuinely frightening: the repetitive, gut-wrenching shocks of grief, and the endless dying of love.

Fred had allowed plenty of time to miss the early evening traffic but there turned out to be very little on the roads, and they arrived outside Conrad's flat half an hour before the time specified on the invitation. A brief argument ensued: should they go up and risk their host's discomfiture at being caught unprepared, or should they fill in the time with a quick drink at Fred and Conrad's lunchtime local? Fred favoured the second option; he seemed embarrassed by the possibility of Conrad greeting them with only the girlfriend present. Ruby, though, objected to the idea of sitting in some dingy bar in her new dress; she'd rather have parked the car in a side street and waited there. In the end, they drove round the streets of Islington three or four times, screaming at each other and attracting the interest of a bemused policeman.

On their fourth traverse of a particularly awkward junction, their shiny red, classic MG – Fred's pride and joy – was scraped by a banged-up silver Toyota. Fred was livid with rage, his contorted face vying with the sunset's raw scarlet and the car's now scarred paintwork of reflective crimson. He'd chosen the colour so carefully; he loved the idea that "red" was part of his name; but now, thanks to that bloody woman's stupid arguing, it was all spoiled: dented and scratched up and unfit to be seen by Conrad's wretched girlfriend. He cursed Ruby, and the Toyota driver, and the girlfriend, with all his considerable command of expletive-laden invective. But Ruby didn't hear; she wasn't listening. All her protecting thoughts had evaporated the instant the two cars made contact, exposing the curdled deposits of shock and grief that still clogged her mind after eighteen long months. Then, it had been no mere scrape but a head-on collision that sent their son Rufus and his best friend hurtling over a cliff-edge to their destruction. They were on the last stage of a European tour celebrating the end of their finals, and had just enjoyed a vigorous week of outdoor activities in the Black Forest, based at a youth hostel in the fairy-tale castle of Kreideburg. Ruby had never forgiven Fred and Conrad for arranging the trip through their connections in the travel business. She knew, though, that she was just as much to blame.

The Toyota driver did not stop to exchange insurance details, and the lightly damaged MG was now blocking the junction. Fred and Ruby were in imminent danger of becoming the victims of a road rage atrocity perpetrated by one or more of the delayed drivers who were sounding their horns with increasingly aggressive intent. Still cursing, Fred manoeuvred his way out of the blockage. Ruby said nothing. They both knew that, early or not, they needed to head straight to Conrad's party.

When they were finally welcomed into Conrad's smart new flat they were still not speaking to each other. Ruby was conscious that she was grinding her teeth and clenching her fingers into her hands – so much so that she was at risk of drawing blood from both gums and palms. Much to Fred's irritation, they were still the first arrivals. Conrad had just put on a CD of 1940s dance music and was in the process of filling bowls with retro-snacks such as Bombay mix and Japanese rice crackers. Rather unnecessarily, Ruby thought, he was slitting open the packets with an ivory-handled dagger. They said nothing about their slight accident. The girlfriend was not in evidence.

The flat was something of a surprise. It must have cost a fortune to buy, and another fortune to furnish and decorate. Ruby couldn't believe Conrad had been able to afford it on anything like the pathetic salary Fred brought home. For the first time in her life, she knew what it was to feel genuine envy. The feeling was so strong that it drove all other thoughts out of her head. It turned out that Ingrid, the girlfriend, had provided most of the cash; not bad for a pick-up and shack-up, Ruby thought irreverently. Fleetingly, she felt some sympathy with Fred's feelings of jealousy; this girl had certainly put his nose out of joint. Conrad assured them that Ingrid would be arriving shortly; she was still busy packing up her own apartment before she moved in with him.

The flat was light and spacious, and was decorated and furnished in tasteful, if rather anaemic, shades of grey and beige, white and magnolia. Instead of making it seem clinical and antiseptic, these restrained colours conveyed a sense of stylish luxury that was far from Ruby's expectations. From her brief encounters with Conrad, she had imagined him inhabiting a dingy, shabby-genteel retreat with frayed curtains and threadbare carpets, like some pale refugee from a Dickens novel. Presumably, Ingrid had taken responsibility for the décor in the new flat. Despite herself, Ruby couldn't wait to meet the mysterious girlfriend who had managed to kindle such jealousy in Fred. She watched him chatting awkwardly to Conrad, his face tight and flushed, and smiled to see him so ill-at-ease with his best friend. She hoped Ingrid would turn up soon.

It was a strained, awkward half-hour until other guests began to arrive. Ruby found herself knocking back glass after glass of white wine, and by the time Ingrid appeared her brain was fairly befuddled. She was dimly aware that Ingrid was strikingly attractive, in a not quite conventional way, with a round, smooth, pale face under a head of thick, bushed-out black hair. She was taller than Ruby and moved with an easy grace, the lines of her body suggested under a silky, full-length dress in deep shades of damson and fuchsia that were perfectly matched in her choice of lipstick and nail varnish. At her neck was a small, silver crucifix which must somehow have got tangled, Ruby thought, since it was clearly hanging upside down.

"How do you like the flat?" Ingrid asked. Her voice was quiet but not weak, pleasantly soft, almost insinuating, with hardly a trace of accent except an un-English tendency to overstress plosive consonants.

"Very nice," Ruby said, trying to sound as if she didn't really mean it. "You and Conrad must have spent a fortune doing it up." She was pleased with the phrase "doing it up"; somehow it put the apartment firmly in its place.

"It did cost quite a bit, I suppose," Ingrid replied. Her purpled lips slipped easily into a condescending smile.

"What do you do, actually?" Ruby asked, trying to free her voice from the sarcastic tone that had crept into it.

"Oh, some modelling, you know; this and that. I have to admit I mostly live off my family."

"Oh?"

"Yes. They have plenty of money to spare; I'm very lucky I suppose. The old European aristocracy – castles, mansions, vineyards, you know?"

Not really, Ruby thought. "So what are you doing over here?" she asked. "Why did you decide to leave all that behind?" (For someone like Conrad, she nearly added.)

"Well, I don't know." Ingrid smiled again. "There's got to be more to life than that. It can be very claustrophobic. How shall I say? A very bloodless existence. One needs to get away from it at times."

"I suppose so." Ruby sounded unconvinced.

"You look lovely, by the way," Ingrid said. "Does your husband know how lucky he is?"

Astonished, Ruby was struggling for a suitable reply when they were interrupted by Conrad, whose face through her wine-fuzzed gaze seemed even more washed-out than usual, his curly fair hair sitting on top of it like a tuft of cotton wool stuck on a potato. He was wearing an old-fashioned beige suit, with an open-necked white shirt. A purple handkerchief puffed absurdly from his top pocket like the bloom of a flagging peony.

"All OK?" he asked. "Another drink, Ruby?"

"No, I mustn't," she protested, conscious that she was slurring her words and wondering if she had imagined Ingrid's last remark. She felt unnaturally hot, and had the odd illusion that her blood was simmering in her veins like one of her signature casseroles. She wished she could turn down the heat by ten degrees or so.

"Oh, go on," Conrad said, topping up her glass with white wine from the half-empty bottle clutched in his left hand. It was useless to protest. As he drew the bottle away, Ruby's sweating fingers slipped on the glass, and wine splashed all over her.

"Oh, your beautiful cream dress," Ingrid cried, and hurried off for a cloth.

"Good job it wasn't red," Conrad joked. "Are you all right?" he added, noticing her dazed expression.

"Yes, yes, I'm fine, thanks." She tried to recover herself and wondered vaguely where Fred had got to.

"Good. We don't want you conking out on us, do we?"

He turned to Ingrid, who was by now dabbing at the dress with a damp cloth, and smiled – a smug, complacent smile, Ruby thought. Something nagged at her clouding brain. She excused herself and went to find somewhere to sit. As she wound her way through the crowded room she casually noted Fred talking to a pasty-faced guy in the corner. He glanced at her and immediately looked away, his face crimsoning with either embarrassment or lingering anger. Her heart sank; she wanted to make it up with him, but guessed he would be in one of his sulks for days. She went into the hall and noticed a door ajar at the far end, into what might be a bedroom. She still felt hot and flushed, and knew she had to lie down for a while. She pushed the door fully open and went in.

The room, like the rest of the flat, was decorated in shades of cream and white, like an Eskimo's vision of snow, yet instead of a sense of light and freshness it exuded only a sickly pallor. Inexplicably, the floor space in the centre of the room was filled not by a rug, but by a large, white sheet of plastic, its edges cut neatly into a perfect rectangle. Ruby could make no sense of it. Looking around for some explanation – fresh paint still wet on the ceiling, perhaps – her eye was drawn to the bedside table, where a single, exquisite, crimson rose was displayed in an elegant, cut-glass vase.

Ruby stepped across the white plastic rectangle and sat down heavily on the bed. She took a deep, slow breath, and the rose's surprisingly dense scent filled her nostrils. Behind the vase she noticed a faded black and white photograph in a silver frame. It was of two children, a boy and a girl, aged about twelve or thirteen. The background was unclear, but there was a suggestion of a castle, with turrets and battlements fading into the whiteness of mist. The children were dressed in what Ruby would have described as late Victorian fashion, and they were both smiling at the camera; smiling directly at her, Ruby felt. She picked up the photograph to examine it more closely. There was no doubt about it: the boy was Conrad and the girl Ingrid; they were unmistakable.

This was mysterious. Had they known each other as children? Ruby put the photograph back in its place, threw off her shoes and lay full length on the bed. She needed to rest, and to stop thinking for a while. She closed her eyes, and was relieved to find she wasn't drunk enough for this to set the darkness spinning. Instead, the voices of Conrad and Ingrid whispered incessantly in her brain, over and over, until she recognised what it was that had been bothering her. It was the way Conrad spoke: not an accent, exactly, just the stress on certain consonants, a slightly un-English emphasis.

For a few minutes, Ruby drifted into sleep. She didn't quite dream, but had the sense that someone was watching her. She woke with a start, sat up and looked around. The room was dim and still, but the muted orchestral swing of Glenn Miller wound jauntily through the echoing laughter emanating eerily from elsewhere. She felt much better now, able to return and face the social awkwardness of engaging in conversation with strangers. She scrabbled in the unfamiliar compartments of her new bag, repaired the carmine sheen of her dry lips and touched up her cheeks and eyes with subtle hints of salmon and coral. For the moment, she had completely forgotten the crimson rose, the photograph, and the whispering voices of Conrad and Ingrid with their strangely emphatic diction.

As she left the room, she collided with the young man she'd seen Fred talking to earlier, with the pale face like a round slab of softening brie. He was returning from the bathroom, and was obviously drunk. His stubby, plasticine fingers were still fumbling with his flies.

"Oops," he muttered, grinning stupidly. "Sorry. Don't think I know you, do I? You've not been to one of these affairs before, I take it?"

Ruby wasn't sure what he meant. She smiled vaguely.

"Nice to meet you anyway," the guy continued. "A bit of fresh blood's always welcome. May see you later." With that, he gave her a meaningful wink and lurched off in the direction of the lounge.

Only at about midnight did this encounter make any sense to Ruby, when she realised this was to be a wife-swapping party – partner-swapping, rather, as not everyone there was married. Swingers, was that it? Her pulse began to race. She'd always assumed these things didn't really happen, that they were nothing but scandalous media fabrications. She'd certainly never expected to find herself at one. She began to notice the guests pairing off – tangled on cushions in corners or slow-dancing in the dim light – with people other than those they'd arrived with. What should she do? The idea was repellent, but a tiny voice in her mind kept insisting that she could bloody well do with a change; she was sick of the way Fred constantly pushed her around and made her feel responsible for everything that went wrong in his life. It had been her fault, apparently, that Rufus had gone travelling in Europe; she should have insisted that he got a sensible vacation job instead of lending him the money to go swanning off on some self-indulgent jaunt with his flaky friend. Ruby felt the truth of this, however unfair it was, but resented his cruelty in repeating it every time their lives hit some new crisis. He was just as much to blame, he and Conrad, for organising cheap accommodation for the boys at the stopping-off points on their itinerary, but she would never dream of saying as much to him. Instead, she let the blame and the guilt fester inside her, pumping their toxic corruption through every vein. She hoped Fred suffered just as fiercely, but somehow she doubted it; after all, he was always telling her it was about time she "moved on". Well, perhaps she would.

She looked around for him, but he was nowhere to be seen. Dragging her mind back to her immediate predicament, she began eyeing up the men who still seemed to be available. When she realised what she was doing, her face flamed with shame and embarrassment. She was aware, somewhere in the depths of her thickening brain, that she was probably quite drunk; but after all, if she was going to enter into the spirit of things, she didn't want to end up with some bespectacled geek.

Once more, she cast an appraising eye around the room and noticed that people were not necessarily pairing off with someone of the opposite sex. A couple of girls were entwined on a capacious armchair and two men were tentatively kissing in the kitchen doorway. For her, this was not good news; it aroused further awkward memories that she was still not ready to face. For a flickering instant she thought she could probably forgive Fred, just about, if only he would get her out of here. Forgive Fred? She must be *very* drunk.

"Everything all right, Ruby?"

Startled, she turned to face Conrad, his face greyer than ever in the semi-darkness.

"I hope you're not shocked," he added. "Don't worry, it's not compulsory to join in."

"No, it's fine," she muttered, trying to stifle her increasing dislike of him. She found it difficult to meet his eyes and, looking down, noticed for the first time that round his neck hung an inverted cross, identical to Ingrid's. He saw her studying it and laughed.

"A family tradition," he said. "It has some significance, I believe: a distant ancestor who repudiated the teachings of the Church."

Ingrid noticed that Conrad's accent seemed different, more Germanic. She found herself fascinated by the cross – largely because she couldn't look Conrad directly in the eyes, so embarrassed was she by how repulsive she found him. He was so pale that she could think only of a dead body on a mortuary slab.

She didn't want her thoughts to take her in this direction and tried to resist, but unstoppably into her mind crashed the memory of her dead son. She and Fred had flown over to Germany to make a formal identification of the bodies of Rufus and his friend. They had made the mistake of staying in the fairy-tale castle with its glittering windows where the boys had been spending the final week of their holiday. The spectacular setting, with its misty forests and gloomy mountains, seemed sinister rather than picturesque, and when they collected the friends' belongings from the room they'd been sharing, they were shocked to discover evidence of a closer relationship than they'd been aware of. Fred and Ruby had never spoken of this again. The next morning they stood side by side in the mortuary as the bodies were uncovered one at a time, stubbornly refusing to hold hands, frightened even of looking at each other. Previously, Ruby's only images of the dead had been of the pallid corpses in the horror films Fred used to drag her along to as an excuse for his teenage fumblings. Those bodies had never seemed real, just laughable parodies of death. But Rufus's corpse looked even less real, as if moulded from suet, flabby and white. In fact, the police were at a loss to understand why his and his friend's bodies appeared to be virtually drained of blood.

The arrival of Ingrid shook Ruby out of her morbid reverie.

"I don't think you've seen round the whole apartment, have you?" she asked. "Would you like to?" Neither she nor Conrad seemed in the least inebriated, and it occurred to Ruby that she hadn't seen either of them actually drinking, though Conrad had never been without a bottle in his hand to replenish everyone else's glasses.

"Yes – that would be nice," Ruby lied. Anything was better than having to go on talking to Conrad without actually daring to look at him.

The apartment was much bigger than Ruby had imagined, with a surprising number of rooms hidden away in unexpected corners. One sitting-room had a balcony with a commanding view across the nearby streets and building sites towards the lights of the City, reflected in fragmented glimpses of the glittering Thames. Broken memories of moonlight glinting on high castle windows flickered in Ruby's mind as she and Ingrid surveyed the spreading panorama, stretched out under the sky's glowing indigo.

"Sorry if the party's not quite what you were expecting," Ingrid said. "Conrad was sure you and Fred would be up for it, but it doesn't matter. Don't go just yet, though – it's still early and there's plenty of food and drink left. At least," she added, "we'll be getting a fresh supply shortly."

Ruby was annoyed that Ingrid had her marked down as boring and conventional, and she determined that she would see the party through to the end, whatever it took. But 12.30 was hardly early, she thought primly. They turned back inside where, to Ruby's surprise, dozens of red candles had now been lit in every room. In the swaying, smoky light it was impossible to make out who was who. Was it Fred that Ruby saw in one room, clasped in an awkward embrace with the putty-faced youth he'd been talking to earlier? She felt neither shock nor surprise; somehow it didn't seem to matter much. Nevertheless, an instinctive flash of anger sent a burning torrent of blood into her cheeks, cascading another wave of vertigo through her pounding head. For the first time, she half-wondered if she might be ill, rather than just drunk; or whether, perhaps, she'd been drugged. But that was ridiculous; it was just a party. As she followed Ingrid back into the hallway, a plaintive voice from somewhere in the crowd called out, "Anything else to drink yet? We're getting thirsty."

"Shortly," Ingrid shouted back. "Some people are so impatient," she added quietly, turning to smile at Ruby.

The tour ended in the bedroom where Ruby had previously taken refuge. She knew in a moment of vivid awareness that Ingrid was going to try and seduce her. In her confusion, she oddly connected this realisation with the white plastic rectangle in the middle of the floor. Despite her anxiety she almost laughed out loud, but instead sought distraction in the photograph on the bedside table. Beside it lay a newly-fallen petal from the crimson rose; unconsciously, she inhaled the rich scent.

"Those two," she began, her voice strained and awkward.

"Yes – Conrad and I," said Ingrid.

"You knew each other as children?"

"Oh, we've been friends a long time. To let you into a little secret, we're cousins."

"Ah." Ruby had half expected this, but she still needed to play for time. "And the Victorian costume?"

Ingrid smiled. "Look at the date on the back."

Ruby picked up the photograph. Her trembling hand brushed the rose and another petal fell. On the back of the picture, in faded Gothic script, was written:

𝕶onrad & 𝕵ngrid
𝕾chloss 𝕶reideburg
1887

Simultaneously, Ruby registered both the date and the name of the castle – the detested place with its high, arched windows glinting in the moon's silvered glance, where her son and his male lover had spent their final night. It's some kind of cruel joke, she thought, and laughed uncertainly.

"Oh yes," she said with a final stab of sarcasm, "a photo of you and Conrad taken well over a century ago!"

Ingrid's smile remained fixed and sinister. Her hand pushed the door behind her; it closed with a click.

"That's right," she said. "Well preserved, *ja*?"

For an instant, Ruby couldn't interpret what was happening. All she knew was that she had never hated Fred as much as she did at this moment. Why had he forced her to come here, despite all her pleading? Dizzy with venom, she dropped her smart new bag on to the soft bed. Her blood had turned to acid, spreading its crimson fire through her whole being until she thought her brain would burst. The wine glass fell from her burning hand and pirouetted on the plastic sheet. With an immense effort of will, she forced her fading consciousness to confront the terrifying reality of her situation. Vampires. The undead. All those horror films she'd always had such contempt for crowded into her head. What could she do? She had no crucifix, no garlic, no silver bullets. What else was there? Out of nowhere, an unlikely memory forced itself into her head, of one film in which the vampire had been destroyed by running water. Instinctively, she snatched up the vase, plucked out the rose and flung the scummy water into Ingrid's face. The thorns pricked her thumb and a globule of scarlet oozed out, vying with the bright red of the dropped petals. At the sight of the blood, a wildness animated Ingrid's pale eyes. She leaped at Ruby, an ivory-handled dagger now mysteriously in her grasp. As the blade plunged into her neck, Ruby was aware for the briefest moment of gouts and spurts of scalding blood spattering her new dress, and a smile of anticipatory relish on the face of her killer. Then blackness closed over her consciousness, to the irregular splat of thick vermilion drops hitting the white plastic, where they hissed and steamed.

The bodies of a man and woman were found just after dawn in a smashed-up MG at the bottom of a deep excavation in the centre of Islington where a new office block was to be built. The driver had evidently lost control of the vehicle and crashed it through the protective hoardings. A police constable reported that on the previous evening he had seen the couple driving round in circles, apparently engaged in a furious argument. Neither of them was wearing a seatbelt, and both had been catapulted through the classic, pre-shatterproof windscreen, causing severe lacerations, especially to the area of the neck and throat. Yet, to the bafflement of the emergency services, there was barely a drop of blood anywhere – in the car, on their clothes, on the windscreen; least of all in the ghastly, pallid bodies of the unfortunate victims.

A few streets away, an ambulance crew had been called to an expensive apartment where the guests at a late-night party had been struck down by a mystery virus. All the victims were convulsively vomiting blood.

Fallen

There wasn't much I could do about it. By the time I was aware of him, he'd jumped. The brow of the cliff, vacated now, pressed its green turf silently against the sea's silvery expanse, which reached in turn towards its own squinting junction with the broken sky. Silence, but for the waves' crashing monotony against the unseen rocks. I didn't dare go any closer to the edge, to risk the vertigo of that immense white drop to oblivion. I didn't need to see his smashed body, the foaming, pink caress of the spent surf.

I suppose I could have acted faster but after all I didn't know he was going to jump, not really. When instinct alerted me, I could have called out, could have pretended to mistake him for a friend. It would have been awkward, but better than this silent horror, this swift slip into a stranger's suicide as the breeze brushed soft against the grass and the gulls swept the sky, screeching indifference.

I looked round, furtively. No-one else had seen him go; what need was there for me to acknowledge that I had? There was no way he could have survived the fall; that's why people came here in particular, to be absolutely sure of success. Along the green verge of the cliff-edge, tiny wooden crosses and poems mounted on sticks memorialised his predecessors in self-destruction, yet the brink remained open for business, unbarricaded against despair. People had a choice, after all.

There was nothing I could do now. Five minutes later and I'd have missed the whole thing. Why didn't I just leave it at that? But I didn't; couldn't. That wasn't how I'd been brought up. In any case, denial would only make things worse; I knew that from Sally. Taking my mobile from my jacket pocket, I was relieved to discover there was a strong signal. I keyed in 999, delivered my message as calmly as I could, and sat down on the rough grass to wait for the arrival of the emergency services.

It was just a couple of months later that his mother tracked me down. She'd gone about it in the right way, made inquiries via the local police, who called to ask if I'd be willing to meet her. It was the last thing I wanted, but yet again my upbringing got the better of me. I didn't see how there was anything I could offer her, although I suppose that was up to her to decide. But I'd put the experience behind me, moved on. I'd already done my duty, and it wasn't as if I'd seen anything other than a young man vanish from the cliff-edge. No plummeting body, no shattering of bones or tearing of flesh. No blood. I should have listened to my instinct, just said no. Instead, I agreed to see her.

After all, it was over six months now since Sally, since the trial. I was fine. That's why I'd been there, on that Sussex cliff-top. My GP had suggested I take a holiday before returning to work, but I couldn't face the hassle of going abroad. I wanted somewhere easy, somewhere familiar, somewhere bracing. I remembered childhood holidays in Hastings and Eastbourne and decided somewhere on the Sussex coast would be ideal. In particular, Sally and I had never been there together; it was free of memories, associations, guilt. I needed to clear her from my mind, and until that day on the cliff-top, it had worked.

I'd returned to my job the following week as planned. I was lucky they'd kept the position open for me; fortunately, they'd found a first-rate substitute who'd proved so talented that she'd now been offered a permanent post. Despite the spoiling of my holiday, I was feeling confident and upbeat. I brought in a couple of new corporate clients and led a substantial rethink of company practice for which I was awarded a not inconsiderable increase in salary. I rarely thought of Sally now – except when she crept up on me at odd moments with a yank at my gut and a pounding of the heart. But I'd learned how to deal with that, without recourse to the medication or alcohol that had kept me going before my breakdown. So, despite my reluctance, I would surely be able to deal with a bereaved mother whose son had slipped from the world before my unwilling eyes. I owed it to her.

We met on a Saturday morning in early October at an old-fashioned tea-shop in Marlborough. There were white linen table-cloths, crisply ironed napkins, lace doilies, china teacups, dark oak beams and leaded windows. She'd travelled by coach from her home in Ross-on-Wye and I'd driven out from Clapham along the M4. My spirits were lifted by the widening landscape of rolling chalk downland, its every detail precision-printed under the sky's uniform blue by the sharp brightness of the autumn sun. We'd decided to meet on neutral territory, if that's not an inappropriate metaphor; I, for one, would not have felt comfortable inviting her to my home, not with all its irrelevant, attendant memories. I'd chosen the venue without thinking much about it, but as soon as I got there I knew I'd made a mistake. I'd forgotten that the memories, the associations, would be there too. Years ago, Sally and I used to break our journey here, stopping off for coffee *en route* to our holiday home in Cornwall. It hadn't changed at all; even the smell, a sweet combination of cakes and starch, was exactly the same.

I recognised her as soon as she walked in. I'd already settled at a table by the window, gazing abstractedly at the High Street's Georgian bustle, brightened beyond its everyday monotony by the sun's dazzle and the sky's misleading blue. She was younger than I'd expected, but I recognised at once that unmistakable air of defeat and resignation. I'd seen it every day in the mirror for months after Sally... Her smile, when I stood up to greet her, was reserved and perfunctory.

"Mrs Foster," I said. "I'm David Helmston."

"It's Debbie," she said. "Thanks for agreeing to see me."

We sat down and, uncertain how to continue, I attracted the attention of a waitress. She could only have been about sixteen and was struggling ineffectually to cast off her habitual teenage indifference in order to earn a bit of extra pocket money. The uniform couldn't have helped her much in preserving her fragile adolescent dignity. She was dressed like a maid from one of those 1930s murder mysteries set in an archetypal English village, but Miss Marple would have marked her down immediately as an imposter, and she certainly looked as if she were harbouring murderous intentions. We ordered coffee and cake, and the girl flounced off to the till to punch it into the system.

"What can I do for you?" I asked, with unintentional brusqueness, after an awkward pause.

Mrs Foster looked momentarily vacant, as if she couldn't quite recall how she'd come to be having morning coffee miles from home with a complete stranger.

"I – I wanted to ask you about Joe," she said. "I just wanted to know some things…"

She trailed off, lowering her eyes to the table in what I read as embarrassment. She looked older than she'd seemed at first, about fifty I thought – not much younger than I was. Joe, her son, had been nineteen. I could only guess what it was like to lose a child in such circumstances; could only imagine, in fact, what it was like to have had a child at all. Sally and I…

"There isn't really anything I can tell you that you don't already know," I said, defeated suddenly by the pointlessness of this whole affair, wishing I'd never agreed to meet her.

"I can understand why you should think that," she said, raising her eyes to meet mine with surprising determination. "But can I just ask you some things? Even if they don't seem very important, or very – rational, to you?"

"Of course," I agreed weakly. It occurred to me that she must hate me for having been there instead of her at the end of her son's life. Perhaps she even blamed me for not having saved him.

"How did you come to be there," she asked after a pause, "on that day?"

This wasn't one of the questions I'd expected and I sensed, wrongly perhaps, something hostile in her tone. I was aware of a slight frown creasing my brow.

"I was on holiday – staying in Eastbourne."

"Can I ask what you do?"

"Do?"

"As a job – a profession."

37

I was baffled by this, and must have bridled with momentary resentment. I couldn't see the relevance; couldn't see what it had to do with her.

"I'm in marketing," I said.

"I'm sorry," she said. "This must seem strange to you. It's just that you're the last person to have seen Joe alive. I just feel I need to know… that it would help to know… a bit about you."

"Well I'm in marketing," I repeated gracelessly, hoping this sounded like a full-stop. End of questioning. What was my life to her, for God's sake? But I went on. "Selling businesses, you know? Corporate identities. Campaigns and strategies. Maximising opportunities at the client/customer interface. Brand recognition. That sort of thing."

I must have sounded dismissive, sarcastic even, as if my heart wasn't in it; but that wasn't true. I enjoyed my job, found it rewarding. And I was good at it. It was what had saved me. During the worst period of Sally's delusions, before…

"Actually," I went on, "I'd been off work for six months. The holiday was meant to get me in shape for going back."

"I'm sorry," she said.

Our eyes met again, and I held her gaze for just a moment too long. Inexplicably cross with myself, I muttered, "Sorry? Why?"

"Seeing Joe," she answered. "It must have taken you back to square one."

I was puzzled. "Square one?" I said. "What do you mean?"

Did she know more about me than she was letting on? Had she googled me, found out where I worked, called the company, talked somebody into telling her everything about me – about Sally, about my breakdown? I began to feel threatened, panicky. I hadn't felt like this for months.

The return of the sullen girl with our coffees provided a calming distraction: a double espresso for me and a decaff cappuccino for her, plus two hefty slices of chocolate cake. In this, our tastes had coincided and I wondered if for her, like me, it was comfort eating, piling the calories on top of that residual core of misery, burying unhappiness under the thick ooze of sticky, dark cream. A comfort and also a punishment, relishing the damage this sickly indulgence would ultimately inflict on our health and well-being. Punishment for not being able to save the ones we loved. "Enjoy," said the girl grudgingly as she turned away.

"Square one?" I repeated when the girl had stalked off, wiping cream-sticky fingers on her short, black skirt.

"Sorry," she said. "I just thought if you'd been off work for that long, something must have…" Again, she trailed off, and I felt irrationally guilty for making her feel awkward.

And so it went on, the questioning. She wanted to know what the weather had been like on that day; what I could see and hear; how rough or calm the sea was. She asked when I'd first noticed her son, whether he'd looked at me before… I thought I was beginning to understand what it was she needed. I began to invent details: a herring-gull gliding over his head as he stood there briefly, contemplating the far horizon; a sudden gust of wind that pressed his thin T-shirt against him on the brink; a particularly resonant crash of the waves; a crow that squawked ominously from some unseen perch just at the moment he vanished from view. She wanted a complete picture, you see, but the thing is, there wasn't one. There'd been nothing; just his disappearance into emptiness at the very instant I'd registered his presence. But I obliged by crafting imaginary details, etching them even for myself into memory: a reimagining, a shift into fiction. I thought it was what she was after.

I did manage to inject a few questions of my own into her interrogation.

"What about Joe's father?" I asked bluntly.

"We – we're not together," she said. "He hadn't seen Joe for a while. They weren't… they weren't in contact with each other."

"Is that why Joe was depressed?" I asked, pushing on crassly in my attempt to gain control of the situation. I sensed that my question had made her uneasy, and she looked away again. We had both finished our coffees by now, and the cake had been reduced to a flurry of dark crumbs and smears of cream on the pretty china plates.

"Sorry," I said. "D'you want another drink? It's my treat, by the way."

As soon as I said it I knew "treat" was not an appropriate choice of word in the circumstances, but I let it stand.

"No thanks," she said, adding after a moment, "that's kind of you."

"No problem," I answered, feeling like a sullen teenager. I might just as well have given a brusque shrug and said, "Whatever." Surely this ill-advised meeting had to be nearing its end. I, for one, didn't feel I could sustain it for much longer. Mrs Foster – Debbie – was nice enough, but I'd given her everything I could. What was the point in prolonging the agony?

"His father abused him as a child," she said suddenly, looking directly at me. "Physically and sexually. I did nothing, tried to persuade myself it wasn't happening." She paused for a moment as tears welled in her eyes, glinting in the brightness of the sunbeams that glanced through the leaded panes. "I didn't believe him – Joe. I thought he was making it up."

Why, in God's name, had I asked? This was no business of mine. She took a tissue from her bag and dabbed at her streaming eyes.

"Sorry," she said. It seemed to be the word of the day. Then, "I let him down."

The girl came to ask if we wanted anything else. Distractedly, I said no and asked for the bill. I knew all about letting people down. Ignoring their pain, pushing it aside, refusing to believe. By the time I lost Sally, it was too late; just as I'd been too late, too slow, to save Joe. It was my fault – again.

Suddenly I wanted to tell Debbie about it, but how could I? This meeting wasn't about me; I couldn't unload my own grief, my own guilt, on to her. But I did have to make a confession.

"When he jumped," I said, "it was all so quick. A minute later and I wouldn't have seen him. For an instant, there on the cliff-top, it might never have happened. For a moment – just a moment, I promise – I thought of pretending it hadn't, walking on, going back down to the Victorian tea-room on the pier for a cream tea. But I didn't."

She smiled – a warm, kind smile that told me it would be all right. "I understand," she said. Then, "Why had you been off work?"

I told her everything. The girl flounced over with the bill, which rested there on its little silver tray, ignored, while I relived for this sympathetic, sad stranger whose son had fallen into oblivion in front of me, the whole story of my failure to save my beautiful wife, my adored Sally, from her own plunge into what I believed at the time to be inexplicable paranoia. I had laughed at her fears: mere childhood terrors dredged up from some rediscovered darkness of nightmare and imagination, I thought. I reassured her, pooh-poohed her insistence that she was being stalked and threatened by some mysterious stranger. And it *was* all fantasy, surely; she could produce no credible evidence, nothing that made any sense. We had long conversations about it that went round and round and never got anywhere, except back to her insistence that it was really happening, and my increasingly frustrated attempts to argue rationally that it was all in her imagination. She had history, you see; a brief but terrifying psychotic episode after our child was stillborn. Something, heaven knows what, must have triggered a recurrence.

She went to the police, who took only a perfunctory interest in her story, but she rejected my suggestion that she should see her doctor, get some kind of counselling for her delusions. To my shame, I actually used the word – delusions. I spat it out like an accusation. I can still see her face, the way it closed down, as if from now on everything would be shut in, locked up, never spoken of again. She stood up in silence and walked out of the room without a word. Ten days later she was dead. He'd killed her.

Debbie listened intently, and with increasing horror, to my story. I suppose it had taken her away from her own grief for the first time since Joe had jumped.

"But who was he?" she asked. "How did he manage to make himself so invisible that no-one believed he was real?"

"It doesn't matter," I said. I was worn out from going through the whole thing. I'd thought it was over, that I wouldn't have to dredge it all up again. But I couldn't leave her with only half the story.

"In London, it's easy to disappear into the crowd," I went on. "He didn't phone her, didn't leave any notes. It was just voices from the dark: whispered threats as she got off the bus after late evenings at work, or sudden noises behind her as she walked down the street. Two or three times she came across dead birds carefully placed in her path – something that could have been nothing more than coincidence, but she knew it wasn't. Twice, something hit her bedroom window at midnight. I didn't hear it, but both times she made me go out and look around: nothing. He was very clever; very careful. Sometimes he spoke to her in a crowd of shoppers, but he was never there when she turned round. I suppose if the police had been more persistent he'd've turned up on CCTV, or someone would have remembered seeing him, but the fact that I plainly thought she was imagining it all didn't encourage them to pursue it. I still don't understand why they didn't think it might be me."

"Did they get him, after she was killed?"

"Yes. At the end, he wasn't quite clever enough. He's serving life."

The conversation faltered, stopped. There didn't seem to be anywhere else it could go. I took the opportunity to slip a twenty-pound note from my wallet and place it firmly on top of the bill on its silver tray. I hoped this would signal that our meeting was over. I needed to get away, to think about why I'd opened up to her so readily, consider the consequences.

"I'm sorry," she said again. "I guess neither of us was expecting this."

She stood up, and the sun shafts from the dazzling street lit up her rich, brown hair and took the wrinkles from her face in a wash of light. For the first time, I saw how attractive she was.

"I'd better go," she said. "I didn't realise it was that time. I've got some shopping to do before I get the coach back."

It wasn't that late; she was obviously making an excuse, extricating herself politely from an uncomfortable situation. Suddenly I felt sorry she was leaving, but didn't feel confident enough to suggest we might stay there for lunch.

"Well, I hope you feel it was worth the journey," I said.

"Yes, very much so. Thank you." She paused for a moment, then said, with a quiet intensity that struck me as just a bit creepy, "You see, I loved him so much." She put on her coat and looked around. "Do you know where the toilets are?"

I gestured towards the far corner of the room and watched her as she walked past the cake-laden counter that offered its tempting, sickly comforts to the lost and alone. The waitress came for the money and smiled for the first time, belatedly angling for a tip I suppose.

"Was everything OK?" she said.

"Fine, thanks," I replied.

My meeting with Mrs Foster – Debbie – affected me more than I'd anticipated, in a variety of unexpected ways. I found myself thinking of her at odd times, wishing we could see each other again when we wouldn't have to talk about Joe or Sally. I realised in retrospect just how sympathetic she'd been – how lovely she was. It was the first time I'd thought of a woman in that way since Sally was killed – as a kind companion; even, I'll admit, a sexual partner. Sex with Sally had been off the agenda for years, and I'd never blamed her for this; how could she be intimate with someone who didn't believe in the terrors she was being subjected to? But with Debbie it would be different. We would heal each other, in every way possible. For the first time in ages, I began to feel I had a future.

I was getting ahead of myself, though. I didn't have her phone number, her email address or any other contact details; all I knew was that she was Debbie Foster from Ross-on-Wye. I couldn't face digging around to find out more, though I guess it wouldn't have been that difficult even if the police were wary of giving me her contact information. I didn't want to seem over-eager, or needy; even less did I want to come across as some kind of deranged stalker. I sat back, thought it over and decided to wait for a while. Perhaps she'd get in touch with me. I convinced myself she'd been attracted to me too, that she'd realise there could be a future for us. At the same time, I told myself I was being ridiculous, and tried to push her to the back of my mind while I got on with my life.

Getting on with my life proved difficult, however. Reliving the whole story of Sally must have triggered something inside me; at any rate, I began to experience disturbing manifestations of my lingering guilt. Arriving home from a late night at the office, I was dazzled by an intensely bright flash of light from my neighbour's garden as I rifled in my pocket for my keys. It only lasted an instant, but as it faded I was sure I heard Sally's name breathed into the damp air. One night, just as I was dropping off to sleep, the phone rang. Dazed and disorientated I rushed downstairs to answer it. A woman's voice, faint and crackly, asked to speak to Sally, but she hung up before I could say anything. I dialled 1471, but the caller's number had been withheld. Back in bed, dozing, I realised I had dreamed the whole thing. One morning I noticed Sally's name fingered in the condensation on the window of my local coffee shop, behind a crowd of people jostling at the door. By the time I got there, it had been wiped clear.

Most disturbing of all, on a Sunday morning in early November I opened my bedroom curtains after a longer than usual lie-in, looking forward, as usual, to the pleasure of the view across the informal patchwork of adjoining gardens. It was a still, bright day, and the few leaves remaining on the clump of lime trees that demarcated my garden from the one beyond hung like yellow pennants on the stark framework of blackened branches. It took me awhile to notice the carefully arranged leaves on the lawn, which had been formed into a sequence of capital letters. This time, the name they spelled out was JOE. I grabbed my dressing gown, ran downstairs, fumbled clumsily at the patio doors and stepped outside on to the cold, damp paving slabs. The name had vanished, the leaves scattered into natural formations that spread unthreateningly across the wet grass. I thought I could make out darker patches, footprints in the dew perhaps, but this was much less likely than that the whole thing had been yet another phenomenon created by my guilty imagination. What worried me more than anything was that my mind had now incorporated Joe Foster into the fabric of my guilt. I was clearly in an increasingly bad way. Perhaps seeing Debbie again would help. I ought to do something about tracking her down.

But I didn't; instead, I let time pass and learned to live with the disturbing hallucinations, which continued on and off for weeks. I felt I deserved to suffer them. It didn't occur to me that I was doing to myself exactly what I'd done to Sally: refusing to acknowledge that what was happening might actually be real. I soon stopped even entertaining the possibility, and they just became part of my inner life occasionally projected on to the real world. Anyway, I could cope; most of the time it was just voices from the dark.

Sometimes I thought about Debbie, but did nothing to advance my hopeless suit. I was busy at work, Christmas came and went and I kept promising myself that in the New Year, some time, I would do something about how I felt. Then, out of the blue, she called me.

She wanted to ask me a favour, she said. Had I realised it was nearly a year since Joe had jumped? I was astonished; it didn't seem possible. Spring had sped by, and most of the summer, and the August Bank Holiday was nearly on top of us. How could I not have noticed? She wanted to meet me on the anniversary of his death; wanted me to show her the very spot where it had happened, so she could plant a poem there. I was surprised she hadn't done this already, but she said she couldn't face it till now. I agreed, of course, though I'd been hoping that next time I saw her we wouldn't have had to talk about Joe, or Sally for that matter. I'd need to take time off work, but that wasn't a problem; they were pretty pleased with what I'd been doing, the new clients I'd brought in. I booked myself into the same Eastbourne hotel that I'd stayed in a year ago and recommended it to her too, but she said she'd make her own arrangements. We agreed to meet for lunch at the Victorian tea-room on the pier; then we'd get a bus up to the fatal location.

The weather was more-or-less identical to how it had been then: warm and sunny with a brisk breeze. Thin rags of white cloud scudded across the pale blue sky and the sea chopped and churned underneath the pier, underscoring our quiet conversation with its restless reminders of mortality. Over our tea and sandwiches we were in a world out of time, a pseudo-Victorian time-capsule of steel and wood and glass thrust roughly out across the waters of the English Channel with waitresses in starched pinafores and ribboned white caps attending to our every need with brisk politeness. I wanted to tell Debbie how I felt, but it didn't seem appropriate. Until she had fulfilled her commemorative intention on the cliff-top, it would be wrong to divert her thoughts to some unlikely future relationship between us. Yet the more she talked, the more I became convinced that that was exactly what I wanted.

"You've written a poem for him then," I said, feeling increasingly frustrated.

"What? Oh, no. I couldn't write a poem. It's by Gerard Manley Hopkins. D'you want to see it?"

"Sure."

I was relieved in a way; I would have hated her to have penned one of those embarrassingly sentimental rhyming tributes such as those I'd seen on the cliff-top that day. They were really bad – the worst kind of greetings-card verses – but to ridicule them for that sparked yet more guilt in view of the circumstances in which they'd been written. It was sensible of her, I felt, to have found something appropriate by a great poet.

She had brought a large bag with her, from which she now took a laminated A4 sheet stapled to a short wooden stake. As she passed it across the table to me, the sleeve of her blouse caught on the spout of the teapot, revealing her wrist and a few inches of her forearm. To my surprise, I noticed a tattoo executed in fierce red against her pale skin. She drew her arm back quickly and pulled the sleeve over it, but not before I'd registered what it was, with a sense of fascinated disbelief. It was her son's name, Joe, in elegant faux-handwriting, with a heart and "my dear boy" inscribed underneath. I pretended I hadn't seen it and looked quickly at the poem, but I felt my

48

cheeks going hot and for some reason my pulse was racing. I didn't dare look at her, so I didn't know whether she realised I'd seen it, and by the time I'd read the poem, both of us had recovered our equanimity.

The poem, neatly typed in Gothic script, was a rather strange choice I thought, though it was appropriate in some obvious ways. It was, I knew, the sestet of one of Hopkins' despairing, final sonnets, in which he desperately tries to reconcile his terrible despair with his deeply-rooted faith in God.

> O the mind, mind has mountains; cliffs of fall
> Frightful, sheer, no-man-fathomed. Hold them cheap
> May who ne'er hung there. Nor does long our small
> Durance deal with that steep or deep. Here! creep,
> Wretch, under a comfort serves in a whirlwind: all
> Life death does end and each day dies with sleep.

Despite Hopkins' characteristically tortured syntax, the strength of his feelings and his desperate need for consolation come through powerfully. As I finished reading it, it occurred to me that the poem was as much about how Debbie felt as it was about the reason her son had jumped – more so, perhaps. But how could the woman who'd chosen this poem also have thought that unexpected, unacceptable tattoo was a good idea? I felt embarrassed for her.

I passed the poem on its stick back to her across the table, and she replaced it in her bag.

"Interesting choice," I said. "Did Joe know the poem?"

"Yes. He did Hopkins for A Level."

"Me too," I said lamely. "I don't think I appreciated at the time what a great poet he was."

Our ability to talk to each other with ease and warmth seemed to have dissipated. I drained the remnants of cold tea from my cup, wondering why a glimpse of Debbie's tattoo should have altered the way I felt about her. I was ill-at-ease, confused. She seemed aware, too, that something in the atmosphere had changed. The sunlight that lit up our table had acquired a chilly glint, the air in the tea-room was thick and still, and the echoing conversations of the other customers boomed in my head like the sea's endless turmoil heard in a shell.

"Shall we go?" I said. She looked directly, challengingly into my eyes.

"That was private," she said. "No one was meant to see it."

– Just as well I saw it when I did, I thought. It had saved me from making a fool of myself.

On the bus, we didn't talk. When we got to the cliff-top, the skies had greyed over and the wind had dropped. Both the rolling land and the stretched-out sea seemed bleached of colour. All I wanted now was to get this thing over with, go back to my hotel, lie down and think – or, preferably, sleep. Such a tattoo, surely, was for a partner, a lover. I wasn't a fan of tattoos at the best of times, but this… I couldn't fathom out what it meant; couldn't face up to the irrational suspicions that had begun to gather like a ripening abscess in my mind. She'd told me Joe's father had abused him, but I began to wonder if I could believe her. Perhaps the truth was significantly different.

We stood for a few minutes, looking out towards the line where the land dropped sheer away. Gulls swirled aimlessly on the soft currents of the air, emitting the occasional, strangled cry. A rook sat complacently on the cliff-edge, contemplating the restless waters that crashed dully, unseen, on the rocks below. Sad markers flapped their disconnected, laminated

50

memorial poems, warped and stained by the weather, in the brief gusts of breeze.

"Show me where," Debbie said quietly.

I couldn't, of course. It was a year ago, and everything was different; I was different. I would have to pretend, reimagine the whole thing, decide on an appropriate spot. As I weighed up the possibilities, I saw – saw, not imagined – Joe and Sally on the brink of the cliff, looking directly at me. They vanished in silence.

"There," I said after a moment.

I led her to the spot I'd chosen. She stepped forward and looked out across the sea.

"Be careful," I said, more sharply than I'd intended.

She knelt down, put her bag on the sparse grass and felt around for a spot soft enough to accept the poem on its wooden stake. As she pulled it from her bag it caught on the handle, loosening one of the staples, but she didn't seem to notice. She also took out a small hammer, placed the point of the stake on the spot she'd chosen and held it firm. Tactfully I moved away, turning into the land, back towards normality, sanity, with the sound of light, irregular tapping in my ears. When it had stopped, I counted to ten and turned to face her. She was standing up, looking directly at me. I raised my eyebrows in an expression intended to inquire if she was ready. She smiled back at me and I felt guilty; what the heck was her tattoo to me? What did it matter? She'd loved her son, just as I'd loved Sally. We should go back down into the town, have a traditional afternoon tea and share a proper conversation, warmly and intimately. I wouldn't feel guilty any more. I would tell her how I felt, and hang the consequences.

As I stepped forward to meet her, her smile twisted into something unreadable. If it weren't a ridiculous idea, I'd have described it as triumphant. Inexplicably, I thought of the leaves on my lawn, spelling out Joe's name. Before I could do anything she turned away from me, took two firm paces forward and vanished from the edge into absence and oblivion. The waves crashed. The gulls cried. The rook fluttered itself into the light breeze. Her bag sat slumped by the loosely staked poem, whose laminated surface flickered in the sky's reflected silver.

I stood there, immobile, fixed in guilt. Finally, I'd received my punishment.

Immortal Longings

It couldn't have gone better. Clockwork wasn't in it. While Bill and Vanessa Prior were enjoying the much-praised production of *Antony and Cleopatra* ("vigorous, athletic, muscular, spellbinding", *The Sunday Times*) at the country's most prestigious regional theatre, Emma and Colin were emptying their house of enough money, furniture and valuables to furnish their new flat and clear all their debts.

It had been Emma's idea, much to Colin's chagrin. As a member of the theatre's box-office staff, she had access to the names and addresses of the hundreds of people who would be at the theatre each night during the current booking period, from April to October. They'd decided to target those buying tickets for the most expensive seats on the assumption that they were more likely to have stuff worth stealing. They'd drawn up a shortlist of a dozen or so possible candidates who'd booked for September performances of *Antony and Cleopatra*; this would give them two or three months to find out what they could about their potential victims' lives. It had to be *Antony and Cleopatra* – at nearly four hours it was the longest show in the season, affording them plenty of time to carry out the robbery. A mere two hours of *The Comedy of Errors* would have been no use at all.

The legwork had been undertaken mostly by Colin, who had time on his hands since he'd been sacked from his demeaning job at a DIY superstore after getting into a violent argument with a complaining customer. That was also the main reason why he and Emma were strapped for cash, and with banks, building societies and utility providers breathing down their necks they needed to do something urgently.

It had been a painstaking and time-consuming operation; there was no Google Earth in those days to facilitate Colin's research. He had checked out in person all the names and addresses supplied by Emma, looking for things such as how secluded each house was, whether it was protected by an alarm system, and if there were any family members likely to be left at home during the theatre visit. Narrowing the list down to about five, he embarked on closer investigations, creeping round gardens, peering through windows, assessing as far as he could the quality and value of furniture and furnishings. Colin found it humiliating that his inability to hold down a job had reduced him to this; whatever happened, his family must never find out. It was only Emma's steady and reliable employment that had secured them a mortgage in the first place, and he felt angrily obliged to show her he could do what was needed to improve their material circumstances. Some days he'd been tempted to break into one of the targeted houses there and then, finding it unoccupied and inviting, but he was not a professional burglar and he had no guarantee that the owners were not about to return, so he resisted the temptation. Finally, he narrowed it down to one: the Priors were the perfect candidates.

Vanessa Prior had retired from the stage in 1982, ten years previously, at the age of 54. As she had done little film or TV work, hers was not a household name. She was regarded, however, as one of the greatest Shakespearean actresses of her generation. Her farewell performance, as Cleopatra, had received considerable acclaim – though not as much as the actress in the production they had seen tonight.

"Frankly, darling, I didn't think she was a patch on you," remarked Bill as he swung the car into the long drive after their two-hour journey home, the headlights carving swathes of scarlet berries out of the dark shrubberies of laurel and pyracantha.

"It *was* a good production, though," she replied grudgingly. "Thanks for taking me."

Vanessa hadn't quitted the stage willingly. Health problems had taken their toll and her doctor had given her dire warnings. Her colleagues had been very generous: they had presented her with a small-scale model of the throne in which she had spoken Cleopatra's glorious dying words, hand-crafted by the production's designer, Klaus Bremmer, and coated with a veneer of gold. It meant far more to her than its monetary value; in it was embodied her immortality as an actress. Sometimes she wished – but that was nonsense; she couldn't go back.

While Bill was putting the car away, Vanessa let herself into the house, looking forward to a mug of cocoa before bed. She went into the lounge to close the curtains and switched on the electric light. At first, she didn't realise what had happened: the half-emptied room seemed to plunge her into a puzzling dream. Then it came to her in a belated flash: they'd been robbed. The television and video were gone, along with the hi-fi and Bill's new-fangled laptop computer; also the coffee table, the pictures, the table lamps, and Vanessa's prized collection of cut glass.

Calling for her husband, she rushed upstairs to their bedroom. Gone were her jewel box, the money she kept at the back of the second drawer in her dressing table – and the precious golden throne, abducted from its honoured position on the cabinet adjacent to her side of the bed.

By now, Bill was at her side. He put his arm round her. "Don't worry," he said. "It might have been worse; they could have wrecked the place, as well as taking our stuff. In any case, it's all insured."

"That's not the point," she snapped, not yet ready to be comforted by his infuriating condescension.

They were too tired that night to compile a detailed inventory of what was missing, or to face the police, so they decided to put it off till the following day. As they sat up in bed with their cocoa – the thieves had at least left the electric kettle, though the microwave had gone – Vanessa was leafing idly through the theatre programme, which she always saved until after the show. Bill was relieved that she had apparently calmed down, until she suddenly let out a cry.

"I knew it," she said.

"What?" murmured Bill, looking up from his book.

"The production tonight – it was designed by Klaus. Look." She handed him the programme. "It was different from the one he did for us of course – except for the throne. I didn't really take it in while we were watching – I suppose I was so involved in the magic of the play – but that throne was identical to the one Klaus designed for *my* performance as Cleopatra."

Vanessa sounded rather hurt, and as she turned involuntarily to the side of the bed, where her miniature replica of the throne should have been, she remembered with a tearful spasm that it was no longer there.

"Klaus obviously felt he couldn't improve on it," said Bill, a hint of sarcasm sharpening his voice. "Come to think of it, I've heard he does that – it's a quirk of his. Every show he designs has to incorporate a feature he's used before, though not necessarily in the same play. I suppose he had fun creating a different design around the same climactic piece of furniture."

Vanessa wondered briefly about the rather contemptuous tone of Bill's remarks, until she recalled that there had once been some awkwardness between him and Klaus. Silently contemplating the irony of the fact that Vanessa's memento of *Antony and Cleopatra* had been stolen while its scaled-up avatar was on stage in front of their eyes, they finished their cocoa.

"I'm going to get it back," said Vanessa with sudden animation, and Bill's heart stopped. For a moment he thought she was referring to the thing that he dreaded most and had worked so hard to discourage. He gave a wry laugh as he realised she just meant the stolen throne.

"What's funny?" she said.

Emma and Colin were determined that their official flat-warming party would be a success. Now that they were solvent again, they were full of confidence about their lives. Colin had two or three job interviews in the offing including, to his secret pleasure, one in the theatre's armoury, while Emma had been promoted to the post of Assistant Box-Office Manager. Their luck had changed, and they wanted to share it with their friends.

Their apartment was in a rather run-down area, well away from the tourist-thronged, picturesque, town-centre streets with their half-timbered quaintness. Despite this, they had determined to turn their home into an island of elegance in an ocean of concrete, graffiti and broken lifts, like a stylish Noël Coward stage-set in a shabby provincial theatre. Colin detested their surroundings, but he consoled himself by calling their flat "The Penthouse", since it was on the top floor of the block, with a panoramic view over the rooftops towards the theatre and the river. Emma soon learned not to laugh when he referred to it as such.

Despite Emma's job, they weren't really theatre people. They never went to the shows, except when the company let its hair down and did a musical or something, and their friends were not drawn from among the actors or directors. They knew one or two of the backstage staff, but only through the local football team for which Colin regularly played; he was an effective goalie, famous for his impulsive flying saves. Emma would have been astonished to discover that Colin had once harboured ambitions to be an actor, so dismissive was he of the town's inbred theatrical culture. Nevertheless, he had invited three or four of his teammates, members of the theatre's stage crew, to the party; they were working on that evening's performance of *Antony and Cleopatra*, so wouldn't be arriving till later.

As Emma looked round the smart flat, swirling with smoke and music and loud conversation and laughter, she could almost forget that they had been reduced to criminal activity to enable them to create this fashionable oasis in a desert of urban decay. Colin had tried to convince her they should repeat the scheme, but she had been sceptical.

"It can only be a one-off," she insisted.

"I don't see why."

"Think. One robbery while the victims are at the theatre means nothing. Another robbery while the victims are at the same theatre is going to look a bit suspicious."

"Not if we pick someone from a completely different part of the country. Nobody'll ever put two and two together."

"Don't you believe it. Everything's cross-referenced on some police computer network these days. No, Col, this was strictly unique. Besides, we don't need the money now. We've done what we set out to; let's leave it at that and thank God no-one's going to find out."

Colin had acquiesced, reluctantly. Emma had no idea he was nurturing visions of making enough money to move away from the area completely. What was the use of a fancy apartment if, to get to it, you had to drive through soulless estates and fight your way through filth and stink up vandalised concrete stairways? How would that show his family that he was actually worth something?

Though Emma was ignorant of Colin's longing for a better environment, her reverie reminded her of their increasingly frequent disagreements. He could be wilful, difficult, and she wondered how well she really knew him. She was frequently surprised by little things he let slip, and sometimes found herself questioning whether she had made the right choice. She often wondered about his family; he rarely mentioned them, but she sensed anger and resentment beneath his dismissive responses to her occasional inquiries.

Her thoughts were interrupted by the arrival of more guests, members of the *Antony and Cleopatra* stage crew who had just finished work on the show. They arrived laden with cans and bottles, anxious to make up for lost partying time and afraid the booze might be running out. Jack Lucas, the Deputy Stage Manager, was particularly effusive.

"Hello darling," he greeted Emma. "Here we are bearing gifts. 'Give me a bottle. Fill up my glass. I have immortal longings in me.' "

His misquotation was totally lost on Emma. As far as she was concerned, Jack was just flirting with her as he always did. Nevertheless, she couldn't prevent an embarrassing pink flush from rising to her cheeks as she became aware that he was studying her intently. He smiled, pursed his lips in a mock kiss, winked at her, and turned away into the braying crowd of increasingly inebriated guests.

Emma felt confused and disorientated. She had drunk too much red wine and eaten too few party snacks. Afraid she was about to pass out, she made her way to her and Colin's bedroom, where she sat heavily on the edge of the bed, sinking into the duvet's soft white folds. She had always liked Jack, but it had never occurred to her till now that he might fancy her. She shivered, and found herself unable to hold on to her thoughts.

Jack waited about ten minutes before he followed her to the bedroom. She didn't notice him until he had slipped into the room and quietly closed the door. Again, she found herself blushing like an infatuated teenager.

"Nice room," he said. "Are you OK?" He sounded concerned, sympathetic.

"I feel terrible," she muttered, trying to shake herself back into a state of alertness, aware of conflicting impulses tugging at her brain and body.

"You should keep drinking," Jack said, finishing off his red wine. "It's like stitch: if you keep running, it goes away. Where's your glass?"

He refilled his own glass, a surprisingly expensive-looking cut-glass goblet, from the bottle clutched in his left hand, and glanced round the room looking for hers. Something on the chest of drawers caught his eye. He went over and examined it, his forehead creased by a puzzled frown.

"When did you have this made?"

She looked up to see him fingering the model throne they had kept from the robbery. Colin had wanted to sell it to an antiques dealer they knew, but Emma guessed correctly that it was unusual enough to be easily traceable. In any case, it probably wasn't worth much.

"Picked it up at an auction," she said quickly, vaguely.

"It's identical," he went on. "What's it made of?"

"I don't know – brass, I suppose. Identical to what?" she added. Her dizziness had passed, and she felt suddenly wary.

"You must have seen it: Cleopatra's throne in the show." He turned it over in his hands. This is more than just brass, he thought.

"We haven't been to see it," said Emma, rather shamefacedly. "Haven't got round to it yet." She was too embarrassed to admit that she found Shakespeare boring and incomprehensible, though, to her surprise, Colin occasionally suggested they should give it a go.

"You should," Jack went on. "It's a bloody fantastic production." Then, "Absolutely bloody identical," he repeated, clearly fascinated by the throne.

"It can't be exactly the same. Anyway, a throne's a throne, isn't it? They all look alike." She was aware that her tone was becoming nervously aggressive.

Jack's voice had by now lost its quality of genial, mocking humour.

"Listen darling," he said quietly. "I've been humping this bloody throne, full-sized version, on and off stage at the end of that play three or four nights a week for four months – including tonight. I know every line, every angle, every squiggle of every fucking decoration. This is it." So saying, he plonked the object with finality back on the chest of drawers.

"Interesting coincidence," muttered Emma, which was actually what she believed, though the conversation had deeply unsettled her. Feeling the need to divert attention from the stolen throne and her guilty discomfort, she took the obvious course by turning the key in the door, switching her tone from aggression to seduction, and offering her guest what he had evidently followed her into the room for.

Vanessa Prior seemed to her husband to have taken the robbery as a personal insult. Weeks had passed and she still couldn't forget it. The insurance company hadn't paid up yet, but Bill and Vanessa had already replaced most of the stuff that had been taken. The golden throne, of course, was irreplaceable. Secretly, though, Bill couldn't help feeling glad that it had gone; that it no longer stood there, night after night, on her bedside cabinet – a constant reminder.

The police hadn't been much help. They suggested the burglary had either been opportunistic, or the work of someone who knew the Priors would be out that evening. They held out little hope of getting any of the stuff back and even less of catching the thieves. "Who knew you were going to the theatre?" That's what they kept asking. Their next-door neighbours; one or two of Bill's academic colleagues; their son and his wife. All these people had been subjected to humiliating interrogation by the police, for which Vanessa felt uncomfortable and guilty. And yet, if it were an opportunist, he – or she – must have been incredibly lucky. Finding the house empty, how did the thief know they wouldn't be returning straight away? According to the stereotypically ineffective police sergeant, most burglars were willing to take this risk, frequently going armed in case they were disturbed at their work.

"Shall I make a cup of tea?" said Bill, interrupting her thoughts. It was Sunday afternoon and the winter darkness was already beginning to invade the house. Bill felt he couldn't take much more of his wife's silent brooding. For weeks he'd been trying his best to cheer her up, to be sympathetic and understanding, to make light of their experience. She ought to have snapped out of it by now.

She didn't answer. She was sitting in the gathering gloom, staring out at the ever-darkening outlines of the trees, listening to the last coarse croaking of the rooks and the odd blackbird squawking urgently as it flew low across the lawn before finding somewhere to roost. Bill clenched his teeth and went to the kitchen to put the kettle on, silently cursing the burglars for stealing his marriage – the marriage he'd had to work so hard to protect all those years ago.

In the darkness of her chair, facing the window, Vanessa sent her mind back along the tracks of memory to her last performance.

> The barge she sat in, like a burnished throne
> Burned on the water.

Not her lines, but the start of Enobarbus's glorious encomium on Cleopatra, for the benefit of the Roman lords. A burnished throne. Her throne.

> Give me my robe. Put on my crown. I have
> Immortal longings in me. Now no more
> The juice of Egypt's grape shall moist this lip.
> Yare, yare, good Iras, quick – methinks I hear
> Antony call. I see him rouse himself
> To praise my noble act. I hear him mock
> The luck of Caesar, which the gods give men
> To excuse their after wrath. Husband, I come.

Husband?

Why had she retired? Her health problems hadn't been that bad; she could at least have taken the odd film role. And now she felt stronger than ever. Yet Bill would brusquely dismiss any half-spoken suggestion of her making a comeback, though he was not averse to telling her at every available opportunity how talented she had been. Had been? Why should she accept that? She had years to live – and a range of Shakespearean parts she hadn't yet tackled. Mad Queen Margaret in *Richard III*, the Countess in *All's Well that Ends Well*, Volumnia in *Coriolanus*, maybe the Nurse in *Romeo and Juliet*. She wanted to do them. Surely Bill couldn't stop her now. Once, long ago, his laughably unfounded suspicions had caused some embarrassment; now he was loving, attentive, considerate – as long as she lived her life according to his implicit rules. She knew the real, unspoken cause of his jealousy: she was, in truth, in love with the theatre – a glittering, expressive fantasy world that could never compete with his dusty old books, his dry lectures, his uninspiring students and embittered colleagues. She had given in and bowed to his demands a decade ago, and for both of them her "ill-health" had provided a convenient excuse, so that the real reason for her retirement need never be voiced between them.

Thinking of the theatre, an idea struck her, projected out of nowhere. When Bill returned with her cup of tea and a plate of her favourite biscuits, he found his wife transformed, if not transfigured. There was a suppressed excitement about her. He put the light on, which had the effect of pushing the deepening shadows out of the room to add to the darkness outside, and saw that her face was flushed. He hoped she wasn't going to be ill. He handed her her tea and she took a biscuit.

"Are you all right?"

"Yes. Bill – "

"What?"

"You know the police kept asking us who knew we were going to the theatre."

"Yes."

"Well, the theatre box office knew."

"Oh come on, Vanessa. Look, it was an opportunist burglar, like the police said. I just wish you'd forget the whole thing and leave it to them."

"Mm." She sipped her tea. "You're probably right."

But Bill knew that, despite her words, she wasn't going to leave this alone. He could tell from the brightness of her eyes, the tension in her body, the delicate rattle of the china cup in its saucer, the force with which she crunched her biscuit, sending a chunk vaulting into her teacup. His heart sank. He knew the signs: this heightened state was just how she used to be immediately before a performance. Perhaps he'd been right to read her determination as being about more than just the wretched bloody throne. His face creased into a forced smile as, inside, he damned the burglars to hell for stirring up feelings in his wife that he knew he was no longer capable of suppressing.

The theatre's end-of-season party was a big event. Everybody came. Directors whose shows had been running for months flew back from opening their latest multi-million-dollar musicals in Tokyo or New York or Adelaide. Designers who'd condemned armies of stagehands to manipulating, night after night, the impossible complications of their intricate scenic effects, breezed in from their latest non-theatrical exhibitions. Actors who'd managed to avoid being in the same productions as each other met to exchange gossip. Even the Artistic Director, whom most members of the company claimed never to have seen in the flesh, swanned around paternally, treating everybody as his closest personal friends, promising actors wonderful roles in future seasons – roles they'd never hear anything further about, but for which they'd live in hope, putting off importunate agents trying to get them to accept less prestigious but more definite offers.

Emma wasn't at the party, despite her promotion. Ever since the flat-warming, she'd been wary of meeting Jack Lucas again. Intrigued by his comments about the throne, she'd taken it into work with her one day and sneaked it backstage while the crew were on their lunch break. It wasn't difficult to find Cleopatra's full-sized throne stored in the wings after the previous night's performance, and she was able to compare the two at her leisure. Jack was right: the design was identical. It couldn't possibly be a coincidence, and the whole thing made Emma feel distinctly ill-at-ease.

Amidst the swirl of increasingly merry partygoers, Jack Lucas carved a path to the exotic figure of Klaus Bremmer, the *Antony and Cleopatra* designer. With his mustard-yellow cravat and blackberry waistcoat he couldn't be missed – or mistaken for anyone else. They hadn't spoken since the first-night party, but they greeted each other like old friends. Klaus always made a particular point of getting to know the crew who'd be working on his sets, and claimed to prefer the company of backstage staff to actors, who, he said, were far too precious about their work.

"I came across something recently," began Jack, "that I thought you might be interested in."

"Oh? And what might that have been, dear boy?"

"A miniature replica of your throne."

"My throne?"

"Cleo's throne. About six inches high, gold-plated, identical in every other respect."

Klaus furrowed his brow in puzzlement.

"Oh. And where was this?"

"At a party. D'you know that girl who works in the box-office – Emma something?" Jack knew her name perfectly well, but preferred to pretend he didn't.

"I've probably seen her," Klaus replied.

"It's hers. Got it at an auction, she says."

"How interesting, dear boy. Coincidence, of course. It can't be identical to the real thing – that, I assure you, is unique."

"I'm telling you it is. I've been humping that bloody throne around for months. I know every bit of scroll and leaf and grape and serpent and cupid on it. It's the same."

67

"If you say so."

"Didn't you tell me you'd used that design before? Last time you did *Antony*?"

"Yes – years ago. And strangely enough I did make a small replica of it – a retirement present for the incomparable Vanessa Prior. Even though I say so myself, she treasures it above all else. She wouldn't have put it up for auction."

"Maybe she was strapped for cash."

"No no no no no. She would sell every stitch of clothing from her body before parting with that throne. She never wanted to give up the stage, you see. Her husband and her doctor got together and conspired to bully her. She clings to that memento as proof that she was, once, a great actress." Klaus knocked back the dregs of his virulent green cocktail. "It wasn't a surprise present: she begged me to make it for her. She identified herself so strongly with Cleopatra, you see." He paused, remembering. "She was magnificent."

Jack hardly knew what to say in response to Klaus's extravagant praise of this woman who had retired from the theatre long before he himself had first tasted its magic.

"Who was her Antony?" he asked lamely.

Klaus laughed, put down his glass and lit a cigar.

"Sadly, not I, dear boy, you can rest assured," he said, deliberately misunderstanding. "Not her husband either." He reflected for a moment. "Too possessive. Easily jealous – even of me, would you believe? No; the stage was her Antony. A passionate affair that ended far too soon."

At this point, Klaus felt a hand on his shoulder and turned to find the small, darkly dressed figure of the Artistic Director, exuding bonhomie.

"Klaus, how are you? How are you fixed for next winter? I'm planning a new production of *Titus* and I'd love you to do the designs. It'll be the first time we've done a full-scale production of it for twenty years. I'm very excited about it..."

Klaus made polite noises, guessing that the world would never see this particular production of *Titus Andronicus*, Shakespeare's notorious gore-fest, and that he wouldn't encounter the Artistic Director again till next year's end-of-season party, when he'd probably be offered the design of something equally obscure like *Timon of Athens* or *The Two Noble Kinsmen*. He was intrigued by what Jack had told him and, impossible as it seemed, was convinced that the model throne must be the one he had made for Vanessa. He wouldn't be able to rest until he found out how it had come to be in the possession of this box-office woman. He turned to ask Jack where she lived, but Jack had melted into the smoke and noise of the party, his own questions about the golden throne still unanswered.

Even though the season was over, the theatre remained open for visiting companies, and the box office continued to do a brisk trade. Jack had a week's break before he was off with the company for a two-month residency in the north-east, prior to the transfer of all the productions, including *Antony and Cleopatra*, to London. Before he went, he was determined to solve the mystery of the golden throne. It had become one of those nagging irritations at the back of his mind, pushing its way into his thoughts at inconvenient moments. The throne even featured in his dreams, in every conceivable size, as a burden to be carted on and off stage in any play he happened to be working on, from *Hamlet* to *The Importance of Being*

Earnest, including a surreal dream-play that had half haunted his restless sleeping patterns for years. In its present manifestation, this dream featured Hercule Poirot investigating the killing of Coleridge's albatross, or sometimes Flaubert's parrot, in a student room at Oxford – a mystical city of bicycles and rickshaws situated somewhere on the plains of northern India. The golden throne had insinuated itself into this tortuous plot as the murder weapon, but the damned thing kept getting lost in the wings so that Jack couldn't set it on stage in the first act, much to the fury of actors and director. He always woke from variations on this dream drenched in sweat, his heart beating in time to the over-amplified ticking of his alarm clock.

Jack decided that this time he would tackle Colin about the throne. He knew from his soccer mates that Colin was out of work again after an unfortunate incident at the theatre armoury, and it was Monday lunchtime as Jack made his way across the dreary estate towards the dilapidated block of flats. Seeing it for the first time in daylight, he realised just how run-down and depressing it was, and he was surprised that Colin and Emma had not ploughed their limited finances into finding somewhere else, rather than merely doing up their flat as if it were a stylish penthouse apartment. It was one of those winter days which is simultaneously bright and dull, the sky stretched taut and white across the bleak vista of concrete, tarmac, brick, mud and gusting clumps of litter. Every so often, a gaunt and spiky tree raised its bare branches as if appealing for a transfer to some more amenable location.

When Jack arrived at the flat, he got the impression that Colin – unshaven, bleary-eyed and surly – had only just got up. He began to feel uncomfortable and couldn't think of an easy way to broach the subject of the golden throne. He'd always got on OK with Colin, despite the evident chip on his shoulder, but now he felt awkward; his prepared excuse of wanting to chat about the football team seemed weak and unconvincing.

"I was about to make a coffee," Colin said ungraciously. "D'you want one?"

"Please."

They exchanged idle chatter over the unpleasantly bitter instant coffee. Jack said he'd been wondering if Colin would be interested in alternative positions in the team, rather than being in goal all the time; perhaps he could take over in midfield while Jack was away with the theatre company up north, and see how he got on. Colin was at first non-committal; then he grudgingly agreed to give it a try. But he was happy in goal, and knew he was good. He particularly enjoyed the sense of performance he got from his dramatic saves – the feeling that, for once, all attention was focused on him.

The conversation petered out. Finishing his coffee with a barely concealed grimace, Jack finally plunged in, as if he were just making casual conversation.

"Emma was showing me that throne thing when I was here before," he said. "I didn't say anything to her, but I reckon it's a lot more valuable than she thinks."

"Oh yeh?" A sharp note of suspicion had crept into Colin's voice.

"Yes. She said you picked it up at an auction."

"That's right."

"Well, I can't imagine… I mean, I reckon it's not just brass. Can I have another look at it? I think you may have something that's worth a fair bit."

"Sure, I'll get it. It's in our bedroom," he added pointedly.

As Colin headed for the bedroom, Jack felt a surge of guilt. He'd been so bound up with thoughts of the golden throne that until now he'd virtually forgotten his one-night stand with Emma at the party. Did Colin know? Or had his suspicions only just been aroused, wondering how Jack had got to see the thing?

Colin returned with the throne. Jack held out his hand to take it, but Colin unexpectedly snatched it back, studying it with a look of intense malevolence.

"Can I see it?" Jack asked, surprised.

"Sure you can see it," Colin replied, switching his expression to a shifty half-smile with the instinctive timing of a practised actor. "But first you can tell me about you and Emma…"

The morning sun streamed through the glass-fronted entrance lobby of the theatre, carrying no warmth from the frosty air outside. Vanessa Prior pushed open one of the heavy doors into the long, tall, art-deco foyer. She was muffled up in a heavy coat, scarf and gloves, and her face was pale. Her bright eyes and firm stride, however, spoke of determination. The box office was not particularly busy, with just two or three people in the queue. She took her place and glanced around at the displays of production photos and posters, including a huge blow-up of the recent Cleopatra, clutching the asp to her breast, her golden throne just visible behind her shoulders – *my* throne, thought Vanessa automatically. It still rankled that Klaus Bremmer had bestowed what was rightfully hers on another woman – the woman who had usurped her own position at the head of this company. It made her angry to feel that she herself was long-forgotten, a mere footnote in theatrical history.

It was one of those moments when coincidence takes on a tinge of fatal inevitability. No sooner had Klaus come into her thoughts than the man himself appeared in front of her, moving away from the box office window clutching a scrap of paper which he was reading over to himself. He looked up and stared blankly into her eyes for a moment before mutual recognition took effect and they greeted each other in warm surprise, hugging and kissing with genuine affection. Vanessa's seething resentment had evaporated in an instant, and she willingly accepted Klaus's offer of a hot drink in the theatre's café; she could pursue her inquiries at the box office later.

It didn't take more than ten minutes, over lukewarm cappuccinos, for them to discover they were on the same mission, and they had soon shared everything they knew. Klaus had been hoping to talk directly to Emma at the box office, but she had left about half an hour before, feeling unwell. He flourished her address, scrawled reluctantly by the box-office assistant on a torn flyer. Klaus and Vanessa knew the most sensible course would be to go straight to the police, but both were so caught up in the chase that they were reluctant to abandon it now. They managed to convince themselves that a visit to Emma's flat could do no harm; maybe when she realised she'd been found out, she'd agree to go with them to the police station.

"To be honest, if she returns the throne I'm happy to leave it at that," said Vanessa. "I couldn't care less about the rest of the stuff, nor whether she ends up in prison."

"Let's go, then."

As Vanessa stood up and began to button her coat, she was overcome by a moment's doubt and a nagging feeling of hopelessness. Why did she worship that throne so much? It symbolised the end of her acting career, but she was still only in her sixties. Why shouldn't she be acting still? The bout of ill-health that had precipitated her retirement had more-or-less cleared itself up, but somehow she'd never seriously considered going back on the stage. She knew that Bill would stop her; he'd always been jealous – even of Klaus once, she recalled with a smile. The fact that Klaus was self-evidently gay had barely convinced him that there was nothing going on between them.

She wondered again about venturing into films. She'd done one or two, of course, in her younger days, but the stage had always been her thing. Yet look at all those great theatre actors who'd had a renaissance through film work in their seventies: Olivier, Richardson, Gielgud, Peggy Ashcroft. Her heart was fluttering in excitement as she and Klaus walked back arm in arm through the foyer, amidst the production photos, publicity leaflets, posters and playtexts, breathing in the rich scent, the magical essence of the theatre. As they passed through the great glass doors into the cold sunlight, neither of them saw Bill, who had been tracking his wife's movements all day, hunched, muffled and tense with anger, lurking under the stark, bare branches of the spreading beech tree that stood silhouetted against the glittering surface of the river.

Colin and Emma's flat was situated in unknown territory for Klaus and Vanessa. Neither of them could have imagined that such bleak architectural uniformity existed in the same town as the world-famous theatre, which stood in a kind of romantic limbo of parks and riverside gardens; of noble Georgian facades rubbing shoulders with olde-worlde relics of Shakespeare's England. Even the modern developments in the town centre –

the shopping arcades in chrome and glass with their cupolas and marble stairways and vast hothouse plants and shop signs in shades of pink, turquoise and cream – seemed to exude an air of hygienic, middle-class comfort, to which these blocks of square, red-bricked, flat-roofed monstrosities were frighteningly alien.

The lifts were not working, forcing them to use the barren, stinking, concrete stairs. Their footsteps echoed strangely in the hollow stairwell, almost as if there were three of them trudging laboriously up towards the top floor. Amongst the depressing graffiti scrawled and sprayed on the walls, one piece caught their eye, proclaiming "SHAKESPEARE IS SHIT". Maybe so, thought Klaus, but at least his name is alliteratively alive in this drab suburb of his home town, even at the dead end of the twentieth century.

They heard the voices as they rounded the turn in the final flight of stairs: weeping and shouting and recrimination, reminiscent of a Mafia movie set in the urban wastelands of Naples. The door to the flat was ajar and the voices clarified themselves into those of a woman, pleading, sobbing, wailing; and a man, shouting, accusing, threatening.

"You'll get the same, you bitch, if you don't get out of here," Colin was screaming.

Emma was backed up against the open door, half cowering, half ready to pounce or to run. She shouted back at him, her voice convulsed with sobs.

"Put it down, Col. For God's sake, let me phone a doctor. He'll die if somebody doesn't see to him soon."

The picture framed in the doorway as Klaus and Vanessa came within sight of it was both melodramatic and terrifying: it would not have been out of place in a production of *Titus Andronicus*. Colin's hand, clutching the golden throne, was lifted threateningly towards Emma, and Vanessa could see that it was glistening with fast-congealing blood. Further back in the room lay the body of a man, his skull smashed in, hands still twitching feebly, moaning in uncomprehending agony. Klaus recognised him straight away as Jack Lucas.

Vanessa felt faint. Klaus grabbed her arm and whispered fiercely in her ear, all his carefully composed theatrical camp dissipated in an instant. "Find a phone somewhere, for Christ's sake. Get an ambulance, and the police. Go on – move," he added, as she stood frozen in horror. He shoved her roughly towards the stairs while he considered what to do. He hadn't been seen yet, and stepped back instinctively into the hard-edged shadows thrown on to the concrete walls by the bright winter sunshine. Somehow he had to stop this guy, whoever he was, from attacking Emma, but how? He didn't want to get himself hurt, but he had to act quickly. He cursed the fact that he'd decided against buying one of those new cellphones, and hoped Vanessa would find a phone box soon, or convince one of the neighbours to help. Breathing deeply, he stepped forward, deliberately resuming his usual mannerisms.

"Put that down, dear boy – the police are on their way. Emma, come over here."

Colin stared at him, baffled but furious.

"Who the fuck are you?" he demanded.

Emma took the opportunity of his change of focus to back out of the door and run towards Klaus, also wondering who he was but vaguely aware that she'd seen him once or twice around the theatre.

"Never mind who I am. Just put that – object – down, eh?"

Vanessa appeared behind them at the top of the stairs. She put out her hand and pulled Emma towards her. "It's all right," she whispered, "I've phoned for an ambulance and the police are on their way."

As she turned to look at Colin, her glance took in a glittering array of her own cut glass, artfully arranged on a teak display cabinet. But it was the sight of the blood-smeared throne that aroused her anger.

"I believe that belongs to me," she said, striding forward, miraculously transformed into a figure of regal authority. "Hand it to me, please." Her voice was crisp, commanding. Instinctively, effortlessly, she had activated the charisma that belongs only to great actors, so that all attention was focused on her alone. Klaus was thrilled – this was her Lady Macbeth, her Rosalind, her Cleopatra.

> Husband, I come.
> Now to that name my courage prove my title.
> I am fire and air; my other elements
> I give to baser life.

Sensing that Colin was calculating whether or not to make a dash for freedom, Vanessa knew she had to capture his attention as she would that of a restless audience. Stillness and control were at the centre of the power she wielded. Though the lines she spoke were banal, she instinctively framed them as two perfect iambic pentameters, infusing them with all her command of vocal technique and accompanying them with a small, impatient gesture of her outstretched hand.

"Don't be a fool: there's nowhere you can run. You stole that throne from me; I want it back."

Completely under her spell, Colin slowly handed her the throne. She grasped it firmly, but otherwise didn't move. Colin knew that he couldn't possibly match this woman's extraordinary performance. Perhaps his family had been right: how had he ever imagined he could be a successful actor? With an immense mental and physical effort, he managed to break free from the spell she had cast. He turned back into the flat and ran to the window. Klaus and Emma raced past Vanessa – who remained immobile, oblivious of the sticky, congealing blood smeared on her fingers.

Colin was outside now, on the tiny, concrete balcony of his laughably unconvincing penthouse suite. Standing there for a moment, he was aware of a vast desert of rooftops, bleak under the blank whiteness of the taut winter sky, stretching around him in all directions. He paused briefly, reflecting just how much he had come to hate this view. But his family would have to acknowledge now that he had at least existed, despite his utter failure to achieve the aspirations they had so derided. Climbing over the rusty metal railings, he launched himself into space as if he were executing one of his famous flying saves. Somewhere down below, the sirens of an ambulance and two police cars blared vainly in the cold air.

Klaus took hold of Emma and pushed her forcefully back into the flat before she could look down to where Colin had fallen. Vanessa still stood there, limp and exhausted yet glowing with expended energy, her eyes bright and sharp. Looking at the bloodied golden throne gripped tightly in her hand, Klaus knew that the media would soon be heralding the return of a great actress to the British stage. Pressed into the shadows on the bleak landing of the apartment block, Bill knew it too; knew that he had lost her forever. Outside, far away across the sad, grey townscape, the flag on the roof of the theatre fluttered jauntily in the cool winter breeze.

Forever

Don't look round. You won't see me, even though I'm right behind you in the darkness. I always keep myself well hidden, even when I'm so close you can feel my breath on the back of your neck. You know I'm here; I can tell from the way you're walking just that bit faster, your heavy shoes clattering in suppressed panic on the uneven paving stones. Take care you don't trip.

I've thought about this for a long time. Not that there is Time in the all-encompassing vapours of my non-existence, yet I still think in terms of hours and minutes, still cling to the illusion of regular, finite markers culminating in the orgasmic release of finality. For me there is no finality; no ending, no conclusion, no closure. I am a continual openness, ever-present, present forever. And I am breathing down your neck.

For you there will be an ending, to this phase at least, before your forever begins. I am the one who will bring it about, because I must. If you knew this, you'd ask me why, but you ought to know the answer. All it needs is for you to remember what you did. Perhaps you do; perhaps you think of it constantly as you go about your daily business, scratching pointlessly amidst the trivial minutiae of your existence. Realistically, though, it doesn't matter whether you remember or not. I remember, and that's enough.

You're relieved to be home, I can tell. You close the door behind you with unnecessary force and immediately switch on the light. You think the winter darkness is now firmly excluded from your domestic refuge, but unknowingly you've let me in. You seem tired and anxious. For the moment, that's good enough for me. It's evidence, perhaps. I watch intently as you throw your jacket over the newel post at the bottom of the stairs, and note the slight wince of discomfort as you take off your shoes and toss them carelessly aside. The stairs; do you remember? You consider the time – a meaningless concept, as you'll discover soon enough. Nine-thirty on a dreary January evening. Too early for bed, perhaps, but there's no point in staying up just for the sake of it, is there? You sort out your medication, wearied by the pointlessness of the nightly routine: potions and powders and tablets that probably do nothing, yet you're afraid to stop taking them. What would happen if you did? I'll leave you for a while; I can tell you're in no mood to face up to my unanswerable questions. But I'll be back.

*

You're looking older. I suppose time has passed, for you if not for me. How long? Five years? Ten? Nothing but an eye-blink. But I need to stay with you now, make sure I haven't missed you altogether next time I'm here. It has to be me, you see. I can't risk you falling into forever through mere decay.

I see that it's summer now. The leaves hang heavy on the sweating trees, clumped threateningly in the warm darkness of your garden. Our garden. You stand in the humid throb of the thick air, letting the bats flit in their jagged spirals round your head. Since before, your hair has grown thin and straggly. You should cut it, crop it close to your flaking scalp. As it is, it looks ridiculous. I wouldn't have let you get away with it.

Can you sense me, as you did last time? Do you read my thoughts as you once did; as you always used to think you could? You said it was romantic that you felt so in tune with me. I acquiesced, not telling you that you invariably got it wrong. I let you impose your wishes on me, let you think it was what I wanted, but it wasn't. As the man, you assumed dominance, omniscience, and I let you. It seemed easier. It *was* easier.

I see you're supporting your weight on a stick, one of those adjustable aluminium and plastic ones you get from social services. Are you that old already? Is it the same one I had, when I was still there? After the stairs? Did you keep it out of sentimentality, or guilt, or just think it might come in useful some day? That, I guess. What else did you keep, after you put me away? There wasn't much, if you think about it. Photographs, maybe. Some of my clothes, perhaps. My favourite mug. I suppose you must have found my diaries. Serves you right.

You're startled when an owl hoots, and look round nervously. Yes, I'm here. Even in the dark, I can see that your face is lined with deep ruts and creases. And you obviously haven't shaved for days. Why's that? Before, you'd never have let yourself go. Is it because of me? Your eyes are hollow, frightened. I almost want to ask you what's wrong – but don't think I'm feeling sorry for you. Just curious.

Stepping back into the house through the wide-open patio doors, you trip, but the stick supports you. Before you have managed to slide the doors closed, I'm in. You stand in the dense gloom for a moment, recovering your equilibrium. You look so old. Of course, you're older than I ever was. I would have grown older, in this house, if you'd let me. It was what I wanted, and you knew that. But you decided otherwise. So many excuses; I couldn't argue, couldn't fight back. When they came, you weren't there. You couldn't face seeing it happen, this thing you'd set in motion. As always, you pretended to know instinctively it was what I wanted. Not romantic any more, was it?

You cough, a thin, guttural, racking cough that goes on for longer than is healthy. You stumble through to the kitchen and get yourself a glass of water. The kitchen light comes on automatically – a phenomenon new to me. The array of jars and bottles and packets on the work surface has grown; how much medication are they making you take? For the first time, I notice something hanging round your neck – a grey, plastic device with a red button. Are you really that old, that ill? I need to work quickly. A confrontation at the top of the stairs, perhaps. Poetic justice.

But I'm beginning to fade, in the electric light's punishing glare. I can't always determine my coming or going. I have no more control now than I ever did. I feel my presence dissolving. You swallow mouthful after mouthful of water, but still your coughing continues, reddening the rough skin of your unshaven cheeks. How old are you? Seventy-five? Eighty? I need to come back while you're still here. I must be the one.

*

Another eye-blink, and I'm back. The house creaks and groans in the violent gusting of an autumn gale. Leaves whirl through the wind's wet slap. The house stands dark and proud amid the hunched and shivering trees. It looks shut up, abandoned, and I realise you're not here. Don't tell me I'm too late.

Without you, I'm not sure I can get in. You have to invite me, even if you don't know you're doing it. But there must be a way – I need to find out what's happened, track you down, deliver you to your fate, if I still can. I've waited too long, no time at all and yet always, to share an ending with you, to craft you into my closure, before forever continues. I scan the house from all sides, hear something clattering in the wild gusts. It's an upstairs window, inexplicably left open, banging and rattling on its metal catch. A lucky oversight – or perhaps you knew I'd be coming, and this is your invitation.

I'm in. It's your bedroom. Our bedroom. Something tells me you're not long gone. Your smell still hangs in the air, and what's that behind it, subliminal? My favourite perfume. How can it have lingered for so long? Or did you keep it, the occasional spray of scent a reminder of me, of us – of your guilt? If I could frown, my brow would be creasing in puzzled reassessment of what happened. The bed is neatly made, the room bare and tidy. There's nothing else here for me.

Downstairs – down those stairs – things are much the same. It's as if your leaving was planned, carefully prepared so that the house wouldn't be left messy and troubled. My presence, unsurprisingly, fails to activate the kitchen light, which means I can stay longer. I don't need light to view this hazy remnant of a previous existence. I can see that, like the other rooms, the kitchen is clean and empty. Your medication is no longer ranged across the work surface, but there is something there – a piece of paper, perhaps. A note.

It's written on a single sheet of A4 in your familiar, sloping hand, shakier than it once was. It's addressed to me.

My love,

I know you'll come back. I hoped it would be while I was still here, and that this time I'd recognise your presence straight away, instead of only after you'd gone. When you first came, shortly after you'd left me, I thought it was just imagination, but when I sensed your love filling the house year after year, always on some anniversary or other, I knew you wanted to tell me something. Why didn't you? I would have asked you but, inexplicably, every time, the moment I knew you'd been there was the moment I knew you'd just gone. Always you left something residual, some trace of our love: a scent or a whisper, a parting touch on my shoulder, the taste of you on my tongue, the briefest glint of your eyes. So, although I went on hoping to catch you before you vanished, I decided to write it down.

My darling, you don't need to tell me; I know. Although at the end you couldn't speak, I chose the course you wanted – the only course possible. You once said you wanted to die at home, but by the end we both knew that was unrealistic. The stairs were a worry, in any case; I couldn't risk being in that position again. Your eyes told me you couldn't cope with seeing me struggle to look after you any longer. I know you would have felt ashamed to be a continuing burden, to be implicated in

*my own deterioration, to watch my love
turning perhaps to duty, then resentment,
even to hatred as I failed to alleviate your
suffering. I knew you wouldn't want me there
when the ambulance came to take you to the
hospice, but I'd got everything ready for your
journey, and also in your new room for your
arrival. Even though you couldn't thank me, I
know you wanted to, and that must have
made you feel you'd let me down. So I just
want you to know you're not to worry. As
always, you're forgiven.*

*Now I must go. I've been ill, you see.
But I wanted you to know you're still mine,
always and forever. I hope you are able to
read this.*

Your loving husband.

I stare at the paper, scarcely believing. He's done it again; the bastard's done it again.

Don't worry, I'll seek you out. If only I had complete control over my visits to this gloomy other-world. Perhaps there's a way, some rite of passage that hasn't yet been explained to me. You seem to think I've visited you often, and perhaps I have, without remembering. Unless it's just you again, getting it wrong as you always did. Perhaps my being the one to confront you, to send you on your endless journey, is a vain hope. Maybe instead I'll find you when you've passed, greet you with a smile in some shady, amorphous arrival-hall wherever it is I spend my intermittent periods of non-existence. As you reach out to me, bewildered, fresh in the realisation that you got it all wrong, all of it, all the time, how I shall relish the moment. Perhaps then it will all be worth it, even though I wasn't able to be the one to bring you here. Never mind. Welcome to forever.

Tidying Up

"Mum, don't put that there, I've just tidied up."

"Sorry, love, I'll move it in a minute. I'm whacked."

Huw's mother flopped down on the sofa next to the offending briefcase and the pile of papers she had tossed there. She kicked off her damp shoes and sank into the cushions her son had just plumped up and arranged neatly across the back, each balanced on one corner, turning the sofa into a panoramic three of diamonds. Matching cushions graced the two armchairs equally spaced on either side.

She closed her eyes. "Any chance of a cup of tea?" she said quietly.

Huw did not answer. He scanned his mother critically: the hair tumbling untidily round her face; the dark business suit, too crumpled to impress; the batch of papers scattered round what had recently been a shiny new briefcase, his present to her; the scuffed shoes, one overturned, next to her perspiring feet; the laddered tights. She always set out to work looking so smart, he thought; how did she get into such a state? Silently, he left the room, righting the upturned shoe as he went, to put the kettle on.

Later that evening, Huw was in his bedroom doing his homework when the doorbell rang. That would be his mother's latest boyfriend – Denis, was it? He clenched his teeth as he heard his mother let the visitor in and their voices retreated laughing into the lounge. Huw pulled his chair closer to his desk, making sure it remained at an exact ninety-degree angle, and finished colouring in the sea around the neat outline of Australia in his Geography book. It irritated him that Australia's shape wasn't more symmetrical; he felt much more at ease with the poise and predictability of geometrical diagrams. The real world was far too untidy.

A few minutes later, his mother appeared at the door. Huw deliberately kept his eyes on his work.

"Huw?" No response. "Denis and I are just popping out for an hour or so. Will you be all right by yourself?"

"Course I will," he muttered, still not looking up.

"There's some cold meat in the fridge if you want to make yourself a sandwich. Be careful when you cut it, though, I sharpened the knife the other day."

"OK."

"We shouldn't be late, but just go to bed when you're ready. Bye."

She moved over to him and stood uneasily behind his chair. She wanted to kiss him, but still he refused to look up at her.

"See you later, then."

"Mmm."

Awkwardly, embarrassed by the lack of warmth between them, she retreated gratefully from the room. As her footsteps padded down the stairs, Huw got up and closed the door after her – not slamming it, but shutting it loudly enough to be recognised as a protest. Then he went back to his desk, restored his chair to its required position, and continued his coastal crayoning round the even more distressing shape of New Zealand.

By nine o'clock the noise in the Golden Lion was, as usual, quite deafening. Alison and Denis had to shout at each other in order to communicate. Alison was drinking more than she usually did, heightening all her senses so that the crowd at the bar appeared larger than life, like characters out of a Dickens novel, their salient features exaggerated beyond reality: the landlord's bulbous red nose, that woman's frizzy hair, the luminously soapy complexion of the guy at the next table. Even Denis's features seemed sharper, unnatural, cartoon-like. She'd never noticed before how the crown of his head shone greasily beneath his thinning hair, nor how his eyebrows seemed to have a life of their own – soft, black caterpillars squirming across his forehead.

"I think you're worrying unduly," he was saying – shouting, rather. "Huw's only fourteen after all. He's bound to have been hit hard by his Dad leaving home."

"I know. It's just that…"

Alison couldn't really explain; Denis would think she was just being silly. She tried another tack.

"Have you been in his room?"

"No – why would I?"

"It's frightening. The bookshelves. He's got all his books grouped according to the colour of their spine – there's even a separate section for multicoloured ones – and then, would you believe, they're arranged in descending order of height within each group. He's never taken to the encyclopaedia I bought him at Christmas because it won't stand upright on any of his bloody shelves. He keeps it on his desk, right in the corner,

89

lined up exactly with the edge. Every time I go in there I feel it's a sort of reproach to me."

"That's just plain silly," Denis said, confirming her prediction of the attitude he'd take. "You should be glad you've got a kid who likes being tidy – most of them are a shambles. And it's great that he's got any books at all; at least he's not constantly glued to a computer screen."

"But with Huw it's almost obsessive," Alison insisted. "He makes his bed in the morning before I'm even up. He has to do the washing-up the instant we've finished eating. And now he's taken to doing the housework when he gets in from school – dusting, vacuuming, the lot."

"I really don't know what you're complaining about." Denis's cheeks looked oddly rubbery as his smile pushed into them on each side of his mouth. "Have another drink and forget about him for once."

"OK," she sighed. "I'll get them this time."

Alison jostled her way to the bar through the Dickensian caricatures with their jangling, reverberating voices and ordered two more drinks. Huw would hate it in here, she reflected, and found herself trying to remember what he'd been like before the divorce – but she couldn't fix an image of him in her mind. Pushing back a few strands of hair that were restricting her vision, she paid for the drinks and made her way dizzily back to their table through the disturbing unreality of the crush of swaying bodies.

Huw was woken up around midnight by the sound of Denis and his mother crashing back from the pub. They were talking very loudly and giggling a great deal, and he guessed from the noises that they were making themselves tea or coffee. He also heard the toaster popping up its jack-in-the-box cargo three or four times; he could imagine the crumbs lying around it, crisp fragments of blackened bread messing up the work surface that he had cleaned so thoroughly after having his own supper. By the time they came up to bed, they had managed to reduce their drunken jabbering to a stage whisper, broken by occasional giggles, but it was a long time before Huw could drift back into sleep. His mind throbbed with irritating visions of Denis, sharply gleaned from the minute observations of two or three meetings: the thin hair and shiny scalp; the podgy, plasticine cheeks and greasy complexion; the patronising smile of the single man unused to being with children. Denis always looked scruffy. He never wore a tie and all his jackets were shabby and threadbare, his shirt collars frayed and grubby, his trousers sagging and shapeless. And now, inevitably, he was staying the night for the first time with his mother – presumably after getting her drunk, which was easily done. Sleep came slowly to Huw as he continued listening to the faint, upsetting sounds from the adjoining room.

Although the next day was Saturday, Huw got up at his usual time of seven o'clock. The first thing he saw, at the foot of the stairs, was Denis's scuffed shoes lying askew where he had cast them off, not even bothering to undo the laces, when he and Alison had arrived back from the pub. Huw wrinkled his nose in disgust and manoeuvred the shoes into a neater arrangement with his foot. In the kitchen he was confronted by two unwashed coffee mugs, two dirty plates and some buttery, jam-smeared cutlery. The coffee jar had been left out with the lid off, as had the milk, its cream congealed to greasy streaks, reminding Huw of Denis's unpleasant scalp. The bread-board was lying at an inappropriate angle across the work surface and there were impertinent crumbs all over the place, including, as expected, a sprinkle of burnt ones around the toaster. It must have been Denis who'd cut the bread, because he'd used the carving-knife from the left-hand compartment of the second drawer instead of the bread knife from the middle section of the top drawer. The knife was still lying there. Huw had certainly put it away after he'd sliced the cold meat the previous evening. It made him mad to think how meticulously he'd tidied up after his supper, while they… He grabbed the knife angrily, thinking that Denis and his mother needed tidying up themselves. They were a mess. They destroyed the order and organisation of his life. It had been wrecked once already, when his father had left, but he'd got everything back on the rails, everything in its place. He wasn't going to let anyone disorganise his life again.

Grinding his teeth until they hurt, he stacked all the dirty things by the sink, cleared the crumbs into the food-waste-recycling caddy, and wiped down. Then he washed and dried up and put everything away – but he left the carving-knife by the toaster, carefully placed at right angles to the front edge of the worktop, the handle towards his hand.

Satisfied with his work so far, he went into the lounge and opened the curtains, only to reveal more wreckage from the night before illuminated by the early-morning sun that filtered through the irregular trees: the sofa pushed back against the wall, the cushions squashed and crumpled; two dirty wine-glasses and a half-empty bottle, its cork stuffed into the damp soil of a spider-plant; both ashtrays half-filled with stinking butt-ends; and an array of cast-off garments – his mother's jumper, a dingy lilac shirt, an odd sock and a frayed black plastic belt. Huw found himself gritting his teeth so hard that his jaw ached, and he felt tears attacking his eyes. How could they do this to him? Suddenly out of control, he picked up the sweat-stained shirt and wrenched it into rags as sobs of anger and frustration racked his body.

Alison lay back in the double bed, alone among the tossed and tumbled bedclothes. Denis had gone down to make them both a cup of tea, and she was glad of the opportunity to think. She didn't have a hangover, exactly, but she certainly didn't feel great. It was unfair to blame Denis entirely for what had happened last night, though he had rather taken advantage of her. Worried as she was about Huw's increasingly eccentric behaviour, she had let herself be comforted with drinks, cigarettes, sweet-talk and toast by a guy who really only wanted to get her into bed. Men were all the same...

Her mouth felt parched, dehydrated. She tried to suck some moisture from her gums and wondered what was taking Denis so long. Huw was already up, she guessed – and suddenly she remembered with a guilty pang the mess they'd left in the kitchen and the lounge. He'd be furious. Still half-asleep when Denis had gone down, she vaguely remembered hearing voices downstairs – raised voices, she now convinced herself. Sitting up, she wiped her gritty eyes with the back of her hand before getting out of bed, grabbing her dressing-gown from behind the door and stumbling out of her room on to the landing. She stood there for a moment, listening. She thought she could hear the kettle boiling, and perhaps the sound of bread being cut. Relaxing, she padded softly downstairs.

Entering the kitchen, she found Huw wiping the blade of the carving-knife, having apparently cut four slices of bread. Why on earth hadn't he used the bread knife?

"I'm making us some toast and tea," he announced abruptly.

"Oh. Good." She paused, glancing around as if expecting to see her lover hiding under the draining-board or in the larder. "Where's Denis?"

"In the lounge," he said casually and then, almost as an afterthought, "It needs tidying up." A thin smile played about his lips.

Alison felt the blood draining from her face and hollow panic welling up from the pit of her stomach.

"What have you done?" she whispered, but without waiting for a reply she rushed from the room, through the hall and into the lounge, terrified at what she knew she was going to see.

On the floor, in the middle of the room, was Denis, dressed only in his shabby trousers and one sock.

On all fours, he was crawling around picking up scraps of torn, lilac-coloured material and putting them into the waste bin, into which he'd already emptied the ash-trays. His scalp glistened in the sun-streaks that were now streaming through the patio window. Hearing a strange gurgling behind him, he looked round. Alison was standing in the doorway, trying desperately to stifle her convulsions of laughter. Sarcastically, he grimaced back at her, before continuing with his task.

"Breakfast's ready," called Huw from the kitchen.

In the Machine

Until tonight, Adrian had never been in his classroom after dark. But it was early November, the clocks had gone back, dusk had edged into darkness during a fraught staff meeting, and before he went home he wanted to finish filling in his pupils' record sheets with their attainment levels, effort grades and a brief comment on each child's progress. This was his first term as an English teacher at the Graystone School, a flourishing comprehensive on the outskirts of a small industrial town in the East Midlands. Built in the 1960s, its most imposing feature was a monolithic structure of concrete and steel and brick and glass, unimaginatively designated the Main Teaching Block. From Adrian's top-floor room, the view stretched as far as the town centre, its imposing Victorian architecture disrupted by the occasional church spire and a grey smattering of angular tower blocks. Nearer to the school, on the other side of a roaring dual carriageway, were the offices of the local newspaper, another monument to the perverse beauty of concrete and glass, transformed now by its brightly-lit windows into a brutalist, fairy-tale palace of glaring rectangles.

Adrian was surprised how eerie he found the teaching block in the concrete chill of the November dark. It was only five o'clock, but it might just as well have been midnight in a deserted fortress. Pushing open the classroom door, he was startled by its shrill squeaking, which he had never noticed during the day, drowned out he supposed by the constantly running soundscape of school life. The room felt oppressive, as if the darkness had squeezed the air out of it. The old-fashioned desks, ranged in irregular rows, sat like hunched creatures shuffled together for warmth. The display boards, crammed with pupils' work, stretched like a tightening band around the walls. On the fixed cupboards at the back of the room perched his battered computer; he had forgotten to turn it off after his last lesson, and its blue screen cast an unearthly luminescence into the treacle-thick gloom. He'd always been disturbed by televisions in darkened rooms, particularly when seen from the street outside: flickering demons of brightness holding their viewers in hypnotic thrall.

Computers were a rare feature of English classrooms at the beginning of the 1990s but Adrian, fresh from his teacher-training college, was keen to embrace all the latest technology. This was a stand-alone machine, a cast-off from the IT Department, completely unconnected to the primitive school network; in truth, it was little more than a glorified typewriter, attached to an antiquated printer. For Adrian it had already proved invaluable, particularly with his less able classes. Unlike some of his colleagues, Adrian found his pupils eager to be taught, but not prepared to tolerate authoritarianism or boredom; anxious to learn, but only in an environment of mutual respect and lively commitment. It was hardly surprising that he was already considered a rising star of the English Department. His rapport with his students was instant and genuine; his interest in his subject passionate and alive, despite the stultifying influence of the educational bureaucrats.

He had those bureaucrats to thank for the task he was anxious to complete tonight before going home. He switched on the lights, which flickered for a while before settling into their uncompromising glare, and sat at his desk, eyeing with distaste the piles of paper and record booklets awaiting his attention. Endless boxes to tick, matching his pupils' achievements against arbitrary statements of attainment, spelt out in interminable lists of impossible detail. Though he was utterly conscientious, Adrian found this a pointless and impersonal exercise, and one that would mean virtually nothing to the kids or their parents. It was all smoke and mirrors, creating an illusion of professionalism and accountability with its incomprehensible jargon, when what was needed was an honest commentary on each pupil's strengths and weaknesses in the subject. With a sigh, Adrian sat at his desk, took out his pen and promised himself he'd be finished by 6.30. He consoled himself with the thought that maybe, by the turn of the century, tasks like this would have been made much simpler by being computerised.

At 6.45, Adrian finally put down his pen and stretched his stiff fingers. This was later than he'd planned; it was his turn to cook the evening meal for his flatmates, three other probationary teachers who taught at different schools, and he hadn't yet done the shopping for the prawn curry he planned to surprise them with. Perhaps he could pick up a takeaway and pass it off as his own. He arranged all his paperwork in a neat stack and shoved it into his desk drawer; he could sort it properly in the morning. He stood up and found that his neck and shoulders were aching; he must try to get to the gym at the weekend. Glancing round the room before he left, he noticed that the computer was still on, and weaved his way through the shabby desks to turn it off and unplug it. As he did so, it made an uncharacteristic noise – an odd combination of a buzz, a whine and a sigh – as the screen faded to grey. Adrian had a peculiar sense that he was being watched and turned quickly to the door, but there was no-one there. Switching the lights out as he left, he decided that in future he'd probably take his school work home with him.

Adrian's Year 10 group the following morning were as lively as ever. A class of average ability, they had nevertheless been motivated sufficiently by Adrian's teaching to be enthusiastically engaged in a variety of projects based on *Titus Andronicus*. Following her normal policy, Judith Spiers, the Head of English, had agreed to buy one new set of texts requested by each new teacher in the department. It was a measure of her confidence in Adrian that her face didn't betray even a flicker of surprise at his request for *Titus*, though she was already composing imaginary letters to angry parents complaining about their children being exposed to a story of rape, mutilation and cannibalism.

The classroom was full of noisy activity – the kind you'd expect from twenty-five fifteen-year-olds working in groups devising newspaper reports on the rape of Lavinia, or rehearsing the trial of Chiron and Demetrius, or writing the last confession of Aaron the Moor, or inventing recipes for various gruesome pies. It was two members of this last group, the least able in the class, who approached Adrian to ask if they could type up their recipe on the computer. He set it up for them and left them to it while he went off to another group to discuss the theatrical practicalities of chopping off Titus' hand in full view of the audience.

"Sir."

"Just a minute."

"Can you come and help us, please?"

"In a minute."

"The computer's going funny, sir."

"What?"

Adrian looked up at Luke's earnest face. Luke wasn't very bright and needed constant attention.

"Every time Cyril types our recipe in, the words go all over the place."

Though he was an enthusiastic technophile, Adrian's computer skills were actually limited to basic word-processing. Technical problems were beyond him, which meant summoning the school's Head of IT, an irascible man with a white beard who always assumed that if things went wrong it was because *you'd* done something stupid.

"All right. I'll come and have a look."

Adrian made his way through the bustle and noise to the computer at the back of the room. Cyril, a tiny boy with spiky black hair, was punching keys. The screen went blank.

"What have you done?"

"I jus' scrapped de lot, sir, an' started again."

"All right. Go on, then – type in the first bit of your recipe."

Cyril's keyboard skills, combined with his limited spelling, did not provide a very coherent piece of work. Laboriously, he typed in:

RESIPE FOR PEPLE PIE
Ingrdience
2 pepole choped up in a mincer
larg JUgg of blud
Pastrie (flower, watter, fat   salt

99

Not for the first time, Adrian questioned his wisdom in introducing his pupils to a play in which two brothers – nasty pieces of work, admittedly – were served up to their mother in a pie. Oh well, he thought, at least I'm introducing them to Shakespeare.

"It looks all right to me," he said. "Water only has one t, though – and you need an e on large." There was no point in drawing attention to too many of their mistakes in one go.

"But look, sir. Every time I get to the nex' line…"

He pressed ENTER to start a new line and began typing again:

Make pastrie by

At that point, however, everything on the screen collapsed in on itself in a heap of jumbled letters. Adrian frowned involuntarily, and all three of them stared as the letters reconstituted themselves into a distinct shape. It was unmistakably a face – a child's face, the eyes sad and staring, the lips moving slowly as if trying to speak. Adrian went cold.

"That's what it did before, sir," said Cyril.

"Perhaps it's a bug," Luke put in, "a computer virus."

Adrian pressed ESCAPE and then Q for QUIT – the quickest way of deleting the file, which the boys hadn't saved.

Are you sure you want to lose your work? asked the screen.

Adrian punched in Y for YES and the menu reappeared on its vivid blue background.

"I'll have to talk to Mr Jacobs about it," he said. "You'd better go back to your places now. Do your recipe in your book and you can type it up next time."

He switched off the computer, checked his watch and began to think about finishing the lesson.

Derek Jacobs, the Head of IT, was busy as usual till the end of the day, by which time, as Adrian knew from bitter experience, he would be bad-tempered and impatient. In any case, it was already darker than usual; a thin fog was closing in, and Adrian was anxious to get home and clear up the kitchen after his previous night's culinary exploits, which had met with notable success. He decided to take home the floppy disk on which Luke and Cyril had been doing their work; this was a thin, flat, square device of metal and plastic that wasn't at all floppy, predating the more sophisticated methods of file storage and transfer that came later. Adrian's parents had bought him a home computer with a smart new printer as a present for getting this job, and he used it constantly to produce worksheets, reports and other materials, as well as for typing up some of the poetry he was beginning to write in odd moments of his rapidly diminishing spare time.

As Adrian walked briskly home in the thickening fog there was a sharp November chill in the air that made him think of hot chestnuts and mulled wine. There were amber haloes round the street lamps, and he had the odd notion that the fog was being generated by the gradual accumulation of misty breath issuing from the mouths of the bustling pedestrians and cyclists as they hurried about their early evening business.

When he arrived home, the house was cold and empty. A three-storey Victorian building, it rose darkly through the wet vapour. Adrian's room was right at the top, big enough for all his needs but with a sloping ceiling that made it seem smaller than it actually was. None of his housemates would be in till later, so he'd be eating alone – but he couldn't wait to try the troublesome disk in his own computer.

His desk was in front of the window, looking out over a long, tangled garden to the rear of the house in the next road. In the distance you could usually see the newspaper building, particularly when it was all lit up on a clear night, with the grim, rectangular teaching block of his school just visible behind it. Tonight, though, you couldn't even see half-way down the garden.

Adrian put the light on, drew the curtains, switched on the fan heater and immediately rifled in his brief-case for the envelope in which he'd put the computer disk. He felt foolish as he set everything up, wondering why he was getting so excited about a computer malfunction. It was odd, though. He didn't see how it could be a virus: it was a brand-new disk, and his classroom computer was totally independent of the school network. How could a virus have penetrated it – unless someone had deliberately programmed it in? He had no idea whether such a thing were possible, or how long it would take. And why should anyone do it anyway? It was a ridiculous idea.

The blue menu screen was glaring at him, offering its various options. He hesitated, then pressed M for MAKE A NEW FILE and his work-screen was ready. For a moment, he couldn't think what to type; then he remembered he had a final question sheet to prepare on *Titus Andronicus*: he might as well do that. He began:

TITUS ANDRONICUS by William Shakespeare

Choose ONE of the following essays. Remember to use brief quotations from the text to support your argument where appropriate.

102

He stopped. The language of this was already too sophisticated for his Year 10 group. Still, the play had been a success – perhaps he'd try it with a more able class next. He continued:

1. Choose the character from the play who interests you most. Write about them, explaining their role in the play and what you thought of them.

As he pressed ENTER, everything he had already typed on the screen collapsed, just as it had in the classroom. Once again, it reshaped itself into the child's face. This time it seemed even more distinct, almost three-dimensional – perhaps because there were more letters available to create it. The eyes, sad and fearful, seemed to gaze in wonder around the room; the mouth was moving, as if trying to speak to him. If he could lip-read, Adrian thought, he'd know what this child was trying to say. This time, he noticed that there were background shapes as well, hovering round the edges of the screen. It was impossible to make out what they were.

His first instinct was to turn everything off. He had gone icy cold, and found he was shivering. He was about to quit the file when he had an idea. His hand veered to the printer and switched it on; it clicked and whirred into life. He pressed ESCAPE, then P for PRINT, and the machine churned into action. Adrian didn't quite know what he was expecting – a print-out of the face, probably. What emerged, however, was something quite different.

At break the following morning, Adrian stayed in his room. When the last of his class had gone, he took a folder from his brief-case and removed from it a single sheet of paper. He had studied the print-out a dozen times since the previous night. He hadn't had much sleep, and the face on the screen had infiltrated his dreams. He read through the words again:

> I am in the builDing. my name is Ste en. I was kille by ONE of the wor men, ritual. Tell my mother. Release me.

The message was clear enough, despite the peculiarities of its presentation. Adrian looked nervously around the room.

> my name is Ste en.

Steven, presumably – killed by one of the workmen who had built the school? It was too fantastic. Nevertheless, Adrian found himself wondering if Steven's remains were anywhere nearby in the walls or floor, or stashed away in some hidden cavity, or maybe ground into a paste, like Tamora's sons in *Titus*, and mixed into the very mortar that held the bricks together. He had to be near – or why had Steven's spirit chosen *this* computer through which to communicate, when there were so many elsewhere in the school? Adrian looked through the steamed-up windows at the lingering fog outside. Across the road, the lights of the newspaper offices glimmered palely. Quite suddenly, it occurred to him that he should go across there at lunchtime. He had to consult their archives.

The fog had come down thicker than ever as Adrian made his way along the street of small terraced houses backing on to the canal. The street lamps hardly penetrated the nebulous darkness, and Adrian was finding it difficult to make out the numbers on the doors. 39, 37 – he was nearly there. He paused for a moment. What would he say? How would he begin?

There was no sign of life at number 33. His heart sank; having worked himself up to this visit, he couldn't bear the thought of being disappointed. But he didn't even know if she still lived here. He opened the iron gate, went up the few shabby stone steps to the front door and rang the bell. The gate creaked shut behind him. After a few moments a light went on in the hall and he began to breathe heavily with relief and nervous anticipation. The door opened to reveal a tired-faced woman in her fifties. Her eyes were tense with suspicion, and Adrian noticed that she was wearing a hearing-aid. Unconsciously, he found himself articulating his words with extra clarity.

"Mrs Webster?"

"Yes."

"My name's Adrian Lewis. I teach at Graystone. I – I have some news for you – about Steven."

Her eyes opened wide with alarm, with a look that said, No, not now, I don't want to know.

"It's a bit difficult to explain; I don't know quite how I'm going to. May I come in?"

The house was small, but tidy and well looked after. Mrs Webster took Adrian through into the living room. She seemed hostile and suspicious.

"I traced you through this."

Adrian took a photocopied sheet out of his brief-case – a front-page newspaper article from 1965. It hadn't taken him long in the offices of the *Gazette* to scan through all the issues from the year the school was built.

BOY STILL MISSING
"Come home" pleads mother

Underneath the headline, Steven's face stared up at them – the same face that had appeared on Adrian's computer screen. He stumbled through his story, not knowing how much she was taking in, and showed her the computer print-out, with Steven's message.

"Why's it printed like that," she asked, "with that capital D and those letters missed out?"

"I think it's because he could only use the letters I'd already typed on to the screen. I was doing a worksheet for school."

"Can you make him speak to me?"

"What do you mean?"

"On the computer. I want to see for myself."

They sat in the darkness at the back of Adrian's classroom, not daring to put the light on in case it was seen by the on-site caretaker. His heart was pounding and he felt like an intruder as he watched Mrs Webster begin to type a message to Steven on to the blank screen. She was evidently comfortable with computers and she typed quickly:

> Steven. If you're there, you must talk to me. Tell me what happened. All these years I've waited for you to get in touch – prayed for you to come back to me. What happened, Steven? You must tell me – I need to know.

She paused here and looked at Adrian.

"Keep going," he said. "It usually happens after about five or six lines of type."

> I love you, Steven. I want to help you, to release you. Tell me how to do it. What do I have to do?

She pressed ENTER to leave a line, but before she could go on, the words tumbled together and coalesced into an image of Steven's face, unmistakably the same as in the newspaper cutting from all those years before.

"It's him! What do I do next? He's trying to speak to me – look!"

Adrian's heart began to race.

"We have to print – to print out what he wants to say. Wait, though – "

Again, Adrian was aware of those indistinct background shapes, almost as if others were standing behind Steven, waiting. He felt the hairs prickle on the back of his neck.

Steven's mother pressed P and the printer launched into action with its usual mechanical scraping. It was operating slowly, as if Steven were having difficulty saying what he wanted from the letters his mother had made available:

> hello mum. It's me, Steve. I've een in such pain – all these years. he strangled me – cut up my body. lack ma ic. pleaSe release me. Type In Some ore and Ill tell you how.

Adrian tore off the print-out and they scanned through it anxiously in the dim light of the screen.

"I can't make out some of it. What does it mean?" Mrs Webster's voice was desperate. "Can you make sense of it?"

"The last bit, yes. I think he wants you to type in some more, so he has more letters available. Why don't you just key in the whole alphabet three or four times?"

While Mrs Webster was doing this, Adrian looked at the face on the screen and compared it to the one in the newspaper. For the first time, his eye was drawn to an adjacent item on the front page, not all of which had been photocopied. The headline was there in full, though:

SCHOOL SITE RIDDLE
Late night ritual disturbs neighbours

He was distracted from this by the printer, which had ground into action again. Steven was giving instructions for how he could be released from his torment. But how? By finding his body and giving it burial? By bringing his killer to justice?

Adrian glanced at the screen. The picture was clearer now. Round Steven's image, in the background, were other faces – faces smiling; old faces; faces that seemed full of the darkest knowledge of things it would be better not to know. The printer stopped, and Mrs Webster tore off the sheet.

"What does it say?"

"There's a whole list of instructions – I have to type in all these things."

"And that will release him?"

"Yes."

"But how?"

"I don't know. I have to do it, though. It's what he wants."

By now, Adrian was feeling distinctly uneasy. Steven's mother started tapping away even more frantically at the keyboard, following Steven's directions. On the screen, Adrian noticed, Steven seemed to have become wild-eyed, panic-stricken. His lips moved, in a series of silent shouts. Adrian instinctively knew what he was saying. He was shouting at his mother, over and over, "No! Don't! No!", but she was not looking – too busy feeding what she thought were *his* instructions into the machine.

Adrian looked back at the half-copied newspaper article:

Residents have complained of occult rituals taking place on a building site in Eastern Way, following the discovery last week of bones and other artefacts dating back thousands of years. Work on the site of the new Graystone Comprehensive School had been halted so that archaeologists could make a full investigation. A police spokesman said that hooded figures had been seen late at night, lighting fires and chanting, but they had gone by the time officers arrived. Ms Jane Smithers of the local archaeological society said it seemed from the evidence so far gathered that the site could once have been a centre of pagan worship. She blamed local children for the recent distur

"Stop!" Adrian shouted; "We're being used!" But Steven's mother was typing madly, as if possessed: strings of incomprehensible words and phrases that would release – not Steven from his spiritual agony, but innumerable dark shapes from their centuries of confinement.

Adrian grabbed her shoulder, made her look at him and shouted, "Look at the screen!" He mouthed the words in an exaggerated way, hitting the consonants with unnatural precision, the way you instinctively do to a deaf person. He had to make her understand. "Look," he said again, "he's telling you to stop. Steven is telling you to stop! He tried to warn us. Black magic – that's what he was trying to say."

He grabbed the last sheet – the one whose instructions Mrs Webster was following. The final command was to print everything she'd typed in. And what would happen then? Adrian had visions of a mass of evil shapes, all those leering faces gathered round Steven on the screen, spewing out of the machine, leaping off the paper in swirls of black ink.

"We have to delete everything. Quit the file," Adrian shouted.

Mrs Webster hesitated, only just beginning to grasp something of what was happening.

"Quickly!"

She looked in puzzlement at Steven's anguished face, his lips still mouthing his frantic pleas for her to stop. Now she knew what he was saying. How many times in his short life had she studied the shapes his mouth made as he spoke, helping her to compensate for the limited effectiveness of her hearing-aid? She pressed the ESCAPE key, then Q for QUIT. Laboriously, the inevitable backup question kicked in: *Are you sure you want to lose your work?* For a moment, Adrian could almost believe he heard screams of fury emanating from the malevolent faces that framed the screen. Then Steven's mother hit Y for YES; the boy's features relaxed as he and the others swarming around him vanished into greyness and the screen became blank and still.

"Let's make sure," Mrs Webster said. Adrian noticed that her eyes were moist. "We'll delete every file on the disk."

Methodically, she did so; it didn't take long.

"We'll have to destroy it completely," Adrian said. "The computer, too. Whatever's got into it will be buried in the hard drive. I'll see to it."

Mrs Webster was crying quietly now, in the cold darkness of the classroom. Adrian put his hand on her shoulder.

"Don't worry," he said, "there's another way to do what Steven wanted – to release him forever. Let's do it."

Adrian stood thoughtfully amidst the dust and rubble of his gutted classroom, surveying the debris. The floor and ceiling had been ripped out, the plaster stripped from the walls, every cavity exposed. It hadn't taken the police long to find Steven's remains, and they had already begun the process of tracking down everyone who'd been employed on the site when the school was built. The murderer must have had access to this part of the building and, alone or with one of his satanic accomplices, had incorporated the dismembered fragments of Steven's body into the fabric of the room. Adrian shuddered convulsively and tried desperately to unimagine the scene he had conjured up. He was glad he wouldn't have to teach in here again for some time, though he did not relish the prospect of months of lessons in a prefabricated hut.

Steven's funeral was to be held on the following day, but whether this would bring peace to his troubled spirit, no-one could say. Perhaps he had in fact been at peace during the long quarter-century since his life had been so brutally truncated, until the installation of Adrian's classroom computer had made him a potential conduit for the release of those dreadful shapes from their dark confinement. They would never be far away, Adrian supposed. He thought of the ever-widening networks of linked computers spinning their webs across the shrinking globe. It was a lucky chance that his classroom computer had stood alone, but even so he had risked transferring its demonic virus via the infected disk to his own machine; perhaps he should destroy that too. His mind raced ahead to the turn of the century and beyond – a new millennium. Within a decade, he felt sure, all human knowledge would be instantly accessible at a click, a word, even a thought. And in a world squeezed hard in the tightening mesh of information and communication, something would surely burst out, some thick, dark pus ejected from that mysterious spirit world whose ever-vigilant forces have sinister designs on our own.

Prelude

Something isn't right. In the past few weeks, I've changed. I don't feel any different, but other people seem puzzled. They pause in mid-conversation, study me for a while with furrowed brows, ask me if I'm OK. It's unnerving. I suppose it could be the first, creeping signs of my Dad's Alzheimer's, but when I think over what I've been saying or doing, I can't see anything untoward. Even the cat seems perplexed. Instead of sidling up to me, soliciting affection, it gives me a sidelong look and pads away, slipping out of the door as quickly as it can. I'm beginning to feel anxious. It's almost like I'm not who I'm supposed to be.

I can't really pinpoint when it started. Maybe it was that conversation with Helena, my fiancée. We were sat in the kitchen, talking about our earliest memories, don't ask me why. For her it was a carnival parade when she was barely a toddler, being lifted up by her Dad to say hello to a clown on stilts with a massive, grotesque head. She screamed and screamed, and her father gave her a good telling-off for showing him up. What is it about fathers?

To Helena's surprise, my first memory was of being born: the glutinous, pulsating darkness giving way to incomprehensible brilliance, a shifting mirage of grinning, threatening faces, stabbings of sharp noise and the uncontrollable switchback sickness of being randomly passed around between unknown entities with some unfathomable purpose in relation to me. I also screamed and screamed.

Helena said I was the only person she knew who remembered being born. She was clearly disturbed by what I'd told her, but it didn't seem odd to me, not at the time; it was just a memory, clear as crystal. When I thought about it later, though, it occurred to me that I'd never remembered any of this before. It was like some microscopic scalpel had probed and picked a tiny cell in the recesses of my brain, releasing long-trapped particles of stored experience. And then it went on happening.

There was that argument with my Mum. She was trying to deny that when I was a kid my Dad sometimes hit me. I have no idea why she was defending him, since he used to knock her about on a regular basis. It was like, now he was in a nursing-home, she'd subconsciously decided to whitewash his character, to completely reinvent him as the perfect husband and father, kind, considerate and affectionate. Maybe I'd never spoken to her before about my memories of his compulsive rages, which admittedly were often fired by my own misdemeanours. As far as I knew, he occasionally hit my sister too, but it wasn't up to me to speak on her behalf.

Anyway, my Mum demanded an example – thinking, I guess, that I would of forgotten it all; forgotten the details at any rate. I could of chosen any one of loads of occasions to remind her of – of which to remind her – but in the end I went for that time when, in my adolescent shyness, I'd made a fuss about being asked to entertain the son of one of my father's French business acquaintances. After all, I was doing French for GCSE, so there was no reason I shouldn't of been able to communicate easily and fluently with this kid. But I was excruciatingly self-conscious, and the thought of having to display my limited command of French was a humiliating prospect. Nothing our French teacher taught us would stick in my head – though, weirdly enough, it's all come back to me recently – and I knew that my French accent was laughably unconvincing. Anyway, I made a scene, insisted I didn't want to meet this boy and they couldn't make me, dashed out of the house and sprinted down the road with not an idea in my head about where I was going or what would happen when my Dad caught up with me.

What did happen was that, in a blind fury, he jumped into his car, an old blue Ford Escort with rusting bodywork, and sped down the street in pursuit of me. My escape lasted exactly five minutes. The car screeched to a halt beside me; he leapt out, red-faced, grabbed me by the arm, just above the left elbow, opened the back door and flung me in like I was – sorry, *as if I were* – a sack of potatoes. It's funny. It's not just the French that's coming back to me, but all that English grammar I was taught that I never really got at the time. What can it be that's probed my mind, scraped all this stuff to the surface?

When my Dad got me home, I was silent and sullen. This must of – *must have* – infuriated him. He shoved me into the back room, away from my Mum, who was stood in the kitchen – *standing* in the kitchen – pretending to get the lunch. He snatched at my shirt collar and lifted me up, so that my feet dangled just short of the floor. I was a scrawny kid at the time, only 4 feet 11 inches tall and weighing just 10 stone. His hot breath in my face stank of the boiled eggs he'd had with two slices of buttered white toast for his breakfast, and the veins on his roughly-shaved cheeks were spreading their beetroot-red fibres across his entire complexion.

At this point in my story, my mother interrupted me. "You can't possibly remember all this," she said, her voice suffused with incredulity. "You're making it up."

I was baffled, furious. "You can't have forgotten," I insisted. "You came into the room just as he hit me across the face. You were in that plastic-coated apron you always used to wear in the kitchen, the one with the daffodil design and that little fabric label that stuck up at the front with the washing instructions on it that would never stay tucked in so you eventually cut it off."

I could see from her face that she remembered, but there was something else in her expression – not shame or regret as I'd expected but a look of puzzlement, like she was – no – *as if she were* beginning to sense something queer, something not quite right in the way I was describing it.

"This was twenty years ago," she blustered. "It's all in the past, and your Dad's – "

I ignored the appeal implicit in her words and carried on relentlessly, determined not only to prove my point but to hammer it home until it transfixed her into acknowledging these long-suppressed truths that had invaded my mind from somewhere hard and deep. I needed her to admit her complicity in my father's bullying, her failure to stand up to him, to protect her children from his whimsical flights of red-veined violence.

"I remember it exactly," I continued. "Every detail. You told him to stop and grabbed his arm but he pushed you away. Don't interfere Marjorie, he said, the boy needs to be disciplined. He threw me into that shabby old chair with the threadbare covers and the disintegrating antimacassar draped

115

over the back. The wooden arm jabbed into my ribs and I yelped with pain. Please Dad, I begged, and you said, Leave him alone Stan, but he pulled me up again and punched me hard in the stomach so that I screamed out and started to cry and he said, Don't start that bloody game you whining brat, you bloody well need to be taught how to behave or you're no son of mine, then he knocked me to the floor, you remember where there was that gap between the fringe at the edge of the carpet and the skirting-board, and I banged my head and he kicked me on the shin and I noticed his shoelace had come undone, it was a black one even though he was wearing his brown brogues and then all his anger seemed to leave him and he stormed out of the room, One day you'll learn your bloody lesson he said as he went, but more quietly like he was exhausted, and you followed him out without even looking at me, calling, Stan, don't; Stan, come back, and I – "

"Stop!" said my Mum, my mother, finally shifted, perhaps, from her habitual stance of denial. For a moment I felt sorry for her, until she backed away, still with that puzzled frown, that air of incipient panic, like she was – *as if* she was – *were* – afraid of me. Perhaps I *had* been getting rather carried away, but the memories were so precise, so detailed, so vivid that I seemed to have relived the entire experience, second by second.

"Don't say any more," she went on. "I remember it. You don't have to say anything else to convince me. Please just stop talking. I'm sorry."

I felt oddly disappointed. I could have gone on. I remembered the flecks of spittle that sprayed from my father's lips as he screamed at me. I remembered the pulled thread on his grey, woollen jumper that curled in an elliptical loop about half an inch in length. I remembered the unswept dust and grit

116

on the dark, varnished floorboards adjacent to the skirting-board on which I'd banged my head. I remembered the dull pain in my ribs and the subsequent blue-grey bruise on my left shin, exactly two inches below the knee. I remembered everything, every tiny detail – yet I had not thought about this traumatic childhood experience for a very long time. For years it had remained buried, deeply embedded in my subconscious, even though it was clearly an inextricable element in the moulding of my character, in what had made me who I am.

I could think of nothing that might have triggered this phenomenon of total recall, after all these years. Is it possible to spontaneously acquire – no, that's wrong, a split infinitive. Is it possible to acquire spontaneously a photographic memory, suddenly to be able to access every detail of everything one has ever experienced, however long-forgotten, however effectively suppressed? No wonder my mother had no wish to hear more. She was disturbed not by having been forced to face up to unpalatable truths about which she had long been in denial. No; it was the queerness of me being able – of *my* being able – to recite every minute detail. It was not right, not normal. If only she had known.

It was shortly after this conversation with my mother that the dreams began. I have always dreamed, of course. I could describe in detail every dream that I have ever had. These new dreams, however, are different. They possess an internal consistency, and weave what seems to be a coherent narrative thread. Their world is not this world. The skies glimmer in shades of mottled gold. Vast conglomerations of artificial structures spread in geometrical patterns across the foothills of great mountains of purple and silver. Legions of skimming craft animate the air, sometimes reflective, sometimes translucent, melting and re-forming, coalescing and separating in a mysterious, unfathomable dance of light. Perhaps they are not craft, but living entities, the shimmering inhabitants of this impossible world. No recognisable creatures have revealed themselves to my dream persona, yet I sense a web of thoughts reaching out to enwrap me, calling me in, drawing me back to this strange place that I have left for some long-forgotten purpose.

These are now the only dreams I have. I dread going to bed, yet just on the brink of sleep's falling, I long to be magicked back to this land of pulsing light whose thought-webs call to me from beyond the realms of known space. One thought-voice has gathered to itself an individual identity, a separation from the generality of awareness that hums constantly in the background. It has an amorphous, paternal quality of stern, unforgiving love. As yet, I have no sense of what this voice might be saying.

When I wake, I lay there – *lie* there – feeling anxious and distracted until the dreams fade. I have had no contact with my mother for ten days, and I have made the assumption that she is avoiding me. My fiancée, Helena, has gone away for two weeks to chair a marketing conference in Edinburgh. For much of the time I am alone, increasingly overwhelmed by the minutiae of my past, by memories and recollections that flood my consciousness, blotting out what little remains of the present. I can no longer control them. They come randomly – unprompted, as far as I can tell, by even the strayest of stray thoughts. They are now my present tense. I see the imprint of my thumb on the leather armchair in our front room, the first time I manage to climb up to it as a toddler. I see my bicycle tyre slowly deflating after I have ridden over a scattering of spilt tacks on the pavement outside our house; I am ten years old. Now I am fifteen, and wincing at the spray of pus on the bathroom mirror as I squeeze the blackhead on my chin. I note the tuft of coarse, dark hairs sprouting from the nostrils of the chairman of the panel at my college interview. I contemplate the blankness in my father's eyes as he looks at me from the rumpled mess of what will surely be his death-bed. As his mind is wiped, so mine is pumped full; a mixed metaphor, as I recall from one of my GCSE English lessons. I do not understand what it all means.

At present, I am incapable of work, so I have taken a week's leave of absence from my job at the Ministry of Defence. The cat has gone, but I do not miss it; I recognise now the sentimentality of our relationships with animals. Perhaps pets will no longer be permitted... what does that mean? This morning I ventured out of my house to partake of a hot drink at one of the local coffee shops... I cannot remember which one. I am forgetting a great deal now – about what is happening day by day, I mean. My mind is filled only with the details of my past life, up to the moment I shared with Helena my memories of being born... there will be another birth soon, I think. Everything I have experienced since that conversation seems vague... confused. That is the reason I have made the decision to write it down. I believe something is about to happen.

In the coffee shop... I cannot remember its name or location... I talked with a woman whom I believe I have noticed there before. We had not previously communicated. We engaged in conversation with apparent spontaneity... she told me she works for the local council. We talked about memories... and dreams. She described her own birth and I reciprocated. We exchanged the recollection of incidents from our respective childhoods, not neglecting the inclusion of circumstantial detail. We described to each other memorable scenes… we demonstrated our long-forgotten language skills, she in Latin and I in French, languages we each believed we had failed to learn whilst we had attended school. We wondered, and speculated. Then we shared our dreams.

They were identical in all but one respect. Her mentoring thought-voice has ventured closer to her than mine and has begun to convey ideas of a complicated, tangled quality that she finds simultaneously alluring and terrifying. A sense of unspecified threat has threaded itself through this evasive, elusive voice. It hints at a flowering, a fulfilment, some desired culmination that comes to her as the violence of bud-burst, a spreading of seed, the strangling incursion of roots and tendrils. She is made to feel that this culmination depends somehow on her, that she has a role she cannot even begin to imagine, a role in the bloom-burst and seed-drop, the crushing, twisting emergence of an alien species. This makes her uneasy, but the night's dreams slip from her mind as she begins the business of each day, making space for the interminable gathering of her past memories, the harvesting of her life's experiences, viewed and heard and felt and smelt and tasted in impossible and overwhelming detail. She digresses to tell me about the sty on her mother's lower left eyelid that terrified her as a child; hums the opening movement of Mahler's First Symphony, to which she was made to listen just once by her stepfather; and recites the whole of the opening chapter of *Great Expectations*.

Who are we? Are we two the only chosen ones or do thousands, millions of us stalk the earth, awaiting our moment: the moment when something will explode into flower, a scattering of seeds will thicken the air and alien weeds crack the soil, their roots rutting deep underground, their twisting tendrils spinning their curling, crushing twine?

I know that when I sleep tonight I shall see and hear more. Perhaps tomorrow I will understand; or the day after, or this time next week. Then I shall have to make the decision whether to resist; to assert my life's history, precious now it is recollected in every fine detail, in the face of whatever change threatens; to abort the promised birth, which is also a dying. Perhaps, instead, I shall decide to accept the role in which I have been cast, to facilitate bloom and seed-burst and the vast flights of opalescent sky-craft, myriads upon myriads of shifting light-shapes dancing under the shimmering gaze of moon and stars. Whatever happens, it will be soon.

Masks

"Where shall we start?"

"Dunno."

"What about the old girl we got last year?"

"What, up Cromwell Street?"

"Yeh. You remember."

Dean sniggered, recalling the fun they'd had a year ago.

"Bet she's got her door barred this year. Letter-box stuck up, anyway."

"Won't stop us, will it? Come on."

The gang moved off, their shadows lengthening on the pavement as they left the pool of light thrown by the streetlamp on the corner where they had gathered. There were four of them, three boys and a girl, all aged about fifteen. Dean was the unacknowledged leader, a short, stocky youth with close-cropped hair.

"Give us a fag, Gail, will yer?"

"I ain't got none. You had my last at school this afternoon."

"Liar. You always got fags."

"No I ain't. Search me, then."

"No way. Don't wanna get my hands mucky."

"Pig."

"Here. Have one of mine," interrupted Nick, irritated by the habitual antagonism between Dean and Gail.

"Ta, mate."

Nick sometimes wondered why he bothered hanging around with this lot, and in particular why he accepted Dean's implicit leadership; he supposed it must be his characteristic laziness that kept him constantly in subjugation – that and the general pointlessness of life.

"Only one left," said Dean, peering into the squashed packet. "Got a light?"

"Yeh."

Dean put the cigarette between his pale lips and tossed the empty container into a nearby garden. Nick reached across with his lighter. Dean's face looked weird in the glow from the flame.

"Smart lighter."

"Yeh."

"Ain't seen it before. Where'd you get it?"

"Nicked it."

"Who from?"

"My old woman."

"Oh yeh? Why?"

"Dunno. Just did."

Nick knew why he'd done it all right. His mother had been going on at him as usual – this time about his mid-term school report. They'd had a row, she'd stormed out and Nick had rifled her bag in a fit of petty vindictiveness. As well as the lighter, he'd taken the then half-full packet of cigarettes and some money, with which he'd bought himself some fish and chips.

The gang walked along without talking for a while. Their feet clattered on the pavement, echoing in the night's dark reaches.

"Ain't this the road?"

The voice was that of Crab – Neil Crabtree, the fourth member of the gang – who had so far maintained his usual silence. The sign on the corner confirmed his judgment: CROMWELL STREET.

"He can actually read," said Gail sarcastically.

Crab felt his cheeks flush and looked down at the pavement, thankful for the darkness.

"Which house was it?" asked Dean.

"Christ knows. They all look the same down here," said Gail.

Nick gazed at the row of gloomy Victorian houses that stretched endlessly along the street, thrusting their bow-windows into cramped, shrub-infested front gardens. He cast his mind back to the previous year's Hallowe'en exploits. 1974, the year his father had finally disappeared for good, his mother had taken to the bottle full-time, and he'd started hanging around with Dean and his gang. They were OK, but something told him he was better than them.

The shrubs and trees looked strange in the mingled light from the moon and the orange streetlamps: the leaves were greyish, the shadows between them deep and black. A gentle wind had arisen and the sound of dry, fallen leaves rustling on the paving stones was unnerving. Nick didn't know why he was on edge tonight; it wasn't like him.

"Ain't that the one?"

Gail pointed to a house about half-way along the street. Unlike most of the others, there was no warm glow of light to suggest homely comforts behind its closed curtains.

"Could be."

They moved down the street towards the house, walking more slowly than they had been. It *was* the right house; Nick remembered it now, as last year's events came more clearly into his mind. Even then, he'd known they were far too old for trick or treat. It was meant to be spookily transgressive fun for little kids, not an excuse for teenage yobs to indulge in intimidation and vandalism. And that's how he saw himself: a yob, a troublemaker, completely irresponsible and entirely lacking in all civilised moral values. The phrases came easily to his mind; he'd heard them so often from teachers, social workers and police officers that he'd absorbed them as indisputable definitions of who he was. Until now.

As he looked up at the dark, forbidding house lurking in the shadow of a tall holly tree, Nick remembered the pale features of the elderly woman who had answered the door to them last year, wary and frightened behind the safety chain, her face framed in the narrow gap.

"Trick or treat?" Dean had demanded.

"What do you want?" she said, in a voice that, though hesitant and faltering, was surprisingly sharp and clear.

"You gotta give us a treat or we play a trick on you," Crab explained dumbly.

She looked blank. Perhaps she was deaf. Or perhaps she didn't know it was Hallowe'en.

"I don't want you here. Go away."

Her voice was angry now, but behind it the fear was plain. She pushed the door shut.

Dean shouted at the closed door.

"We'll be back then. We gotta play a trick on you now."

The four of them had retreated sniggering down the gravel path, emerging on to the pavement muttering obscenities and giggling stupidly.

Two hours later, at midnight, they had returned, rapped loudly on the door and posted two lighted fireworks through the letter-box, before running for all they were worth back to their own territory.

As Nick recalled all this he felt strangely detached from it, as if he himself had not been involved. It seemed stupid to him now; childish; just as it seemed childishly spiteful of him to have stolen the things from his Mum's bag. The whole of life seemed pointless to him really – nothing but bitterness and hate and pain. In twenty-five years' time it would be the end of the century: the year 2000. This had always sounded unreal to him; and as for the word millennium, it suggested nothing less than the end of the world. It frightened him. How old would he be then – 40? His parents were older than that now. Would he be facing the apocalypse as miserable and broken as they were? He might just as well be dead long before the time came.

His thoughts were interrupted by the voice of Crab, daring to speak for the second time that evening despite his previous humiliation.

"What we gonna do, then?"

"Dunno. What d'you suggest, brainbox?"

Crab fought back the incipient blush this time, largely because the comment came from Dean, not Gail; he could always cope better with insults from his own sex.

"Let's just see what happens when we knock on the door," Gail suggested.

"Why don't we – " began Crab, but stopped when he found everyone looking at him.

Nick felt sorry for him. "What?" he asked encouragingly.

Some hidden reserves of courage urged Crab to continue.

126

"Why don't we put our masks on first? That'll get her." He giggled.

"Hey – yeh. Go on." Thus Dean expressed his astonished approval of Crab's idea. "Dunno why they keep him in the dummies' group at school; he's got brains after all." Throwing his cigarette stub to the pavement, Dean pulled out from the pocket of his anorak a squashed looking piece of rubber attached to a length of elastic. Pulling this over his face, he was transformed into a misshapen and unearthly creature, grey-faced, with red, staring eyes and bulbous cheeks. Two fangs dripped blood over his protruding chin.

Crab followed suit with a mask that represented the Incredible Hulk, a face that sat incongruously on his slight frame, its vivid green transformed to a sickly greyish-brown in the orange light. He faced his rival monster and they emitted experimental growls and roars, sizing each other up and clawing at each other menacingly. Gail, meanwhile, had covered her entire head with an old nylon stocking. When the others saw her, they curtailed their performances and fell back in silence. She presented a far more terrifying spectacle than either of them, her own features visible but distorted through the nylon, like a face pressed against glass.

"Where's yours?" came Dean's voice, muffled through his mask.

Nick found himself barely able to reply. He still felt edgy, as if something unpleasant were about to happen to him.

"In my pocket."

"Come on then. Get it on."

Nick's unease turned quickly to nausea. There was now a cold breeze blowing, which made his nose tingle and was beginning to give him earache. The taste of the fish and chips he'd had earlier came back to him, sickly and unpalatable.

"What's the matter?" Gail's voice cut clearly through the chill air.

Nick felt he had to say something, to explain his anxiety, but the words wouldn't come. How could he tell the others he didn't think they ought to be doing this? They'd laugh at him; worse, they'd accuse him of cowardice and spread his shame throughout the school. He resorted to a half-truth.

"I feel sick. Must've been those chips I had."

"You gonna puke up?"

"Think so."

"Get away from me then, filthy devil! Come on, let's leave him to it." Dean pushed open the wooden gate and entered the garden of the silent house, followed by Gail and Crab. Nick forced himself to stop them with a shout.

"No!"

"What?"

They turned and looked at him. There was a moment's pause, during which the sound of children's laughter, streets away, mingled eerily with the wind.

"Nothing."

Nick turned away and staggered a few yards along the pavement. What was the matter with him?

The other three looked at each other for a moment, then went up to the front door.

Nick could contain himself no longer. A convulsive shudder doubled him up and he was violently sick. He coughed and spluttered, wiping his mouth with his sleeve. Slowly, he pulled himself upright. His face burned, yet beads of sweat ran down it like slivers of ice. He turned to look back towards the house.

His three companions stood at the door, the hand of the Incredible Hulk raised to knock. The sound of the sharp rapping reached Nick as if from a great distance, through the gently whispering wind. The door opened and a pale, old face appeared in the gap. The woman showed no surprise at seeing the three hideous creatures confronting her. Maybe her eyes weren't that good.

"Trick or treat?"

The familiar words came clearly to Nick's ears, as did the woman's reply in her strange, sharp, quavering voice.

"Oh yes. Come in. I've got a treat for you this year. Come in."

She unlatched the safety chain, and the door opened wider. Nick could sense the uncertainty and confusion of his friends. He heard Crab's familiar, endearing giggle.

"Come on."

Crab disappeared into the house. The other two followed. Just before the door closed behind them, Nick saw Dean's face looking back, staring directly at him, a bloated grey mask of horror. He shivered.

An hour later, Nick was feeling genuinely ill. Waves of nausea and vertigo kept gathering inside him until he felt sure he was going to pass out, but he didn't. Instead, his heart battered away at his ribs and his brain seemed to be lifting the top off his head. The others were still inside the house; what the hell could they be up to in there? He should have gone home and left them to it. But he couldn't face his mother, not yet. The habitual mask of hatred that he felt obliged to put on for her benefit was just too much of an effort, and he couldn't cope with the inevitable interrogation about the theft of her things.

"What's up, son?"

Nick jerked his head up to be confronted by the dark outline of a uniformed policeman.

"What?"

"What's up? Not feeling well?"

"Oh. No, not very."

"You responsible for that?" the policeman demanded, indicating the pile of vomit on the pavement, glistening in the congealing grip of a fast-developing frost.

Nick nodded.

"Drunk too much?"

"No – I ain't 'ad nothin'."

"Wouldn't you be better off at home?"

"Nah – I'm all right."

"You don't look it. What exactly are you doing here?"

Overcoming his ingrained reluctance to respond to a policeman as if he were a human being, Nick found himself stammering out his unease.

"I'm waitin' for my mates."

"Where are they?"

"In there." Nick jerked his head in the direction of the house.

"Oh yes?" The policeman began to look suspicious.

"They ain't doin' nothin' – nothin' wrong," put in Nick hastily. "She asked 'em in."

"Who did?"

"The ol' girl what lives there."

"I see." The policeman obviously didn't believe him.

"It's true. They ain't broken in or nothin'."

"There isn't anyone living there, son. So tell me another."

"Yes there is. She opened the door an' they went in."

"Listen son – what's your name?"

"Nick."

"Listen, Nick. I know this area. It's been my beat for eighteen months, right? The old lady who used to live in that house is dead. She died, oh, nearly a year ago I reckon. Apart from some squatters a while back, the house has been empty ever since."

"No it ain't! She opened the door an' let 'em in!" Nick was almost shouting now. "Same as she did last year – only she didn't let us in then," he added feebly.

"Last year? When?"

Nick realised he'd said too much, and dropped his eyes to the ground.

"I don't remember," he said sullenly.

"Yes you do. Let me tell you something. That old lady died in hospital. Exactly a year ago, some sods shoved fireworks through her letter-box. Actually, it was her daughter that was injured – they went off in her face." The policeman's voice was charged with feeling, as if he were talking about his own family. "She was badly disfigured, the daughter; but the shock of the whole thing killed her mother. She died a couple of weeks later; had two strokes, one after the other." He paused, reaching into himself for firmness and authority rather than compassion and anger. "What do you know about it, eh? Was it you? You and your mates?"

Nick felt his insides churning. Only by concentrating very hard could he stop his mind from floating out through the top of his head. He forced his eyes to stay open, to stop the terrifying, whirling vertigo. The policeman's voice cut sharply through the roaring in his ears.

"Was it? Eh?"

"No! I tried to stop them." His voice sounded thick and incomprehensible to him, but the policeman seemed to have understood.

"All right. So it was your mates." He thought for a moment. "What did you come here for tonight, then?"

"I – nothin'. I – dunno."

"You say they're in the house now?"

"Yeh."

"How did they get in?"

"I told yer – she let 'em in."

"All right. She let them in. How long ago?"

"Dunno. 'Bout an hour."

"Why didn't you go in with them?"

"I di'n't want to. I di'n't feel well."

Nick was unable to articulate his motives any more clearly.

"Strikes me, son, they've done a bunk and left you in the lurch. They probably nipped out the back."

The same thought had already crossed Nick's mind. But what about the old woman? What had happened to her?

"I'm gonna want you to come down to the station with me. Talk about last year. Strikes me there might be criminal charges."

"I told you, it weren't me."

"Then I'll want the names of your friends."

On a sudden impulse, Nick replied, "I've told yer: if you want them, they're in there."

For the first time, the policeman looked genuinely puzzled.

The individual frost crystals sparkled on every exposed surface, from the gravel of the drive to the bark of the holly tree. The breeze which had earlier created an eerie whispering through the suburban laurels and cypresses had died away, giving place to a chill silence. Distant traffic hummed, like an echo of another, far-off world.

Standing in the hallway of the house, accompanied by this disreputable youth, Police Constable Fenwick felt like an idiot. They had broken in through the French window at the back and now stood listening to each other's breathing in the semi-darkness. There was something odd, he had to admit, about the atmosphere of the house. He recalled that the squatters who had taken it over, having resisted all attempts to remove them, had suddenly left for no apparent reason. Maybe they'd felt it too.

Nick, meanwhile, was surprised to find that his nausea had passed and he felt much calmer, though his heart was still beating faster than it should. He, too, was conscious of the atmosphere that enveloped them. He'd felt the same sometimes in the stillness before a violent storm. He looked around, peering into the molecules of gloom that seemed to close in on them.

Through the frosted glass panel of the front door, above the letter-box, the orange streetlamp was transformed into a huge, amorphous glow which lent an otherworldly luminescence to the narrow hallway. On the right, the stairs led up into darkness; to the left was a door to the lounge. Fenwick was about to open this when he felt Nick's hand on his arm. He turned to him inquiringly. Nick was pointing to a coat draped over the stair rail.

"Dean's," he whispered, his heart beginning to race even faster.

"You sure?"

"Yeh. It's got 'is badges on, look."

Fenwick took a deep breath. He began to feel anxious; what the hell was going on?

"They must be here. He wouldn't leave his coat," whispered Nick.

Fenwick said nothing. He had a growing suspicion that Nick's friends were playing a trick on them, that suddenly they'd leap out from their hiding place, frighten the wits out of the two intrepid investigators and make him, P.C. Mark Fenwick, look a complete fool. With a sigh of resignation, he opened the door to the lounge.

It was very dark inside. The curtains were closed and the holly tree outside obscured any light that might otherwise have filtered through. Fenwick shone his flashlight quickly around the room: chairs, sofa, a coffee table, pictures on the wall, a fireplace, ornaments on the mantelpiece...

The beam of his torch returned to one of the ornaments, placed dead centre, above the fireplace. What was it? It seemed to be a mask of some kind, propped up against the wall. He recognised it from somewhere: the Incredible Hulk, that was it. Strange. Nick was also staring at it.

"That's Crab's mask."

"What?"

But Nick was fighting to understand. How was the mask supported? When removed from the wearer, it became just a wrinkled bundle of rubber. He knew now his mates were trying to scare him. Anger began to take the place of his fear as he strode across the room, grabbed hold of the mask and picked it up. Then, with a choked cry, he flung it down and backed away, his hands dripping with warm, sticky blood as he watched Neil Crabtree's severed head rolling gently backwards and forwards in the shaking light of Constable Fenwick's torch.

Fenwick recovered himself quickly. Appalled and sickened as he was, his professional training kicked in. Roughly, he took hold of Nick's arm, dragged him out of the room and shut the door behind them. His mind was racing. What should he do?

"Nick."

There was no answer. Nick's face was grey and blank. He wanted to be sick, but he'd already vomited up everything he had inside him. He was shaking, and felt hot and cold at the same time.

Mark grabbed him by the shoulders and shook him roughly.

"Listen. Get out of here now. I'm going to take a look upstairs, then I'll come out to you."

He pushed Nick towards the front door, unclipping his two-way radio from his lapel. "Go on."

Vaguely, Nick stumbled towards the door and tried to open it; his mind was still reeling and he could hardly focus on what he was doing.

Suddenly, he stood stock still. Fenwick had heard it too: a loud creak from upstairs. They stared at each other.

"Go on. Out," muttered Fenwick, but part of him wanted Nick to stay with him. Nick managed to detach the safety chain and open the door. A cold draught entered the hallway and the curtains fluttered. Replacing his radio temporarily, Fenwick began to climb the stairs. Nick watched him. Something kept telling him to get out of the place before it was too late, but he knew he could not let the policeman go up alone. Leaving the front door open, he started to follow him up.

Reaching the landing, they stood in silence for a moment or two, listening. There was no repetition of the creaking sound, nor was there anything else to be heard. Perhaps it had just been a floorboard contracting. There were four doors confronting them, all closed. Fenwick thought carefully, then turned round to Nick. He was glad the kid hadn't left him, but he was still responsible for his safety. He took out his truncheon and handed it to Nick.

"Be ready for anything," he whispered. If necessary, he himself could use his flashlight as a weapon. For the first time in his career, he regretted not being allowed to carry a gun.

He guessed that the door on the left was the bathroom. He opened it carefully and shone his torch in and around. Lying in the empty bath was the body of a girl. The stocking with which she had covered her head earlier that evening, with the intention of frightening the life out of an old lady, was wound tightly around her neck.

Gritting his teeth, Fenwick closed the door and looked at Nick, who had caught a glimpse of Gail's body. His face showed no response but remained grey and drawn, his eyes staring and vague. Fenwick hoped he wasn't going to crack up just when he needed him. He was about to open the door on the right, to the front bedroom, when there was a noise from one of the other rooms, as if something had been knocked over. He tensed. Nick also seemed to come back to life: his face became alert, his eyes lost their vacant stare. Fenwick motioned him down a couple of stairs. Whoever – or whatever – had killed these two kids – possibly three kids – was in there, with no way out. The constable knew his next move. He unclipped his two-way radio.

"This is P.C. Fenwick," he said quietly. "Shut up and listen. I need backup at 54 Cromwell Street now. Two kids have been killed. I've got the culprit trapped in a bedroom. For Christ's sake, hurry."

136

He switched the radio off, and turned to Nick.

"We're going to wait," he said. "If you want to go, get outside now. I'm staying here. But – "

He broke off as the bedroom door, behind which God-knew-what lay concealed, slowly creaked open. Fenwick drew in his breath sharply and tensed himself, ready for anything – anything except what he saw in the beam of his torch.

Standing directly ahead of him, against the far wall of the room, was a figure, about five feet tall, human in shape, but with the most gruesome features. Its face was green and bulging, its hair was black, two red eyes protruded from deep in the fleshy mass, and it had fangs from which blood dripped down on to its chin. The creature didn't move. Fenwick remained frozen in terror until he was released by Nick's voice whispering in his ear.

"It's Dean. What's the matter with him?"

Scarcely had the first wave of fear passed than it was overtaken by another. The figure moved forward, fell away from the wall and collapsed in a crumpled heap on the floor. The handle of a large carving knife could clearly be seen sticking out of Dean's back.

Time seemed to stand still. From somewhere, Nick became aware of a clock ticking loudly. With a start, he realised it was his own watch. His nerves were stretched tight, to the very limits of their sensitivity. He could almost hear the blood racing through his veins, the blood that gave him life. He knew then what he had never known before: life was good; he didn't want to lose it. He didn't want to be like Dean, and Gail – and Crab. He couldn't bear to think of Crab's bodiless head and the blood still sticky on his hands. He didn't want to be dead like them. He wanted to live.

Suddenly there was a piercing screech. In the doorway, illuminated by the torch beam, appeared a small, frail, female figure, grey-haired and wrinkled, with steel-rimmed spectacles perched on her sharp nose. Fenwick was too startled to react. He just stared. The old woman screamed again, then rushed forward with astonishing speed, lifting something above her head, something gleaming in the torchlight and red with congealing blood. The axe that had struck Crab's head from his body descended on Constable Fenwick and buried itself in his chest. Blood spurted over his uniform, his flashlight fell from his hand and the look of surprise on his face flattened into a blank stare. Darkness fell and the groans of the dying man mingled with the woman's screams as Nick struggled frantically to get down the stairs to the front door. Half-way down he felt the woman's body fall heavily on top of him. He shouted, kicked, screamed in terror, grabbed at anything he could find. Flailing out in all directions, he felt a sharp pain in his hand as he inadvertently grasped the axe blade. Thinking quickly, he reached for the handle, trying to wrest it from the old woman's grasp. He tugged harder: the axe came away from her hand and flew down the stairs, smashing into some piece of furniture at the bottom, which fell against the open door, pushing it closed with a crash. In the same unbalancing movement, the two struggling figures also tumbled down the stairs and into the hallway, where they were illuminated by the light of the streetlamp shining through the door's frosted glass panel. They clawed at each other, scratched and kicked, each trying to get the upper hand. The woman's strength was phenomenal. Nick found his hand on her face; he grabbed her glasses, pulled them off and nearly died of shock as her features crumbled away, disintegrating to a piece of shrivelled rubber in his hand.

The two antagonists stared at each other. Nick was looking into the face of a middle-aged woman, disfigured by scars and blotches and warped by hatred.

"You did this to me," she said, her quiet voice contrasting with her former harsh screams; "and you killed my mother. You'll pay like your friends did."

Nick forced his voice out.

"No! It weren't me! I tried to stop them." But it was a lie, and they both knew it.

The woman was distracted by the sight of the axe, embedded in a shattered cabinet at the foot of the stairs. She made a leap for it, but Nick beat her to it. He grabbed the handle, yanked it free from the broken shards of wood and swivelled round to face her.

"I'll kill yer," he hissed. "Keep back."

She looked uncertain.

Into Nick's mind flashed the image of a severed head – the head of someone who had once been his friend. He moved towards the woman, raising the axe and gathering all his energy ready to strike. She backed away, snarling. Nick looked at her scarred, disfigured face. He and his friends had done this terrible thing to her, and for what? For nothing; for "fun". He thought of her mother, dying slowly in hospital, fading into the blankness of forever, distressed and alone. He thought, too, of his own mother, and tried desperately to hate her. Instead, he ached to be close to her, as she used to be; as *he* used to be. He needed the comfort of her soft touch, the soothing balm of her warm breath. He thought of Gail, lying strangled upstairs in the bath; and of Dean, spread-eagled across the bedroom floor with a knife wedged in his back.

With a shattering cry of confused anger, terror and pain, Nick swung the axe round his head as the woman shrank back into the shadows and flung it with all his strength through the translucent panel of the front door. Trailing slivers of shattered glass in its wake, the axe curved through the night air, silhouetted against the orange glow, before descending on the gravel of the front drive, where it came to rest in a raised cloud of stones, dust and glittering crystals of frost.

The woman sat huddled in the corner of the hall, crying now. Upstairs, Constable Fenwick lay still and quiet.

Deliberately, Nick bent down and picked up the crumpled rubber mask. Taking his mother's lighter from his pocket, he flicked the mask into curling flame and threw it back to the floor, where it burned itself out in a few brief seconds. He leaned against the wall and smiled faintly. He knew now that there was still hope for him; knew that when the century ended and the new millennium dawned, he would be ready to face its challenges, whatever they may be, with courage and integrity. He listened calmly to the sound of a police siren growing louder and louder in the chill emptiness of the night air.

Assignation

Jamie blinked as the air before him shimmered into a new screen layout, responding to his unspoken request. The implant on the inside of his left wrist began to itch but he resisted the temptation to scratch, knowing he would regret it – as he ended up regretting most of his decisions. This new technology was still settling down and the holographic screen, seemingly assembled from the very atoms of the air, was subject to unpredictable wobbles and clouds of dim vapour that made Jamie's eyes water. Words and figures were the worst, blurring into the flickering background of violet phosphorescence that fuzzed his vision. He rubbed his eyes and tried to focus on the instruction, displayed in electric blue lettering amid jauntily dancing graphics.

STATE PREFERRED GENDER

He was aware of his heart's nervous, guilty thudding as he thought his response: *Male*. The letters within the screen corkscrewed ostentatiously into the next command. Briefly, he looked away, his watery eyes drifting aimlessly over the indoor plants that filled his room with their myriad shades of green and infinitely varied leaf designs.

Jamie breathed in the stress-easing scent of his pot-bound rosemary as he considered this. Stupidly, he hadn't anticipated the need to be specific. He found his hand shaking and turned to grab the whisky bottle from the table at his side. The screen swivelled disconcertingly to match his head movement, provoking an attack of vertigo. He cursed, turned back more slowly, established the screen's location where he wanted it, and thought, *Fix screen in this position.* His hand shook so much as he poured his drink that he spilled most of it. Amber droplets pooled themselves on the glass surface of the table, like sluggish globules of mercury. Thoughtlessly, he wiped them with his sleeve and knocked back the whisky in one gulp. The glass rattled as he replaced it on the table, and the bottle vibrated – but not because of his shaking nerves. The whole house was shuddering as a jumbo-transport skimmed the rooftops of the estate before coming in to land at the adjacent US base. Jamie hardly noticed the roar as he thought his response to the screen's insistent demand, which still hung accusingly in the congealed air. *Seventeen.*

Jumbo-transports operated at the lowest end of the technological spectrum, like lumbering dinosaurs clinging to existence well beyond their allotted era. From seven in the morning till nine at night they hauled their cargoes of life's mundane necessities backwards and forwards across the rounded world, but in a rare act of "considerate legislation" they had been banned from operating during the ten hours during which most people slept, necessitating some intricate scheduling to take account of varying time-zones. They no longer revived painful memories for Jamie, and he took no more notice of them than he did of those other technological fossils: the central heater-cooler with its irregular hum, or the food-prep unit and its whirring buzz.

Seventeen. Did he really mean this? The screen was demanding confirmation of his choice. Idly, he supposed his answers were being instantaneously logged in his security profile, monitored automatically by some arcane program at ECIA headquarters, along with everything from his shopping lists to his choice of reading. But so what? This wasn't illegal. It was a freely available service, no more questionable than downloading a vidstory or ordering a meal. Everything was available that could provide consumer satisfaction, and this new hire-site, tactfully called COMPANY4U, had already become a globe-wide phenomenon and would soon be raking in billions for its founding genius. Yet Jamie couldn't entirely shake off the antiquated moral scruples instilled in him in his distant childhood. What made him any better than one of those creepy, contemptible paedophiles whose activities regularly exercised public outrage? Nevertheless, he gritted his teeth and thought, *Yes*.

He poured himself another whisky, more carefully this time, as he waited for the floating screen to cast him its next instruction. He supposed he would be asked for his racial preferences, or would this be forbidden under the equality laws? He sipped his drink, reflecting that the program seemed to be operating more slowly now, perhaps accommodating itself to his own pace of thought. Then, with a pointless swirl of accumulating green letters, the next message materialised in a flash of purplish light. He found himself unable to read it clearly and dabbed at his damp, stinging eyes. This didn't help much. Reluctantly, he issued a thought-command, *Enable vocal backup*. None of the downloadable voices had sounded remotely human, and he'd eventually selected an unashamedly electronic option, with its smug artificiality and sing-song American accent. As it spoke now, it was reassuringly free of any emotional resonance. No empathy, no pity, no blame.

PLEASE RATE EACH OF THE FOLLOWING ON A SCALE OF 1-20

Almost immediately, the screen switched to a series of promotional films extolling the merits of ten young men of the age he had specified. He felt entirely indifferent to the first two, largely because of the brash over-confidence of their self-publicising commentaries, underscored by syrupy background music and unthreatening soft rock. Jamie decided he'd be better off concentrating on the visual impression made by each of the candidates. *Cancel soundtrack*, he thought.

The image of the third youth consolidated itself within the atoms of the airy screen. He stood on the diving-board at a swimming-pool, perfectly poised. He executed an impeccable somersault and stabbed the water cleanly, rising through the ripples a few seconds later and swimming strongly to the side. He hauled himself out and swivelled round to sit on the edge of the pool, shaking the droplets from his fair hair as the visuals slowed to a lingering appreciation of his glistening body. As the camera completed a slow zoom-in to his head and shoulders, he grinned broadly and waved, before dematerialising in a measured fade. Jamie found himself unexpectedly aroused and his cheeks flushed instinctively; but the boy's physical prowess was too intimidating for his taste.

PLEASE AWARD YOUR SCORE

Without hesitation, Jamie thought: *14.*

The fourth candidate was first seen from behind, dressed in a red tracksuit, jogging across a field. As he vaulted a gate, the camera angle switched to a low-level view, framing his head and shoulders in a self-consciously casual pose. He was a good-looking, dark-haired lad with oriental features; like the previous contender, he grinned and waved. Wondering if all the choices would be presented in various modes of athletic accomplishment, Jamie thought him a score of 12. Physical strength and sporting prowess were not quite what he was looking for, whatever COMPANY4U's market research might have suggested. Unthinkingly, he scratched his wrist, with the inevitable result that the itching became more intense.

It was number 8 that grabbed his attention. It wasn't just that this fresh-faced youth was the first one not to be engaged in physical activity (he was in fact reclining in the open window of a smart country house, an old-fashioned book in his hand, surveying a view of rolling hills); it was more the suggestion of a wistful intelligence behind the grey eyes and the lop-sided half-smile. There was something oddly familiar in his pale, lightly-freckled face, but his most striking feature was a thatch of auburn hair, not fuzzy or frizzy but smooth and straight, hanging thickly over his ears. When he smiled, it was as if he were smiling for Jamie alone. Jamie resisted the urge to rewind the scene with the commentary reactivated; he didn't want to risk disappointment. Without hesitation, he thought into the program a score of 20. Full marks.

When Jamie had awarded a score of 11 to the final candidate, a black kid playing the clarinet, there was a slight pause. Then:

YOU HAVE AWARDED FULL MARKS TO NUMBER 8. DO YOU WISH TO MAKE A BOOKING?

It was done before he knew it. Date, time and location were agreed. Jamie's line-bank was relieved of 3000 euro-dollars. The airscreen was shut down by a mere thought, to the accompaniment of a tinny jingle that had already netted its composer a fortune in royalties. As Jamie picked up the empty glass from the table, his sleeve brushed against the rosemary in its confined pot. Its sweetly pungent scent filled his nostrils. He took the glass through to the sentient kitchen that hummed with readiness to minister to his every need. His wrist was now itching unbearably. He stared out of the window at the dead streetscape, hardly noticing as the house was shaken by the day's final jumbo-transport skimming the rooftops.

At regular intervals during the following day, Jamie considered cancelling the arrangement, or at least revising his gender option and booking a female companion instead. The choice he had made seemed like a double betrayal. He had loved Caroline a great deal, though they had both been aware that in some ways their marriage was a sham. After her death, his feelings for her had ossified into a disingenuous, automatic faithfulness that had kept him lonely and celibate for thirteen long years. He had no social life. Even though, unlike most people, his job required him actually to travel to a place of work, he rarely saw his colleagues and had never met in person the elderly lady with whom he shared his position at the TransLib Center. Here, he spent three days a week surrounded by dusty, antique books, acquired from the holdings of yet another defunct aristocratic family, transferring their contents online for the benefit of potential researchers and archivists. The books themselves were then atomised. Every time he thought of this word he replayed in his mind that final image of Caroline that was imprinted on his every brain cell. Caroline – and Jake.

On his days off, he stayed at home, mostly recumbent in front of his mindscreen, immersing himself in ancient movies, or solitary games of chess or bridge. Sometimes he would try one of the virtual sporting activities on offer – the ones where you didn't even need to get up off the couch. There was a limit, though, to how much time could be satisfyingly passed in this way. His collection of house plants needed regular attention, but they had long ago become a habit rather than a hobby. Against all the rules, he occasionally brought home one of the books he had been working on, having made a false entry in the atomiser records. His spare room was filled with an unhealthy collection of crumbling volumes, crammed with dust-mites and spores. He particularly enjoyed early 20th-century fiction – Forster and Lawrence, Conrad and Joyce, H.G.Wells and Virginia Woolf. He could have chosen to read all these in a range of digitised formats, but there was something about the books themselves that he found irresistible. He couldn't explain it, but their narrative and intellectual content was somehow embodied in their physical existence as objects. They had a solidity that all five senses could appreciate, even to the light flick of the turning pages or the musty infusions of ink, paper, leather, cardboard and glue that infiltrated the mouth and nostrils, smelling and tasting of the past.

When he felt particularly restless, he would take a walk round the estate where he lived, looking for signs of individuality in the identical house-blocks fronted by their concreted parking spaces. It pleased him to come across the occasional house that still had something approaching a front garden, with bright flowers in tubs or exotic grasses erupting from a gravel base. Rear gardens were generally given over entirely to access – for refuse trucks, recycling drones, emergency vehicles, security vans. If he saw other people on his walks, they eyed him suspiciously and looked away. When the weather was especially damp and gloomy he would sometimes venture as far as the airbase; he had learned to stop at a point just before his presence would activate the lights and sirens, though there was no escaping the cameras. He stood there now, four hours before the assignation, still puzzling over whether to go ahead. He kept telling himself that there was nothing to be ashamed of; he was simply taking advantage of a popular consumer service. He knew there was no stigma attached to same-sex liaisons; at least, there was not supposed to be. When it came down to it, he was simply paying for the company of this young man for twelve hours – from nine this evening until nine the following morning. People did it all the time.

As he gazed at the dark criss-cross of the base's perimeter fence etched against the damp, grey sky, the clouds roared and parted as the late afternoon jumbo-transport thundered in from the west. For once, the noise got to him. Usually he was indoors when they passed, but seeing the dark shape lumber towards its ungainly landing like an airborne sperm whale, roaring and screaming as it hurled itself into an unfamiliar and hostile environment, he was racked by a convulsive shudder. At the same moment, his conscious mind finally acknowledged what had been troubling him; his own son would have been exactly the same age as the youth he had booked for the night. Jake, his son, vaporised along with his mother at four years old. They had been visiting Caroline's elderly parents on the outskirts of Exeter. No trace of them had been found in the dust and rubble of the wrecked street. Atomised, like the redundant books that were stacked up every day for his attention. His son, a mere footnote in the virtual records of his life.

His wrist-comp buzzed, startling him out of his painful reverie. Who could this be? Nobody ever contacted him in this way.

Screen, he thought.

The air in front of him fizzed like a carbonised drink as the screen materialised, blotting out in a violet haze a large portion of the base's intimidating wire fence. The word LIVE hovered in the air as the face of the boy he had hired for the evening materialised three-dimensionally amidst the glistening raindrops, smiling in that same, lop-sided way.

"Hi, Jamie," he said. "This is Euan. I'm really looking forward to meeting you tonight. I'll be there at nine. See you later. 'Bye."

The image faded, overwritten by the legend, LIVE LINK TERMINATED in letters of luminous green. Jamie logged off with a thought, and the screen shrank to a tiny dot of light that popped into nothingness to the strains of the infuriating jingle.

It was obviously too late now to cancel the arrangement. But, Jamie decided, he and Euan would just talk, order a take-in maybe, share a drink. But nothing else.

The greet-bell buzzed at exactly nine. Jamie quickly checked his appearance in the reflective wall and spoke the door-command: "Open." As yet, he had not upgraded his household technology for thought-response, aiming to see how things went with his mind-driven wrist-comp. As the door slid smoothly aside, he welcomed his guest.

"Hi. Come in."

The boy responded with a ready smile, utterly natural and unforced.

"Thanks."

"Let me take your coat."

It was evidently still raining outside. The boy's fake-leather, hooded trenchcoat was speckled with drops that began to slide and coalesce as Jamie hung it in the cloakroom alcove. He led his guest into the lounge, embarrassed by the artificiality of his behaviour. He felt like a character in a RealTheater show, where the actors were actually present in the same space as the audience. Paradoxically, this physical proximity always seemed to result in far more stilted performances than in vidstories or even antique movies. Yet the boy seemed perfectly at ease. Just well-trained, perhaps.

"Can I get you a drink? Euan, isn't it?"

"That's right. I'll only have a drink if you're having one, Jamie."

Jamie couldn't get used to this seventeen-year-old's easy and assured use of his first name. At that age, he himself had been invariably gauche and tongue-tied in the presence of adults.

"I'm having a whisky," he said. "Same for you?"

"You realise I'm not eighteen? Yes, of course you do. I'll just have a fruit juice, thanks."

"Sure. Sit down."

Jamie reflected briefly on the laughable hypocrisy of Euan's being considered old enough for the job he was doing but too young to drink alcohol. The law remained as stupid and confused as it had always been.

Euan placed himself casually on the sofa, leaving plenty of space for his host to join him, but Jamie held back. He hadn't anticipated just how much he would be attracted to this young man, and knew he would need to steel himself against his driving desire if he were to stick to his resolution. All his life he had been aware that he was strongly drawn to certain members of his own sex, certain physical types especially. Until now he had rigorously repressed his feelings and found ways of avoiding too close encounters. Caroline knew, of course; she knew everything. But she'd never forced him into admitting his secret, and it had not hindered them from enjoying a moderately fulfilling sexual relationship, of which Jake had been the only product.

Jamie handed Euan a glass of cranjuice and sat down on the chair opposite, nursing a tumbler of whisky. It occurred to him that he should probably avoid drinking too much. As Euan lifted the glass to his lips, Jamie noted the embedded wrist-comp and felt oddly disappointed. He had thought that, for once in his life, he was at the forefront of technological progress, but these devices seemed to be spreading like blown dust. Someone had once told him he was allergic to the modern world, and he had been determined to prove them wrong. Nervously, he scratched at his itching wrist and instantly regretted it.

"Nice house," observed Euan. "I know they all look the same from outside, but you've made it very – individual. I like all the plants. Unusual."

"Thanks. It's… I suppose I've tried to make it how my wife would have liked it."

"Oh."

"Does that surprise you? I expect you thought…"

"I didn't think anything. Relax."

"Sorry. I'm finding this quite difficult. I've never…"

"Don't worry. They prepare us for all this. Lots of clients are anxious, ill-at-ease. COMPANY4U is still a fresh idea; people haven't quite adjusted to the fact that it's actually legal."

Euan paused, suddenly aware that he was sounding too much like the training manual.

"Sorry," Jamie repeated. "You've obviously encountered customers like me before." He was aware that his choice of the word "customers" sounded all wrong, and he gave what he thought was a wry smile. He felt as if he were the teenager, Euan the adult.

For once, however, Euan looked as awkward as Jamie felt. "Actually," he admitted, "you're my first. So you see, I'm probably as nervous as you are."

There was a pause before they both relaxed into laughter. Jamie felt he had made a good choice; there was no feeling of pressure on either side. But how on earth did a kid of Euan's age end up doing this? What kind of family did he come from?

Jamie's relaxation was short-lived, however. Without a trace of embarrassment, Euan said, "Look, don't be afraid of asking me for sex. After all, you're only getting me for twelve hours; I wouldn't like to think you've wasted your money."

Jamie turned beetroot red, wondering irrelevantly if Euan would have heard of that extinct vegetable. With a shock of disgust, he found himself visualising the boy's training sessions in the nuts and bolts of his job. He felt revolted, by the situation, by the world in which he lived, but mostly by himself. What he was engaged in was nothing short of exploitation.

"Sorry if I embarrassed you," Euan said, breaking into his slanted smile.

"No, no. But there's no hurry. I'm happy just to talk. For now."

"That's fine. We're told to be upfront right from the start. Some clients are apparently too reserved to ask for what they want until it's too late. But if you'd rather just talk all night, that's great too."

Considering this was his first job, the boy was doing really well. He was a natural. Jamie refilled the glasses, then asked bluntly, "Are you allowed to talk about yourself?"

For the first time, Euan seemed uncertain.

"Well – up to a point," he answered. "But I'd rather talk about you. You mentioned a wife." Immediately, he knew this was the kind of prompting he was supposed to avoid.

"Yes. She's dead. And our son," he added. "Are you surprised that I was... I mean, that I've chosen a male companion?"

"Not at all. It's more common than you'd think. Anyway, we don't judge, even to the extent of being surprised. We're taught to be prepared for absolutely anything."

"So how long did your training take?"

"A couple of months. It's mostly virtual instruction, but there's physical training as well, fitness, role play, first aid." Euan paused. "And the sexual stuff, of course. Then at the end we do our promotional films. Two minutes max."

"Most of the others I looked at were doing something athletic," Jamie observed.

"Yes – there's a lot like that. We don't get much say in it actually, but they do make some effort to fit the ads to our personalities."

153

"It was the book that clinched it," said Jamie.

"The book?"

"You were reading a book. At least, you had a book in your hand."

"Oh, yes. They didn't much like that. Too retro. It was my idea."

"Do you have books? Real books?"

"Some. Poetry mostly. People think I'm strange."

Jamie laughed. If people knew about his own illicit reading habits, they'd think he was more than strange. Early 20th-century fiction!

"How did you get into this line of work?" he asked, cursing himself yet again for his inept choice of words. "I'd have thought you'd still be at college."

Euan considered for a moment just how much he should reveal about himself.

"I dropped out of school a couple of years ago," he said. "It was a pretty rough one, down in the West Country. I decided if I was going to be bullied and exploited, at least I'd make sure I was in control of it. And getting paid."

He stopped, aware that he had probably said too much. It was tantamount to accusing Jamie of exploiting him. For the briefest of moments, his façade of self-assured ease evaporated.

Jamie didn't seem to notice. "What about your family?" he asked.

This was easier, and Euan was able to slip back smoothly into his repertoire of practised responses to personal queries.

"I don't really know anything about them; I was brought up in a council institute for orphans. I suppose my parents died, or abandoned me or something; I was taught not to be too curious. Anyway, when I was 15 I walked out on it all, ended up in

London doing various jobs, saw the advert for this, and here I am." He smiled broadly, his genial self-possession securely re-established.

Jamie too felt more confident and relaxed, and pursued his questions, genuinely interested in this personable young man he had invited into his home.

"How much do you earn from this?"

"Sorry?"

"I'm paying 3000 euro-dollars for your companionship. How much do you get out of it?"

Euan laughed. "I don't get any of it, as such. Just my keep. Somewhere nice to live, food, clothes, entertainment. Bonuses for positive feedback, tips – I hope – from satisfied customers." He grinned warmly at Jamie. "Sorry!"

"Someone," Jamie observed, "is making an enormous profit."

"Of course," Euan laughed. "That's how society works."

When they finally went upstairs Jamie noticed, as the blinds rolled across the raindrop-spattered window, that there was a single car parked a little way down the street, just outside the circle of violet light cast by the nearest streetlamp.

"Yours?" he asked.

"No. Well, yes, I suppose. It's my driver," Euan replied.

Jamie's heart jumped. He hadn't expected this; stupidly, he now realised, it hadn't even occurred to him to wonder how Euan had got here.

"Surely he's not going to stay there all night?"

"Yes, but don't worry," Euan said with a laugh. "He's a robot."

Despite his anxiety, Jamie was impressed. Robot cars were a recent technological development, building on the success of the recycling drone. Although they didn't actually need anyone, or anything, in the driving seat – or even a driving seat, come to that – people liked the sense of a humanoid-form in control. These vehicles cost a fortune; someone, somewhere, was certainly netting an awful lot of money.

"More plants," Euan said, changing the subject as he glanced around the room. "I love the cactuses. Or should that be cacti?"

"Whatever. My little boy used to like them. But he could never get it into his head that if he touched them they'd hurt his hand. Always getting pricked, never learning."

Jamie fell silent. Cacti. Who knew the Latin etymology these days? He had taught it to Jake. "Daddy, the cactuses hurt me again," the child would say. "Cacti," he would correct the boy, and explain why, simultaneously reflecting on the pointlessness of being so pedantic in the world as it now was.

Euan knew better than to enquire further. Never ask the clients about their lives; listen and respond non-commitally to what they tell you. He had already forgotten the correct etiquette once this evening. So he made no comment on the room's double bed, assuming that it was a relic of Jamie's married life. He wondered what had happened to the wife and child.

"Euan."

"Yes?"

"Do you mind if – will you be offended if we just – sleep together, and not… ?"

"Don't be silly, Jamie. Whatever you want." He pulled his sweater over his head and began to unfasten his shirt. "But just make sure you get your money's worth."

Hesitantly, glad of the tactful, strawberry glow of the bedside lamp, Jamie began to undress. In the car, waiting silently in the darkness of the shining street, Jamie and Euan's conversation was relayed from Euan's wrist implant via the robot driver to COMPANY4U's virtual headquarters, along with that of dozens of other employees and their clients.

As morning edged slowly over the world's rim, the pale sun pressed its soft gaze through the bedroom blinds, casting a diffused sheen on Euan's tousled hair and freckled complexion. Jamie had been awake for hours, his mind teeming with troubling reflections. Like the world he unwillingly inhabited, he was made up of a tangled mass of contradictory programming. Just as the technology by which the world operated was an inexplicable mixture of the magical and the mundane, so people's impulses were stuck paradoxically in different centuries. In a nominally secular state, power lay largely in the hands of religious fundamentalists. Though tolerance and equality were enshrined in the law, social attitudes were often bigoted and reactionary. Sexuality was entirely a matter of personal choice, yet anything that departed from the heterosexual norm was still regarded with fear and distaste – hence Jamie's conflicting responses to his uncertain desires; his avoidance of "coming out" even in a society that had long ago espoused same-sex marriage. He felt both cowardly and hypocritical, yet he was glad that, at his insistence, he and Euan had remained partially clothed as they lay side by side in the bed he had never before shared with anyone but Caroline. Even so, he had found it nigh on impossible to keep his physical arousal in check, and when Euan sensed the tension in his body and placed a comforting hand on his chest it was almost more than he could bear. Now, he risked gently stroking the sleeping boy's head. Running his fingers through the smooth, auburn hair, he was surprised to note in the day's increasing brightness that at its roots it was just ordinary, mousy brown, like his own thinning strands.

Something began to nag at Jamie's mind. He looked around the room, taking in the almost obsessive collection of plants – herbs and cacti and ivies and spider-plants and others whose names he had long forgotten. A half-remembered line of something or other floated through his consciousness. "Rosemary – that's for remembrance." He felt an enormous flood of relief and thankfulness at his powers of resistance; he knew that if he had succumbed to his physical impulses he would have felt guilty, and soiled, and morally culpable. He wondered, not for the first time, if his increasing attraction to men – let's be accurate, to young men – was just a fantasy, a desperate urge for something different, something irregular, something that, to him, still felt dangerous, forbidden.

Euan stirred and opened his eyes. Jamie quickly removed his hand from the boy's soft head.

"Morning," he said.

"Hi," Euan replied through a leisurely yawn. "What's the time?"

"Seven, just gone. Do I have to give you breakfast?"

"No, no, it'll be ready in the car. But we've got another two hours. I'll just go to the bathroom while you decide what you want to do."

158

Jamie's eyes followed Euan as he left the room. In his black cotton briefs, lit by the pale, unflattering light of morning, he seemed more slight and frail than he had as they'd undressed at midnight in the shaded, pinkish glow of the bedside lamp. He was certainly less muscular than the diving boy in the promotional film, his body less tanned and toned. His arms were thin, and his pale skin was disfigured by pink blotches and the faint remnants of scars. His legs were stronger, and covered with a soft down of light hair that made him seem boyish and fragile. In short, he seemed less attractive than he had at first appeared, for which Jamie felt immensely grateful. He relaxed fully for the first time since Euan's arrival; again, he offered thanks to some non-existent deity for helping him to resist the overpowering physical sensations that had punctuated this ill-judged assignation. He was absolutely certain now that all he wanted was company.

When he heard the sound of the auto-flush from the bathroom, Jamie pushed himself up into a sitting position. Feeling embarrassed now at his own flabby semi-nakedness, he reached down and grabbed his shirt from the floor where he had dropped it the previous night. He was struggling into it as Euan returned.

"Ah. I take it you haven't changed your mind about sex," laughed Euan.

"No. Let's just lie here."

In the brightening light, Jamie noticed with interest the reason for the boy's slanting smile: there was a thin, pink scar at the corner of his mouth. Focusing more closely, he became aware with a start that the freckles that covered Euan's face were actually tiny flecks of healed skin. For a moment or two he became lost in thought.

The intense golden glow seeping into the room promised a fine day, a rarity in this dim world of damp grey. Despite the impossible idea that was beginning to crystallise in his mind, Jamie felt strangely peaceful. Somehow, things seemed to have become clearer. Even his itching wrist had eased, and his eyes hadn't watered since the last time he had been peering at his mindscreen. They lay in silence for a while, neither of them feeling the need to stir the still air with words.

Then, with a roar, the house shook as the day's first trans-Atlantic delivery lumbered and thundered across the estate, sinking into a laboured dive towards the landing strip. The bed vibrated, the cactus pots rattled on the shelves, the windows hummed like trapped wasps. Euan shot up in bed, his eyes wild, his face drained of blood.

"Jesus! What was that?"

"It's okay. It's just a plane coming in – one of those jumbo-transports. There's a US base right next to the estate. I hardly notice them anymore."

Euan's breath was coming in quick gasps and his chest was heaving convulsively. Jamie began to panic.

"Are you all right? You're shaking."

"Yeh – I – I'm okay. God! I thought it was the Bomb."

There was something unnerving about the boy's terror, which seemed more than just the shock of an unexpected noise. It was as if some repressed memory had been triggered. Instinctively, Jamie put his arm round him.

"It's all right; it's all right. Let me hold you."

They lay back on the bed, Euan clasped firmly in Jamie's arms like a small child desperate for comfort after a nightmare. Gradually, his breathing slowed, his body stilled and he regained his composure.

"Sorry," he said. "Wow. I don't know what happened there."

He relaxed, and they lay together in silence for a time.

"When can I see you again?" Jamie asked.

Euan frowned. "You can't. We're not allowed to see the same client more than once. It's in the small print. You were supposed to read it before you ticked the boxes."

"I don't mean that. I couldn't afford another 3K anyway. Can't we just meet somewhere? There are things I'd like to talk to you about."

"It's not allowed."

"Why not?"

"Forming attachments with clients is frowned on. It could lead to – complications, I suppose."

"Do you have a girlfriend? A boyfriend?"

"No. That's not allowed either. It's one of the things we have to agree to before we get the job."

Jamie was outraged, but he knew his outrage was largely selfish. There was something special about this boy, something deserving; perhaps it was the trace of Caroline that hovered about his smile, the hint of her intonation behind his light West Country accent. He needed more time with him, but they only had another hour together. What could he do in an hour? Finally, trembling, he spoke the unspeakable thought.

"Does the name Jake mean anything to you?"

"No. Why?"

There could be no answer to this; it was a stupid question. This couldn't possibly be his son; it was inconceivable. Coincidence could never be so fantastic; he had let his imagination spin out of control. He had been alone too long.

Somewhere in the complex mesh of information passing through the ever-expanding COMPANY4U database, the name Jake was being processed, and matched against all available information on Jamie and Euan. An alert buzzed automatically on the airscreen of one of the few actual people in the system. This needed a human decision, a human response from the desiccated, middle-aged operative still designated by the archaic term, Personnel Manager.

"Oh my God," he muttered. "How the fuck did we let this get through?"

As Euan walked through Jamie's tiny front garden to the waiting car, he turned, looked back and waved.

"Hope you got your money's worth," he called.

Jamie was frozen to the spot. His mind was racing, his pulse thumped, but he was incapable of movement. The walk, the turn, the wave; it was Caroline. It was his last image of her, the one that still haunted his dreams. Forever in his memory she was walking to the taxi with their young son. She stopped, she turned, she waved, while Jake continued to trot childishly towards the vehicle's opening auto-door. The taxi drove off, heading for Caroline's parents' home in Exeter – in the West Country. That was their final day – all of them. Late in the evening, a jumbo-transport failed to make it to the airstrip and crashed in the middle of the estate. Obliterated. Atomised.

But he knew now. Jake had escaped, somehow. A miracle. Euan was Jake – there could be no doubt. The shock of the aircraft's intolerable roar: the boy had never experienced the passing-over of a jumbo-transport since that unspeakable day because after the disaster the routes had been altered permanently as a mark of respect – considerate legislation, they called it. Changed by 200 miles. Changed to pass across the distant home of the bereaved husband and father.

Jamie's body finally freed itself from its paralysis as the robot car pulled away from the kerbside with a quiet hum. He ran after it, shouting and screaming frantically. Blinds twitched momentarily in the neighbouring houses. An elderly woman walking her muzzled dog switched direction and strode quickly away. The car turned off the estate at the end of the road and vanished from sight.

Jamie stopped running, and cursed himself. Why hadn't he listened to his instincts? Why had he talked himself out of his suspicions? But he would track his son down; he would chase up COMPANY4U and demand answers, demand to see Euan's files, demand his son back.

But he felt sick. His stomach heaved. He couldn't believe he had done it. After keeping himself in check throughout the night, why had he finally let his desire overrule his resolution? Why had he allowed himself, desperate at the thought of their final hour together, to submit to Euan's persuasion? Even though he had known; inside, he had known. Empty, distraught, he stopped running and stared down the bright road. He rubbed roughly at his watery, stinging eyes and scratched violently at his fiercely itching wrist. The embedded control device began to loosen and shift its position, and a thin trickle of blood ran into the palm of his hand – the same hand that had touched his son forbiddenly, his own son, stroking, caressing, stimulating, arousing, allowing the boy to respond in kind with hands, with mouth, with the whole of his body. Jamie stopped breathing and fell heavily to his knees. Something inside him crumbled to dust.

Inside the robot car the instructions were received in silence. Euan relaxed in the back seat, thinking over the events of the past night. He had handled it well, he thought – until this morning, that terrible noise; what had all that been about? As regards the sex he was indifferent; that was the job. But he had felt sorry for Jamie; a good man, consumed with grief and loss. Cactuses? Or cacti? Oh well, at least he had received a substantial tip. He swallowed his breakfast pills with the hot, strong coffee and pressed the plastiboard carton into the disposal slot. His wrist implant buzzed; this would be his instructions for tonight's assignation.

Activate, he thought.

As the screen swirled into its purplish existence in front of him, he was aware of a faint hissing sound. Before he could even wonder what it was, the passenger module was filled with carbon monoxide. Euan slumped heavily across the seat, the airscreen collapsing into invisible atoms before his closing eyes.

Humming quietly, the robot car drove on.

Forgeries of Jealousy
A Tale of Academe

The fact that it was just like all the other third-rate comedies of the period was neither here nor there. Here it was, a newly-discovered Elizabethan play, in printed quarto form with a title-page date of 1597. As always with such discoveries, there was a compulsive heart-leap of excitement: could it be an unknown Shakespeare? Even a cursory reading of this one, however, confirmed that the Bard's hand had come nowhere near it. It was typical dramatic hackwork of the period, self-evidently a lively stage-piece but virtually devoid of literary merit. Nevertheless, it was an important document, and it was his.

He'd acquired it by an almost laughably stereotypical route: the totally unexpected bequest of a period cottage with an inaccessible attic left unvisited for generations. It was a miracle the small volume had escaped the ravages of damp and mould and insect infestations. Well, it hadn't entirely; one corner had rotted away, fortunately not damaging any of the printed text, and the pages were initially difficult to separate, requiring the services of an expert. But the most astonishing coincidence was that, at the very moment this lost playscript was restored to the world, Sam was about to begin his studies as a mature student at the Warwick Academy of Renaissance Drama, and was scratching around for a suitable subject for his MLitt dissertation. It was like a gift from the past, saved up for centuries for him, and him alone.

He had stayed up till the early hours of a hot summer night, sweatily hauling boxes of bric-a-brac and other paraphernalia down from the dark attic into the overpowering humidity of the poorly-lit cottage. Heavy clouds built ominously in the crackling air outside, pushing up into the sky's purple vault. Sam had no-one to help him. His estrangement from his family had been exacerbated by his unexpected and, they felt, undeserved legacy. And he had no friends with whom he could have shared this arduous task. His late mother was the only person who had ever really liked him, and she had loved him not wisely, but too well. In fact, he was glad to be alone, particularly when he opened the lid of one of the boxes, noticed the small volume and turned over its dank cover. The play's awkward title, revealed in the half-light to his excited gaze, seemed like a deliberate reference to the fruits of his labours: *A Faire Nightes Pickings*.

He didn't know then, of course, that this could turn out to be a lost play, a valuable relic of early modern theatre. The fact that he had never heard of the title before meant nothing; while researching possible dissertation subjects he had become only too well aware that there were hundreds of dramas of the period that he had never heard of, many with the most unlikely titles: *When You See Me You Know Me*; *If You Know Not Me, You Know Nobody*; *If This Be Not a Good Play, the Devil Is in It*.[1]

---

[1] *When You See Me, You Know Me*, by Samuel Rowley (1604); *If You Know Not Me, You Know Nobody*, Parts 1 and 2, by Thomas Heywood (1604-05); *If This Be Not a Good Play, the Devil Is in It*, by Thomas Dekker (1611).

(The last of these, he subsequently discovered, wasn't a good play – and the devil *was* in it.)

There was, inevitably, a long process of investigation and authentication. This was carried out by Chettle and Haughton, an agency recommended by one of the Fellows of the Warwick Academy. During this process, Sam was reluctantly obliged to allow his precious discovery out of his hands. While it was gone he was anxious and fretful, given to restless pacing and compulsive clenching of his fingers, and completely unable to get on with the task of clearing out the rest of the cottage's contents – none of which proved to be of any particular interest. His main consolation was that the agents were not concerned with reading the play, merely with authenticating the quarto as an historical object. Even so, he kept his fingers tightly crossed lest they should notice the bombshell on the final page.

It took an inordinately long time. Chettle and Haughton had to liaise with the Bodleian and the British Library. The book had to be checked against what was known of the printing-house, its equipment and its working practices. The paper had to be subjected to rigorous analysis of its age, its quality and its watermarks. The chemical composition of the ink had to be matched against that used in contemporary texts produced by the same printers. Finally, the authenticated artefact went for valuation to a major auction house, though Sam insisted that it was not for sale under any circumstances, and he demanded that Chettle and Haughton keep his identity secret until he had decided exactly what to do with his unlooked-for treasure. He just kept on hoping that no-one would bother to read the text of the play too closely – not to the very end, at least.

Before handing over the play for analysis, Sam had discovered that it was otherwise unknown, making it both more problematic and more exciting. Not only was it a lost play, but it was a play no-one knew was lost until he had found it. The title page's claim that it had been "sundry times acted" was made less convincing by the uncharacteristic failure to name the performing company. More likely was the assertion that it had been "never before imprinted". Its title should in theory have been known from the Stationers' Register, the list of all works submitted for publication, yet it was apparently not mentioned anywhere in those densely-written pages. [2] No author was named on the title page, but this was not unusual; even many of Shakespeare's plays had first been printed anonymously.

The plot of the play, such as it was, concerned a disgraced knight, Sir Baltimore, who undertakes a series of robberies during the course of one eventful night, the title thus referring to his ill-gotten spoils: a fair night's pickings. In a predictable twist, this ambiguously attractive rogue turns out to be something of a hero, targeting for robbery only those who have successively ill-treated the inhabitants of his native village. And, for good measure, he is finally restored to knightly status, and to the girl who had rejected him, when he proves to be innocent of the misdeeds for which he was cashiered, having been framed by the evil Mordred.

What gave the play its modicum of dramatic effectiveness was the combination of verbal wit and slapstick vigour with which Baltimore's night-time exploits were animated. Unfortunately, its structure was weakly episodic, with a number of frustrating loose ends, and the crude, demotic energy of its prose was vitiated by reams of insipid and pedestrian rhyming verse. Nevertheless, when Sam paid Chettle and Haughton

---

[2] In fact, some printed works, such as the First Quarto of Shakespeare's *Romeo and Juliet* (1597), do not feature in the Stationers' Register.

considerably more than he had expected for the folder of documents they handed over in support of the quarto's authenticity, he felt it was worth it. This play was going to make his name.

The Warwick Academy of Renaissance Drama was a postgraduate institution affiliated with a distinguished American university. It was romantically situated on a semi-cobbled street, its vintage red-brick elegance partly abutting on to the stern walls of Warwick's magnificent castle. It had once been the home of a minor Regency novelist, as attested to by the blue plaque outside its front entrance. There had been some talk of a change of name, to avoid confusion with the enormous number of schools, including at least two in Warwick, that were being granted "academy" status, but the only suggested alternative, the Warwick Institute, made it sound like a prison, or perhaps a secure hospital for the criminally insane. Some wag suggested this would be entirely appropriate.

Sam couldn't wait to start work there. He had been provisionally accepted as a research student, but needed to fix on a dissertation topic appropriate to the advanced degree of MLitt – Master of Letters. His mother, an expert in her time on the writings of Virginia Woolf, would have been proud of him; so would her brother, his academic Uncle Jack, whose work on the plays of Shackerley Marmion was much admired.[3] When Sam finally put in his dissertation proposal – to produce a scholarly edition of the play – there was considerable rivalry among the Academy's Fellows to be his supervisor. He had, of

---

[3] Shackerley Marmion (1603-39), known for three plays from the reign of Charles I: *Holland's Leaguer* (1631); *A Fine Companion* (1632); and *The Antiquary* (?1635).

course, submitted the authenticating documents supplied by Chettle and Haughton. Inevitably, there were those who said the discovery was far too important to be handled by a mere research student, but Sam was adamant: the play belonged to him and he had no intention of letting anyone else, however eminent, get their hands on it. He caused some consternation when he insisted that the existence of the play, and the nature of his research proposal, should be kept secret from all except the Academy's teaching staff, but an accommodation was soon reached. Eventually, his supervision was taken on by Dr Merton Wittings, the Academy's acknowledged expert on obscure Renaissance plays. At first, Wittings hadn't seemed keen to work with Sam, but he showed much more interest on learning that he was the nephew of Jack Ford, the respected Marmion expert. He instantly endeared himself to Sam by suggesting that, in view of the cultural significance of his discovery, his research degree should be upgraded from MLitt to PhD. If all went well, after a few years' challenging work, he would become Dr S. Craftwell; that would be one in the eye for his family. Like his mother, he would sport just the initial; she'd been known simply as Dr O. Ford – using her maiden name, of course.

Everybody at the Academy referred casually to Dr Wittings as "Professor", and so he should have been on account of his distinguished academic record and the brilliance of his published work. However, he had recently been accused of plagiarism by a fellow academic, and though the charge was patently ridiculous, it hung over Wittings like a smudge of grey cloud in an otherwise clear blue sky, casting its insidious shadow over his career. On the surface he remained the genial eccentric he had always been, with his half-moon glasses and garish bow-ties; occasionally, though, students and colleagues were shocked by an outburst of venom and bile for which he would instantly apologise. The Academy's pompous Director, Professor Chapman, even spoke to the students, trying to persuade them that under the circumstances it was rather tactless to refer to Wittings as "Professor", but the habit was so ingrained, particularly with the American postgrads (for whom all university teachers were professors), that it was impossible to enforce.

It was a typical sign of Merton Wittings' scholarly acumen that he was able to point out to Sam, without even needing to check, that while *A Fair Night's Pickings* was not a title that graced the Stationers' Register, that invaluable document *did* have an entry for an otherwise unknown opus entitled *A Fair Knight's Prickings*. "Look it up," he suggested.

Sam was astonished, hardly able to believe it at first. But it was perfect, and fitted incredibly well with the play he had discovered. The fair knight was Sir Baltimore, of course, and "prickings" contained a satisfying *double entendre* (or more correctly, he thought, *double entente*) that was entirely appropriate to the play. As in the opening lines of Spenser's *Faerie Queene* – "A Gentle Knight was pricking on the plaine" – it meant "riding", from the "pricking" or spurring on of a horse. Here, perhaps, in its plural-noun form, it suggested Baltimore's night-time journeyings on horseback from one exploit to the next. Indeed, his horse, Glanders, managed to be one of the play's most entertaining characters without ever appearing on stage. As Baltimore's downtrodden comic squire, Bluebottle, remarked at the outset, "A mare with the glanders is like a maide in *Flanders*: all swoll'n o'er, and ne'er a goer".[4] The play contained a great deal of such obscure, low comedy that Sam would have to wade through and explicate in his edition of the play, but the rewards would be worth it.

"Pricking" was also suggestive of the sexual adventures and misadventures engaged in by Baltimore during the course of this memorable night – something that disturbingly soured the play's supposedly joyous romantic denouement. If Sam were directing the play, he would definitely want to leave the audience with a nasty taste in the mouth after the closing scene of Baltimore's betrothal to his restored lover, Amelia; she was, after all, set to marry a rapist. Shakespeare, of course, was the master of such ambiguous, edgy resolutions, as in *Measure for Measure* or *All's Well that Ends Well*: "All yet *seems* well".

Six weeks into the Autumn Term at the Warwick Academy, when the trees in its secluded gardens had almost completed their alchemical transmutation into burgeoning gold, Sam had made virtually no friends. This didn't bother him, as he had deliberately courted privacy to diminish the risk of his fellow students finding out about his discovery and his work. If asked, he just told people rather vaguely that he was editing an obscure play, and changed the subject. Very few people asked.

Even Dr Wittings had been granted only limited access to the precious text, confined to a selection of photocopied pages – not including the last. Sam had resisted the inevitable pressure to make any complete copies of it, for fear it should become

---

[4] Glanders is an equine disease that causes swellings beneath the horse's jaw and nasal discharge. The swellings of the Flanders maid are, of course, quite differently located; why she should not be "a goer", despite her attributes, is obscure and inexplicable.

common currency before he was prepared to launch his scholarly edition on what he fondly imagined to be an eager world that would by then be champing at the bit, rather like Sir Baltimore's horse. At one point he had toyed with the idea of offering to direct the play, with judicious cuts to its final speech, for the Academy's drama group, but immediately realised that to do so would vitiate the very secrecy he craved and put his play into the public domain before the time he intended. Consequently, he was perfectly happy to be regarded as distant, superior, unfriendly and awkward. People diagnosed his condition in whispered conversations that were just outside his hearing. Did he have OCD? Was he autistic? Delusional? Cripplingly shy? Eventually, he didn't even merit discussion; he was just that rather smelly, bearded, bespectacled nerd who hid himself away day after day in the cramped attic room that served as the top floor of the library, emerging occasionally to access various books and documents that he needed to consult.

It didn't take long, however, for the attitude of Sam's fellow students to shift from indifference to antagonism. A certain amount of envy had reared its head when Sam used some of his considerable fortune to buy a handsome town house a few streets away from the Academy, while everyone else had to make do with sharing cheap lodgings in Warwick's insalubrious suburbs. What particularly got up people's noses was that he didn't even throw a house-warming party. To compound this unforgivable sin, he refused to let his play be read by the Academy's play-reading group, which met every Tuesday evening in term time to read obscure and forgotten specimens of early modern drama under the lively chairmanship of Dr Wittings. Usually, this was a great opportunity for those students who were editing texts to "test run" their editions, but

Sam was so possessive that all Wittings' persuasive powers could not convince him to introduce the play to a wider audience. It was a stupid and dangerous decision to alienate his PhD supervisor. In his naivety, Sam didn't realise that slighted academics make dangerous enemies. But then, Sam had a lot to learn about many things.

Sam soon sensed a certain coolness on the part of his supervisor and decided to do something he'd hoped to avoid. He emailed his Uncle Jack – to speak to him, even on the phone, would bring back memories that were too painful to contemplate – and asked him if he knew Merton Wittings and, if so, could he put in a good word for him. His uncle replied quickly, saying he'd do what he could. Uncle Jack, or Professor Ford to give him his proper title, didn't much like his nephew, but had always indulged him for his late sister's sake. On this occasion, however, pressure of work – among other things – caused him to forget all about his promise.

In the early months of his PhD studies, Sam was mainly concerned with researching the background to late 16th-century drama, absorbing everything he could about theatres, playing companies, playwrights, actors, performing licences, printers and the whole panoply of socio-political contexts in which his author might have worked. He kept referring to the play as being "anonymous", until Dr Wittings put him right.

" 'Anonymous' implies that the name of the writer was deliberately withheld. It's more accurate to say that the authorship is unknown."

Sam had become used to Wittings' sharply astute observations, but had never successfully worked out when to take him seriously. There was always a nagging sense that he was just having you on. There was his name, for example, which he enjoyed claiming as evidence of his inherited intellect.

"All the eldest sons of my family have been christened 'Merton' since the early 16th century, after the Oxford college they traditionally attended. Actually, though, I was the first member of the family for three generations to be accepted there."

Neither Sam nor any of the other Academy students knew whether to believe this fantastical story, always recounted by the doctor with a fey half-smile and a twinkling eye. Fatally, Sam failed to notice when Merton's ocular twinkle shifted from star-bright to diamond-hard to steel-sharp.

It was the middle of January when Sam finally took the plunge and started to type up the text of his play on his laptop. His intention was to reproduce the spelling and punctuation of the original quarto, as Merton was strongly in favour of what academics call an old-spelling edition. He insisted, however, on removing such presentational quirks as the interchangeable u/v and i/j, as well as the confusing ſ symbol, or "long s" which was so easily mistaken for an f. Eventually, though, Sam was determined to overrule his supervisor and produce a modernised version which would be more accessible to ordinary readers out in the waiting world. He had become so used to working in his own cosy alcove of the library's attic room, next to the roaring warmth of a wall-mounted heater, that he didn't really think of undertaking this new stage of his work anywhere else. Occasionally, other students would come up to consult a volume of Elizabethan public records or some arcane study of medieval demonology, but few ever settled there to work; even fewer if Sam were there, since the heater's warm air tended to waft his acrid body odour into the confined space. Outside, the season's grey light filtered through the denuded trees, barely penetrating the misty gloom from dawn till nightfall. With a sharp intake of invigorating breath, and a self-satisfied smile briefly creasing his normally taciturn features, Sam began typing up the play's Prologue.

> Our sharper *Muse* must now laie down her speare
> While lighter notes divert your gentle eare,
> Wafting their harmonies of red hued *Mirth*
> Through this great *Play-house*, figured like our *Earth*.
> Midwifes to *Laughter*, we delivere ryghte
> Our craftie *Authors* newly wrought delight.
> But, save you lift us from our tender'd knees,
> Our *Project* falls, whiche onlie was: to please.

To describe this Prologue as unsophisticated would be over-generous, to say the least; but Sam's editorial brain was already at work, commenting, explaining, annotating, speculating. There was the standard trope of the inspirational muse; the faux-modesty; the audience-flattering tone; the stereotypical metaphors of music and birth; the matter-of-fact wordplay; the dual meanings of "deliver", "crafty", "tendered"; the facile rhyming couplets. But there were also more intriguing features. Was the opening line intended to suggest that the dramatist's previous play had been a tragedy, or a history play perhaps? And then there was the image of the theatre, "figured like our Earth". This was suggestive of the Globe – yet that famous playhouse was not built until two or three years after the ostensible printing date of the quarto. Perhaps this was no more than another familiar and conventional metaphor: theatre-as-world, world-as-theatre. Finally, there was the question of textual accuracy: was "our project falls" in the last line a printer's error for the more obvious "fails"? If it were, then the mildly witty conceit that the actors would fall down if not helped up from their knees would also collapse. Sam reflected wryly that if every eight lines of the play provoked the same amount of commentary, he'd be working on his PhD for the next ten years.

What Sam could never have predicted was that he would fall prey to the attractions of Merton Wittings' partner, a junior fellow at a nearby university that enjoyed a friendly and productive rivalry with the Academy. She was younger than Merton but much older than Sam; not conventionally pretty but undeniably alluring; slightly intimidating, perhaps, but with unexpected flashes of sympathetic humour. She was an irregular member of Merton's play-reading group, which is where Sam first encountered her, and in the wine-filled intervals – which always served to render the plays' second halves more richly enjoyable – they would chat about everything from their respective educational backgrounds to their emotional back-catalogues. Though Sam was rather lacking on the latter front, he invented a varied array of non-existent former girlfriends. In fact, Bianca was the first person, apart from his late mother of course, with whom he had ever been romantically involved. He was flattered by her attention, and too naïve to conceal their developing affair from Wittings, who after all, as Sam argued to himself, was not actually married to Bianca. His fellow students, apparently oblivious of what was going on when in the presence of this odd triangle, nevertheless gossiped avidly among themselves. What *did* she see in him? What did they find to *talk* about? How could she bear that *smell*? To all outward appearances, Merton went about his academic purposes, scrutinising textual minutiae or poking about in antiquated documents, blissfully unaware of any untoward developments in his private life.

By an odd coincidence, Sam and Bianca were destined to have their first, rather limited physical encounter just as he was in the process of typing up the first of Sir Baltimore's vigorous sexual exploits, which saw him seducing the maid at an inn whose landlord had overcharged and mistreated a poor couple from his village while they were *en route* to collect the body of their son, killed in the Dutch wars, from Deptford.[5] (As in all the episodes, this was not revealed until the play's denouement.) The climax of the scene struck Sam as being excruciatingly different from his own botched attempts to get Bianca from his lounge to his bedroom.

> Knight. Nay come, faire wench, hold hard an if thou wilt;
> Grasp firm my sword and heave it by the hilt
> To ease me of its grosse encumberment
> That wee may better close for our content.
>
> Maid. O sir, I'm sure your tongue doth more than speake
> Of swords and hilts. My apprehension's weake,
> And wots not what your *Honor* truly means;
> Your language is moore fit for trulls and queans
> Than for an innocent and humble maide
> Who never yet e'er thought so to be laid.

---

[5] In the early 1500s the Netherlands became a province of the Spanish Habsburgs, but later in the century Prince William of Orange led a Calvinist-inspired revolt against Spain, in which many British soldiers took part. The northern provinces broke away and established independence in 1579. It may seem odd that this conflict features in a play ostensibly set in legendary, Arthurian times, but such inconsistencies are common in the drama of the period. Shakespeare's *Cymbeline* (1610), for example, seems to be set simultaneously in Ancient Britain, classical Rome and Renaissance Italy.

> Knight. Dissemble not with falsly honied breath:
> I know thou know'st too well that little death
> That fades in sighs, expires in joyous floods,
> Shivers exquisitely thro' *Springs* fresh woods,
> Quivers thro' stoutest tree-trunks, bushes wilde,
> Makes *Man* a wanton, *Woman* pleasure's childe.
>
> Maid. Your tongue hath charmed my simple maiden's ear;
> Hie to my chamber and we'll to this gear.[6]

This wasn't quite, Sam reflected, how his own amorous encounter had gone the previous evening. Perhaps he should have essayed some of Baltimore's grossly unsubtle sexual innuendo.

In the text, however, there was an odd coda to this dialogue that Sam found particularly interesting. While Baltimore exited with priapic enthusiasm to his anticipated pleasure, the "wench" remained behind, and was given a brief soliloquy:

> Maid. He knows me not, nor guesses yet how neere
> I am to him in birth: his sister deere.
> Long have I worshipt him, thron'd in my heart,
> Ne'er dreaming that I'd play a nearer part.
> What though his veins do streame with brother's
> blood?
> I love him so, that sinne shall turn to good.

When he'd read this for the first time, Sam had found his cheeks burning. Looking at it now, though, its oddest feature was that it was never followed up in the play. The maid, named as Melinda in the *dramatis personae*, did not appear again, as if

---

[6] The characters in the play, while generally named in the list of roles or in the dialogue, are referred to in speech prefixes only by their generic identities – a not uncommon feature of the period's printed play texts.

179

she were one of the playwright's half-ideas that had not quite reached fruition. This could perhaps be used as evidence that the play had never been performed: if it had, then surely either the speech would have been deleted or some follow-up would have been demanded from the playwright.

As the weeks went on and snowdrop season passed into daffodil time, no such natural process of sprouting and blooming took place in Sam and Bianca's relationship. His lack of experience told against him. He didn't realise that, generally speaking, you don't tell your partner your entire life-history on a first date – even with certain crucial omissions. Bianca had persevered despite Sam's endless reminiscences about his wonderful mother and her encyclopaedic knowledge of Virginia Woolf. The low point of their ill-matched affair was embarrassing for them both, shameful and humiliating for Sam. This was when Bianca told him of his body-odour problem. It took some courage on her part, and she fully expected it to mark the end of their abortive fling. Sam, however, once he had clambered out of the pit of self-loathing into which her revelation had flung him, concluded that only someone who really loved him could have told him such an unpalatable truth. He saw his doctor, took advice, shaved off his beard, improved his personal hygiene and determined to beat his previously unsuspected affliction. It seemed to work; their relationship appeared to be rebooting, other students became more willing to share their academic progress with him and, for the first time, he felt able to open a Facebook account. When his online "friends" numbered eight, he felt inordinately pleased with himself – something that inevitably lost him two of the virtual acquaintances he had so recently acquired. Despite these ups and downs, he and Bianca achieved sexual consummation as the tulips in the Academy's gardens burst blood-red through the green shells of their fat, juicy buds. That was when Merton decided, finally, to act.

Sir Baltimore's adventures, in Sam's laborious typescript, were approaching their end. As the night went on, he and his associates – squire and horse – grew wearier and wearier, and the knight was increasingly careless in managing his assignations. In the final scene of Act 4, having robbed the house and raped the daughter of Sir Barnsley Barnadine, Baltimore discovered to his horror that she had previously been forced into a sexual relationship with her wicked father. [7] Leaving her callously to her fate, he was forced to flee what he called "foul *Incest*'s castle" and head back to Camelot for refuge. Only later was Baltimore's motive for robbing Sir Barnsley revealed: he had failed to send aid and succour to Baltimore's village when it was struck by plague. However, the rape of the ironically named Virginia was not exactly the knight's finest hour. Like the brother-besotted Melinda earlier in the play, she was given a soliloquy which steered the action momentarily towards tragedy, though the insistent jogging of the rhyming couplets worked against the despairing tenor of her reflections.

> Daughter. My bloud is tainted with the foulest blot:
> Incest and Rape have been my lifes sad lot.
> No man is safe from *Lust*'s consuming flame:
> Nor *Father* nor bold *Knight* deserves my blame,
> For tis my beautie tempts them so to falle:

---

[7] This seems to be a foreshadowing of the father/daughter incest strand of Shakespeare and George Wilkins's *Pericles, Prince of Tyre* (1607), which itself derives from various versions of the ancient story of Apollonius of Tyre.

> Beautie so bitter turneth bloud to gall.
> That no more men shal slip perforce to sinne,
> Tis fytte I end my life e'er more beginne.
> Wrongèd *Lucrece* shal now my pattern be:
> I'll end my troubles 'neath the swelling sea.[8]

This was pretty strong stuff, and would not do for our more enlightened times; particularly the idea of the rape victim who blames herself rather than her abuser. As far as Virginia's suicidal intentions were concerned, the play was silent about whether or not she carried them out – yet another of its irritating loose ends.

The whole of this episode soured the comedy of Baltimore's narrow escape, something exacerbated by the intrusion of odd gobbets of more serious blank verse into the play's characteristically jaunty rhyming and vigorous, colloquial prose.

> Knight. *Bluebottle*, hie thee, saddle my sad mare.
> The house is up and we, I feare, descried.
> Yet droop not, *Boy*, the moneybags are got
> And sweete *Revenge* hath ta'en her cunning course.
>
> Boy.
>
> O maister, I feare your sad mare will be a sadder mare if e'er she be saddled more, so sore she be with pricking. La you now, she has more prickes in her flanckes than a porpentine in his pranckes; more welts on her backe than peas in a sacke; less fire in her belly than pits in a cherry. She'll ne'er go more, your mare, till she go brave to her grave.

---

[8] The classical tale of Lucrece, raped by Lucius Tarquinius, was well-known in the period, and was retold by Shakespeare in his narrative poem, *The Rape of Lucrece* (1594). Unlike Virginia in the play, who determines to commit suicide by drowning, Lucrece stabbed herself.

Knight. Alas, boy, spend no further breath in speech;
       Saddle my mare *instanter*, I beseech.
       When we be well awaie from louring harme,
       Then, tell her, she'll be rested, fed and warm.
Boy.

       No words more, maister. *Bluebottle* shall hie, fast as
       an arrow flie; *Glanders* shall be saddled, however
       raddled; and all shall scape from toe to nape; heads
       too if we be both pluckie and luckie.   *Exit.*

Knight. (*solus*) Now *Night*'s dark deeds dissolve in
                           Morning's dew
       And dawn disrobes my cloakèd villainie.
       But harke, the house is rais'd, the servants crie,
       The *Lord* doth rave and stamp *Revenges* coin.
       Tis fit I flie from *Virgin*'s forcèd blot
       And *Father*'s ire; I'll speed to *Camelot*.   *Exit.*

Sam decided to take a break before launching into Act 5.
Normally, he would have gone to the local Starbucks for a
coffee; now, however, he was determined to avoid dog-breath
by drinking only herbal teas. As he passed through the
Academy's listed Edwardian conservatory, with its
unseasonably early splashes of scarlet geraniums and its lush
camellia dropping half-rotted lumps of pink flower on to the
terracotta floor, he passed Merton Wittings giving the usual
schtick about his name to a gaggle of prospective students.

"And then there's the surname – a good old Middle English
word, naturally. We still have 'unwitting' in Modern English, of
course, but 'witting' is more than just its opposite. It's clear
from the contexts in which it occurs that it signifies a
combination of skill, knowledge, cleverness – and a sense of
mischief," he added, glancing at Sam as he passed with a
sharper than usual twinkle in his eye. "Interestingly, it was used

more as a noun than an adjective. 'Wittings' might be translated as 'clever and witty deeds'. Look it up."

Nobody ever did look it up, just as these awed and baffled new students wouldn't. To find that his name did indeed mean what Merton suggested would be a disappointment; to find that it didn't would provoke complete disillusionment. Either result would only serve to pluck out the heart of his mystery; to diminish the perverse, ambiguous mystique of this infuriatingly likeable sage. Essentially, he was unreadable: a wavering signifier of something inherently unknowable.

In fact, no students ever looked up *anything* Merton told them. He was such an acknowledged authority on the drama of the early modern period that whatever he said was automatically assumed to be true. He still couldn't believe, though, that Sam had so far failed to discover that no such title as *A Fair Knight's Prickings* actually featured in the Stationers' Register. If he did find out, Merton would simply make the excuse that he had misremembered it. He had been playing these games for years, spicing up the plodding dullness of his scholarly endeavours.

Sam found the structure of Act 5 especially interesting. Carefully built around a series of false endings, it teased the audience with a sense of repeatedly deferred closure, emphasised by a sequence of apparently conclusive rhyming couplets. At first it appeared that Baltimore's safe arrival at Camelot, with squire and horse in tow, would end the play:

> Knight. Now we'll to rest, our labors all are done;
> Tomorrow we'll enjoy that wee have won.
> See *Glanders* safelie to his bedde of straw:
> No servant for his master could doe more.

Then a procession of complainants arrived at Camelot, demanding redress for Baltimore's nefarious nocturnal activities. The knight was summoned before the King's Chief Justice, and defended himself by revealing the crimes each of his victims had perpetrated against the people of his home village. (In another loose end, no mention was made of Sir Barnsley Barnadine's incest.) The charges against him were dismissed and he was granted a pardon, provided the proceeds of his robberies found their way into the King's exchequer:

> Justice. Youre faults are pardon'd, but your gains are lost:
> So *Justice*' balance mingleth heate with frost.

Again, the play seemed to have ended; but more was to come, in the form of the evil Mordred's confession that he had framed Baltimore for the oddly unspecified, non-knightly conduct for which he had originally been demoted. Mordred was hauled off to prison and the restoration of Baltimore's knighthood promised:

> Justice. *Gaoler*, to prison with this caitiff wretch
> Whose villainies no *Mercie* thence shall fetch.
> Now *Baltimore*, great feasting is toward,
> Thy *Honor* and thy *Knighthood* both restor'd.

Finally, with the reunion of Baltimore and Amelia, and King Arthur's unexpected intervention, the drama's playful teasing arrived at a genuine resolution.

Time passed, and Sam was able to tell Merton he had finished typing up his basic text. Merton already knew that Sam wasn't going to let him see it, but that was OK; he could bide his time. Sam and Bianca had long ago ceased to be an item, and Sam had reverted to frequent cups of coffee and infrequent showering. His beard was slowly re-growing but his Facebook friends had dropped to one – his Uncle Jack. Sam had long ago concluded that Professor Ford had neglected to put in the good word on his behalf that he had promised. If he had, it had had no appreciable effect on Merton Wittings' cool attitude towards him. Nevertheless, he tried again, firing off another email to the professor, wondering if this time he should add urgency to his plea by hinting at what he knew of his uncle's relationship with his own, much-missed mother. He decided that he would. As far as he knew, only she had noticed Sam spying on them on that fateful day.

He was in his usual place in the library, giving his word-processed text a final check prior to transferring it to his brand-new, top-of-the-range iPad, when the fire alarm sounded. It was shortly before the library's closing time, as April dusk dropped its damp dark through the pregnant branches, packed to bursting with spring's green promise. With a huffing of resigned annoyance, Sam abandoned his work in mid-check, logged off, shut down his laptop and tramped heavily down the cold staircase to the ground floor. You weren't supposed to take anything with you, but he was always overcome by a sick, clammy anxiety when he was separated from his work. As the emergency exit door closed behind him, he failed to notice Merton Wittings slipping into the library's lift. Sam's mind was elsewhere. The email to his uncle had brought it all back: that dreadful day, all those years ago. The shock; the summer's unbearable heat; the cruel betrayal by those he loved most; the unforgettable, imagined picture of the closing waters; the soft undulations of gentle, inevitable ripples.

Sam joined the scant evening staff of the library and a thin straggle of students under the dripping trees while, presumably, the appropriate fire-safety procedures were put into practice. Glancing up at the window of what he now thought of as "his" alcove, he saw a shadow flit briefly past: the duty caretaker, he assumed, giving each floor of the library a cursory check before pronouncing the all-clear. By the time the false alarm was over, it was chucking-out time, so he collected his bits and pieces together before briskly walking home through the glistening streets. As he turned the corner to cross over the road in front of the Academy's main building, he noticed there was just one room still lit, on the first floor. Not surprisingly, it was Merton's study, a book-cradled haven of lonely academe, whose creaking shelves slanted precariously at a variety of crazy angles. His supervisor was well known for working obsessively till gone midnight when he had a major project on the go. Sam thought crossly that Bianca would be free – if only she hadn't broken off their relationship when sexual delight had become transmuted into little more than mechanical coupling. For him, there would be no harmonious reunion with his lover as there was for Baltimore in the final scene of his play. He glanced back up at the dim light lurking behind Merton's shabby floral curtains.

Wittings: clever and witty deeds; and mischievous.

Sam turned his coat collar up against the chill drizzle and thought briefly about his mother as he headed for home. He'd loved her unwaveringly – even her stupid nickname, Phillie – and believed she loved him with the same overpowering single-mindedness, until…

When he got home, the first thing he did was to check through the play's final scene, from the point where the fire alarm had cut short his labours. In it, Baltimore and Amelia expressed their mutual love in the form of a (rather bad) sonnet – not an original idea, and evidently "borrowed" from *Romeo and Juliet*. Its romanticism was considerably undermined by Baltimore's habitual, almost compulsive use of sexual innuendo: too subtle, perhaps, for the average member of the audience to pick up.

> Knight. Through all this night I've labour'd long and hard
> Righting the wronges my village hath endured;
> But if thou love me not, my labor's marred,
> My shafte mis-aimed, my *Soules* deare light
> obscur'd.
>
> Lady. Leave to protest, my dearest *Baltimore*,
> And know my heart hath always cherished thee.
> I ne'er did credit *Envies* slandering jaw,
> But knew not how to bringe the *World* to see.
>
> Knight. Thy wordes restore me to my long-lackt joy
> And sow my breast with *Hopes* renewing seede.
> Now thou'st enfranchised me from base annoy,
> I'll serve thee knightly; so our *Love* shall breed.
>
> Lady. Then heere I kneele to thee and pledge my *Life*,
> Never to rise till thou dost call me *Wife*.

Too subtle for poor Amelia too, perhaps. Could the playwright really have intended her to be oblivious of the *doubles ententes* in "long and hard", "shaft", "serve thee", "knightly/nightly", "seed" and "breed"? More food for his critical commentary. Closing his laptop, Sam cast a glance outside at the cobbled street, as moist and shining in the lamplight's sour glow as his own perspiring brow. He decided to indulge in an early night, pleasuring himself in the absence of the only girlfriend he had ever managed to attract.

Merton Wittings was determined to work all night if necessary. He was an experienced textual editor and a notoriously quick and accurate worker. As soon as he had downloaded Sam's laboriously keyboarded playtext from the memory stick on which he had copied it, he got to work on the task he had persuaded Sam not to do, converting it into modern English spelling and punctuation. In little more than three hours it was complete. Even while doing this, his sharp intellect was running through possible authorship candidates who might prove a match for the play's style. Dekker, Heywood, Greene: all were capable of writing this badly.[9] It could, of course, be a collaborative work, a possibility Sam hadn't even considered. But it was not until he reached the very end of the play that Merton became aware, in a flash of scholarly excitement, just how significant this text was. The final scene was set in Camelot, with King Arthur, in his only appearance, performing the role of *deus ex machina* to bring together the sundered lovers, Baltimore and Amelia, and effect what was supposed to be a romantic resolution. The King's status granted him the privilege of the play's closing speech which read, in Merton's modernised version, as follows:

> King.   Come hither, man, and kneel before our sword;

---

[9] Thomas Dekker's best play is his comedy, *The Shoemaker's Holiday* (1599). Thomas Heywood wrote the brilliant domestic tragedy, *A Woman Killed with Kindness* (1603), and claimed to have had "an entire hand, or at least a main finger" in over 220 plays. Robert Greene, best-known for his attack on Shakespeare as an "upstart crow", was a third-rate dramatist whose plays include *Friar Bacon and Friar Bungay* (?1589) and *James IV* (?1590).

Once more we dub thee knight, and are thy lord.
Thy deeds, performed for Justice, we forgive,
So long as thou in truth and faith dost live.
Take up thy lady, kiss her proffered hand,
For soon ye both before the priest shall stand.
Cherish her, Baltimore, her life's thy care,
Her love thy gift, her son-to-be thy heir.
Now gleam the stars in pale Diana's realm,
Casting their lustre on thy knightly helm.
Thy trials are ended, thy delight's begun:
As said our court's chief bard: love's labour's won.

Merton could hardly believe his eyes. There it was, in black and white: only the third known reference to Shakespeare's mysterious lost play, *Love's Labour's Won*, mentioned in passing by Francis Meres in 1598 as one of Shakespeare's most pleasing comedies, and thus providing an endless source of academic speculation. [10] Herein lay the true value of Sam's discovery, which Sam himself seemed to have missed entirely. Or had he? With Sam, it was difficult to tell; he kept his cards close to his chest. Merton thrust his right fist vertically into the musty air of his lamp-lit academic retreat and uncharacteristically vocalised a triumphant if monosyllabic ejaculation: "Yesss!!!"

He paused briefly to consider whether this new discovery should affect his plans, and decided it shouldn't. Some weeks before, he had called in some favours and set up a fake email account through one of his American colleagues, an IT lecturer at the Academy's mother-university. It should be secure for a while, though he had no doubt that, if anyone were so inclined, they could trace it back to him; anyway, it didn't really matter. Revenge was the name of the game; let Nemesis approach later.

---

[10] Francis Meres, *Palladis Tamia: Wit's Treasury* (1598).

Now, at the click of a mouse, he could email Sam's precious play simultaneously to interested parties across the world. He had hundreds and hundreds of contacts already lined up: universities, colleges, theatre companies, publishers – and the media. He had composed a brief, anonymous covering letter, assuring his audience that expert testimony could vouch for the genuineness of the original quarto – collated by the very agents, as it happened, that he had himself recommended to Sam. Chettle and Haughton.

It was now five in the morning, and a grey light was preparing itself just over the horizon, ready to offer a dim validation of day to April's damp streets and soggy trees. Merton smiled, yawned and clicked on "SEND". As he did so, the door of his study creaked open and Bianca peered quizzically inside. She had her own, illicit access card to the building.

"OK?" she asked.

"Oh yes," he replied, leaning back on his chair and stretching his arms into a symmetrical pair of acute angles on either side of his head. "I have done the deed – with a vengeance." He laughed, and yawned. "Sam's play has just been recast; I'm Sir Baltimore now – and I get the girl."

She moved to him, leaned over and gave him a long kiss. "I was right then?" she said.

"You were. Your assumption about his password was spot on. Ophelia, his mother's name, but spelt backwards, suffixed by the year of her death. It was divine. The fire alarm was perfectly timed, too. And I've found something else, to boot. Something good."

She stood back, eyeing him speculatively.

" 'Love's labour's won'," he pronounced cryptically. "All in all, a fair night's wittings, I think you'll agree."

She laughed, pleased with his joke, and with her part in his success. She didn't admit that she'd actually *seen* Sam entering the password on his laptop, as well as having had to listen to endless tales of his mother's many virtues and her tragic suicide. Freud would have had a field day. She preferred to let Merton think she had outdone Sherlock Holmes in deductive reasoning; and the fact that when he attempted to access Sam's work he couldn't be sure that the password would actually function simply added to the frisson. The whole thing had only been made possible, though, as a result of Merton's entire lack of interest in sex, so that his and Bianca's relationship was utterly uncluttered by sexual jealousy. But her fling with Sam had been a huge sacrifice; apart from anything else – the smell…

"Sam's still got the quarto, though," she said, her mind switching, as it habitually did, to a different track. "Maybe we should have stolen that too."

"No need," Merton observed casually. "He'll have to hand it over to someone with academic credibility in the end, particularly if he wants his name associated with it. If I'm the lucky recipient, so much the better. The main thing is, we've stolen his thunder, as well as his work. Oh, by the way," he added mischievously, "speaking of plagiarism, I was summoned to a meeting with our great Director yesterday morning. The odious Jack Ford has finally retracted his accusations. I'm getting my professorship." As an afterthought, he added, " 'Tis pity he waited so long: what a shame we had to destroy his nephew's work."

*

192

Within forty-eight hours, *A Fair Night's Pickings* was an internet sensation, exploding well beyond the bounds of the international academic community. Editions of the play were planned on every continent, though the more scholarly of these would have to wait on the facsimile of the original quarto that Merton had promised in his mass email. The play was to be translated into eleven different languages. Stage productions, amateur and professional, were conceived in Britain, the USA, Canada, Australia, Germany, Poland, Israel, India, Japan, South Africa and Brazil.

Within forty-eight hours, too, Sam knew that his work had been stolen, his precious, secret play clicked into virtual ubiquity. One glance at the headline in the arts pages of *The Times* was enough:

New evidence of Shakespeare's lost play

Instinctively, he knew who was responsible. Everything fell into place with a horrible, brain-numbing clarity. Carefully, he closed the newspaper and put it back neatly on the rack in the Academy library. He looked around, casting his eyes contemptuously over the few students who were working away on their own petty projects. This explained the awkward, shifty half-smiles he had been getting all morning from people who would normally have ignored him. He felt suddenly hot, and unpleasantly sticky under his heavy clothes. Picking up his laptop and his back-pack he went out into the gardens, where a weak April sun was lighting up the rich, pink blossoms of the flowering cherries that were daring to unfold their frail petals with the promise of spring.

Finding a bench in the mild, thinly filtered sunshine, he sat down and thought for a moment, still not entirely clear why Merton Wittings had done this to him. Then, oddly, he smiled. He hadn't expected ever to have to reveal the truth but perhaps, after all, it would be better out in the open. His smile broadened as he ran silently through a range of possible strategies for announcing to the world that *A Fair Night's Pickings* was a forgery, its precious Shakespeare reference a cynical con.

When Chettle and Haughton, the firm he had engaged last summer on Merton's recommendation, had reported back to him that the quarto was a fake, he had been, as they say in the media, devastated. But he was not to be so easily thwarted in his intention of outdoing his Uncle Jack in academic distinction and thereby claiming back in his imagination his dead mother's love and admiration. He soon found that everyone has a price, and his considerable legacy readily covered what the agents demanded for supplying their own fake documentation attesting to the genuineness of a fraudulent artefact.

He had been puzzled, though. Apparently, the quarto actually dated from the early nineteenth century; but why should anyone want to forge a mediocre comedy by an anonymous playwright? Surely it was only worth creating a fake Shakespeare play, or at least a new Marlowe or Ben Jonson. And why hadn't this forgery ever been unleashed on a gullible world?

Sam thought he had worked out the answer. The unknown forger had evidently planned to pique the interest of the academic community with the intriguing if clumsy reference to *Love's Labour's Won* at the play's conclusion. And then, Sam decided, the *real* revelation was to be made: a forged version of Shakespeare's lost play itself. What had then happened it was impossible to guess. Perhaps the forger had died before getting any further with his scam. Or simply didn't have the skill to imitate Shakespeare as convincingly as he could one of the Bard's less talented contemporaries. Or perhaps a fake text of *Love's Labour's Won* was, in fact, waiting to be discovered in some other mouldering attic. None of this mattered. Forgery it may be, but Sam had determined that, as far as the world would ever know, *A Fair Night's Pickings* was a genuine Elizabethan comedy, concluding with a revelatory reference to a lost Shakespeare play; and he, Sam Craftwell, would gain all the academic kudos of having discovered and edited it.

Now, though, a mere nine months later, Sam's focus had been twisted, thanks to Merton Wittings' treachery. If all that was left for him was to expose Merton as an envious and embittered old fraud, and to humiliate him as the renowned expert who had been taken in by a blatant forgery, then that would have to suffice. He began to look forward to it, only regretting that he wouldn't be there when Merton discovered the truth. Sam shivered as the pale streaks of spring sunshine gave way to watery grey clouds, and the vibrancy of the pink blossom fell prey to an unexpected power cut.

Merton knew that Sam would soon put two and two together and work out who had stitched him up, stolen his work and wrecked his career. He was half-expecting Sam to come storming up to his study, shaking with rage; indeed, he was almost licking his lips at the prospect. When nothing happened for three or four days, and he hadn't seen Sam creeping round the Academy as he usually did, Merton assumed that he must have locked himself away to lick his wounds. But there would be consequences, he had no doubt; and he thought he knew exactly the form they would take.

He was dead right. A week later, the world's media was full of the shock revelation that the recently discovered reference to Shakespeare's lost play, *Love's Labour's Won*, was part of an elaborate forgery. Sam had confessed all, yet despite the shattering of his academic credibility, he was quietly satisfied; in time, Merton would be totally discredited, and there was no way he would now be able to claim he had won whatever perverted game he thought he was playing.

Sam gloated quietly, revelling in Merton's future humiliation. As yet, he had told no-one of his suspicions about Merton having stolen and broadcast his work, though this would come in time: he thought he might open a Twitter account for the purpose. Meanwhile, it was enough to imagine his former supervisor's discomfiture; the recriminations that would no doubt be tossed around between him and Bianca; the grim certainty of his forthcoming academic downfall. Sam enjoyed mouthing the word "*schadenfreude*", with a sly smile. Merton was finished.

Bianca thought so too, and was at a loss to comprehend Merton's cheerfulness as he went about his everyday work, finalising his radical new edition of the works of Shackerley Marmion, the publication of which would at last knock Professor Jack Ford off his academic perch. As far as Bianca could tell, Merton was completely indifferent to the fact that Sam had turned their victory on its head.

"What's going on?" she asked.

"I wondered when you'd ask," he replied with a sly grin. It was obvious he'd been dying to tell her something for days, ever since the revelation that *A Fair Night's Pickings* was a forgery.

"Well? Give."

"Ah, my dear, how inexperienced is the ambitious young student in the winding ways of academe. Fired with the single purpose of his own prospective elevation to scholarly eminence, he is utterly blind to the devious, internecine brutality of the academic community. I knew from the start he was Ford's nephew; knew I needed to put a spanner in his works for his dear uncle's sake. Chettle and Haughton owed me a favour, and with a few extra inducements, well... If Sam's precious quarto was a forgery, they could tell him so. If it were genuine, I persuaded them to tell him it was a forgery. I had no particular plan, just the satisfaction of setting the odd explosive charge for activation whenever it seemed most entertaining. I could never have imagined in a million years that it would all have worked itself out so perfectly."

Bianca stared at him, wide-eyed and open-mouthed. This was something new; this was not Iago's motiveless malignity, but random mischief-making: tossing a handful of pebbles in the pond to see where the ripples went, how they coincided and intersected before resolving themselves into short-lived placidity. And he hadn't confided in her...

"The play's genuine, of course," Merton concluded. "Chettle and Haughton will magically reveal the truth, sometime soon. It's been a bit complicated for them, poor souls," he added, "but I made it worth their while. They handed over all the authenticating documents to Sam except for the clincher, the paper analysis. Instead, they substituted a forged version, dating it as no earlier than 1790. They'll simply tell him the analysts got it wrong first time round and have subsequently reassessed it as late 16th century."

"But you won't get anything out of it," Bianca protested, her head spinning.

"Oh but I will. I already have," Merton whispered with relish, utterly failing to observe an expression of bilious distaste creeping across her face. "Such fun," he added, turning back to the neatly stacked file of papers at his side, his dusty old books, and his humming laptop. On his desk was a newly-engraved nameplate for his office door, pronouncing in gold-etched capitals on a tasteful maroon background:

PROFESSOR MERTON WITTINGS

A fitting epilogue, Merton reflected, to his devious adventurings – and much more concise than the play's actual Epilogue, a typically toadying piece of cringe-making fake humility that somehow seemed even more insipid in Merton's modern-spelling version:

> So now all's well, or seemeth so;
> Good Wit's defeated Vice's tricks;
> Our knight hath vanquished every foe,
> Gained Love's reward, spite of Life's pricks.
> If we have pleased with our poor skill,
> No more reward do we request,
> And yet it would not serve us ill
> Were you to will us this bequest:
> Let your kind hands complete our plot
> And bring us safe from Camelot.

*

It was on an unseasonably hot afternoon in early May that Sam Craftwell walked into the deepest stretch of the River Thames near Henley, his pockets filled with stones – along with the only extant copy of an obscure Elizabethan comedy, *A Fair Night's Pickings*, author unknown. This was the exact spot where, fifteen years previously, his mother had slipped quietly into the water, just an hour after Sam had discovered her in bed with her own brother. Sam's death merited a brief report in the local paper, but otherwise went largely unremarked. Only two people attended the cremation: Sam's ex-lover, Bianca; and his Uncle Jack. As the recorded organ music played itself out in the crematorium chapel, they walked arm in arm between the ranks of dark conifers under the hot blue of a cloudless sky.

A hundred miles or so away, among the cool shadows cast by the towering walls of Warwick Castle, a new revenge plot was being formulated in a dim and dusty academic retreat whose crazily-angled shelves were crammed with steadily decaying volumes of desiccated scholarship.

Time-Knot

The room was faded and shabby, but recognisably the same room. The translucent door of the machine slid noiselessly aside and Caryn stepped out, a surge of anxiety curdling her gut. As her eyes grew accustomed to the familiar, windowless gloom, she was astonished to see the lab still in place around her, its careless scattering of equipment stranded as always in a tangle of cables. Her laptops, tablets and other electronic devices remained where she had last seen them, which made no sense at all. Yet there was a dullness draped about everything, a feeling of disuse, of abandonment. Decades of dust had settled, the paint on the walls had flaked and fallen, the display-panel on the desk-clock was grey and blank, and the shrivelled corpses of long-dead insects lay shrouded in disintegrating webs.

In the centre of the lab, sturdy as ever, stood the solid oak table with its random array of books and the single, sad photograph of her children. A collection of used mugs and crumbed plates, thick with filth, awaited the weekly visit of Anya, the cleaner – deferred indefinitely, it seemed. The screwed-up blot of a dead spider caught Caryn's eye at the bottom of her favourite mug under a greasy blanket of grey dust, ringed with a desiccated brown smear of coffee. She stood still, baffled, troubled. She scanned the table more closely, swallowing back the slither of panic that rose and spread like a cobra bracing itself for the kill.

There was no doubt of it. The mug was exactly where she had left it, what, less than an hour ago. That morning's local paper still lay where she had tossed it aside, now crisped to a yellowish-grey, its edges falling to fragments, its printed news illegible under the detritus of disintegration and decay. She knew without looking that it was still folded open at the article she'd been reading earlier, an interview with her ex-husband, who talked about his anti-ageing research in that infuriating, unbending tone of absolute certainty from which she had thankfully extricated herself five years ago. But how could it be there still? How could the lab, with all its contents, still exist, just as she had left it, but for the depredations of time and decay? It was only minutes ago, true; but seventy years had passed.

Caryn had given careful thought to her first time-trip, the test-run of the world-changing invention that would nudge her ahead of Justin to Nobel laureateship. There would be no venturing into the past, running the risk of sparking even minuscule changes to the world as it currently existed; no rash sampling of the far future, thrusting herself unprepared into an alien unknown. No; she had studied the theoretical fictions of dystopian literature and had no intention of inadvertently stamping on a Jurassic butterfly or straying into some terrifying future of cultural fragmentation. Her much-thumbed copies of Bradbury and Wells, she noted, still lay on the table alongside the more reputable tracts of theoretical physics that dealt with the paradoxes and potentialities of time travel. She had decided to move with, rather than against, the stream of time; to aim for a future near enough to be recognisable, she hoped, but safely beyond the date of her own death and that of her contemporaries. Yet for seventy years, it seemed, her lab had remained utterly untouched.

Nothing in Caryn's reading had prepared her for the anti-climax of the "journey" itself. Instead of the gradually accelerating, kaleidoscopic phantasmagoria of time's passing posited in speculative fiction, with its blurring vertigo and psychedelic disorientation, there was nothing. She simply strapped herself into the padded, black plastic seat that she had modelled on her patio recliner, set the required date on her dashboard display and pointed commandingly at the START button. Nothing happened, except that the operating light switched to green for a fraction of a second before reverting to red as a buzzer sounded. Surely that couldn't be it? She squinted through the misty, perspex screens, unable to perceive any alteration in the dim forms of the surrounding room. She gave vent to a muttered obscenity; the machine had failed. Her Nobel Prize slipped embarrassingly from her mind's grasp and she blinked away an image of Justin's complacent grin. Releasing her safety constraints, she tensed herself for disappointment and moved to the door, which slid silently aside to disclose the scene already described.

Caryn's mind chased after some explanation, any explanation of the scene in front of her. Idly, she reached out for the photo of her children, their smiling, unknowing faces swathed in decaying strands of broken webs and specked with the dark blots of long-dead flies. Tears welled in her eyes, which must have caused her to misjudge the distance, as her hand failed to make contact with the tarnished silver frame. Instead, she went to pick up the disintegrating newspaper with its incensing headline, BOFFIN BOASTS AGEING BREAKTHRU, and watched in horrified amazement as her hand passed straight through it and sank into the sturdy wooden table. She snatched it back, her brain instinctively generating a tingling in the tips of her fingers, but in reality her hand was unaffected by its impossible spatial collision, and the newspaper did not even quiver in response to the invasion of its space.

A quick pulse of panic propelled Caryn unthinkingly towards the chair she'd been sitting in just moments before, as it seemed, composing auto-timed messages to be dispatched in the event of her failure to return. But she made no contact with it, dissolving into its lack of substance with flailing arms until she came awkwardly to rest, one chair-leg protruding painlessly from her stomach and her buttocks buried a few centimetres below floor level. Briefly, she lost consciousness; when she came to, she struggled quickly to her feet, trying desperately to extricate herself from the objects intersecting with her bodily space. She stood, shaking, and realised there was nothing she could grab hold of to steady herself. Looking down, she observed with astonishment that her feet had sunk into the vinyl floor-covering. She lifted each in turn, as if freeing herself from a quicksand's sucking grip or the sludgy pull of glutinous mud, and restored herself to a precarious balance. She felt stranded, an Arctic explorer adrift on a vast shelf of unstable ice. Stepping with exaggerated care, she made her way unsteadily back to the machine. The translucent door slid open at her approach; it at least still recognised her physical presence. She stepped in and it closed silently behind her. Her legs were shaking and her stomach was knotted with pain. Before collapsing into the reclining seat, she touched it gingerly to make sure both she and it were dimensionally coexistent. To her relief, it felt softly supportive.

For a minute or so she sat there, unmoving, unconsciously reconstituting both her composure and her dispassionate scientific curiosity. It was clear to her that she had two options. She could beat a shameful retreat, rewinding her personal chronology to the moment she had activated the machine's controls. Or she could stay in this future world, unnerving as the prospect was, exploring its disturbing peculiarities and drawing some preliminary conclusions about her unstable relationship with it. A ground-breaking academic paper began to write itself in her head, along with her Nobel acceptance speech. There wasn't really a choice, was there?

Before venturing out of the machine for a second time, Caryn reflected on how embarrassingly ill-prepared she was for her expedition to the future. The problem was, she hadn't really considered it as an expedition so much as a technological experiment. She was in her everyday working clothes and had neglected to supply herself with food, medication or toiletries, anticipating a quick, exploratory visit of just a few hours. She had nothing, electronic or otherwise, on which to make notes; her new compact-tablet still lay where she had left it, webbed thickly in dust and grease. She could hardly expect it to work after seventy years – and in any case, she realised with a jolt, she wouldn't be able to pick it up. She cursed her stupidity and decided that her priority in this virtual future was not to investigate the abnormality of her relationship with her surroundings, but to discover why the room she had been working in just a short time ago remained exactly as she'd left it, despite the passage of seven decades.

She stood up, animated suddenly by a fragile determination. Dark thoughts crowded at the fringes of her mind, but she pushed them aside; refused to contemplate the panic of knowing that, if her room was exactly as it had been seventy years in the past, then clearly she had never returned to it; *would* never return to it. A wave of claustrophobia smothered her in stifling heat. She had to get out of here, explore the world outside the mystery of this impossible room. The machine's door slid aside and she strode with a tentative confidence to the fire exit, tucked in a corner of the lab. She reached out to push the release-catch and grimaced when her hand passed straight through it. She stood in thought for a moment and inhaled deeply, taking in air from – when? This would be another puzzle to ponder in due course; perhaps in this disembodied state she didn't need to breathe at all. Summoning all her limited reserves of courage, she stepped forward and shimmered through the closed door into the street outside.

The journey to the library was a swirl of uncomfortable sensations and colliding impressions. Unlike her lab, the streets around the house were not mummified in time's smeared bandaging of dust and grease, though Caryn was not really paying attention to the dispiriting townscape as she passed, ghostlike, amidst its unfolding layers. All her energies were focused on negotiating her disconcerting progress through the impedimenta of urban life, struggling to maintain her balance on the insubstantial paving stones and absorbent road surfaces. A brisk wind sent scraps of paper and tin cans spinning through the air and scuttling across the cracked pavements, and gusts of gale-strewn leaves flung autumn at her in rushes of yellow and gold. Every time a flapping grey fragment or a twist of corkscrewed foliage hurtled in her direction she flinched unnecessarily as it passed through her, undiverted by her presence. The world's volume control had been turned to zero; the wind and its effects were eerily silent, the infrequent, battered cars glided by without a sound, and when she experimentally spoke Justin's name in a burst of resentful, ridiculous anger, it registered only as the subliminal suggestion of tongue on palette and a slight, decisive movement of her jaw. The streets were drab and empty, with only an occasional shabby, slumped pedestrian labouring by, oblivious of her passing. To her horror, one man veered drunkenly towards her to avoid a puddle that filled a ragged pothole with rippling black glitter. Unable to avoid him, she shuddered to a halt as their existences briefly coincided and let out a scream of panic and disgust that sent no sound-waves shivering through the silent, turbulent air. Already she was regretting her decision to venture out into this nightmarish maelstrom of half-familiar unreality. Irrationally, it was all Justin's fault; why had he pushed and pushed her with his casual superiority, his insouciant arrogance, his cruel, demeaning love into this desperate need to outdo him, to cheat him of the glory and celebrity he craved? Why had she ever wanted to meet him? Why had she decided, against all advice, to marry him? Why, when he persisted in humiliating her with that calm, smug self-assurance and that stretched sneer, hadn't she grabbed the nearest solid object and smashed it into his stupid, brilliant head? The children, of course…

By now it had started to rain. Caryn remained still, catching at her breath, straining to inhale the air from whatever atmosphere sustained her existence. She held out her arm and watched as the slivers of thickening drizzle slipped through it

206

smoothly and painlessly. She had no plan of action for when she reached the library. She could ask nothing of anyone, separated as she was in an invisible loneliness far worse than the isolation she was accustomed to in her lab. She would be powerless to operate any computer, or to pick up any book or newspaper, if such things still existed. This entire venture had been a woeful mistake; she should have stayed in the machine and back-tracked seventy years to the time and place she'd occupied just an hour or so ago, where she could have given proper consideration to planning a more organised visit to this questionable future. Bloody Justin!

Still, she was here now; she would allow herself at most an hour in the library before beating an inevitably ignominious retreat. She stood for a moment more, oddly enjoying the experience of the damp wind's whip and whirl buffeting round her and through her, screened as she was from its effects in a protective bubble of non-existence. For the first time, she looked with interest at her surroundings. This morning, that impressive building opposite had been a car park. Only yesterday she had left her car in the space now occupied by an unusual statue in brightly-coloured fibreglass, evidently representing some local dignitary. There was something odd, though. While these new additions to the urban landscape stood proudly in their commanding positions at the centre of the street, both they and the surrounding buildings conveyed a discouraging impression of neglect and disuse. Windows were cracked and smeared, paintwork scratched and flaked, bricks mossed and crumbling, roof slates missing, clumps of grass and twisted branches spouting from guttering and drains. She looked more closely at the pock-marked road surface and broken paving slabs, brushed with a drifting sheen of blowing wet, and wondered what had happened to the world. Unaware of Caryn's presence, a woman walked past, stooped and despondent under a frayed umbrella. She looked about forty, but her demeanour spoke of age and weariness. Caryn's curiosity was aroused; briefly forgetting her immediate situation, she determined to use her visit to the library, assuming it still existed, to investigate the history of the past seventy years, to find out why both the animate and inanimate worlds seemed so drained of hope.

The library was still there. She passed into the main reading room and stood – or, rather, settled herself as best she could on the yielding, carpeted surface – casting an eye over the familiar but altered scene. Nothing had changed, substantially at least, yet everything seemed different. She hadn't been here much, not since she used to bring the children to the weekly sing-alongs and storytelling when they were toddlers – before the "accident". Tables and shelving had been rearranged since she was last here; hardly surprising in seventy years. Yet, to all appearances, they were the *same* tables and shelves. They were bent, battered, scraped and smeared by decades of use. The black leather covers of the familiar chairs were frayed and split, with tendrils and carbuncles of pale, stained foam slowly disgorging into the dim light. A few people sat hunched at tables, poring over torn and faded books; others peered myopically at the shelves, apparently indifferent to whatever might attract their attention. There seemed to be only one library assistant on duty, and she sat isolated behind the service desk, idly flicking through a dog-eared magazine.

Caryn knew, though, that there was something odd about the scene, which she couldn't at first identify. Then it came to her, in a double epiphany of puzzling import. There were no old people or children in the library; everyone here seemed more-or-less middle-aged. And, more surprisingly perhaps, there were no computers. The last time she'd been here, a year or so ago, the place had been buzzing with the eager, anxious hum of pensioners discovering the joys of social networking or exploring the rich wealth of online information. In what had been the children's area, empty now of all activity, a ceiling-light flickered forlornly above the largely empty racks. All this was rendered dreamlike and unnerving by the total silence in which Caryn was enveloped. Remembering something, she glanced round, looking for the rotating stand where current newspapers were displayed. There it was, still untidily stuffed with badly refolded pages of news and comment. She could hardly believe such artefacts still existed, but at least she'd be able to scan the visible headlines and begin to make some sense of this distorted world.

She moved closer to the stand, unafraid now of passing through irrelevant intervening objects. The familiar titles still clamoured for attention: *The Times*, *Daily Telegraph*, *Guardian*, *Daily Mail*, as well as the local rag she'd been reading with increasing annoyance earlier that day. Only a few of the headlines were completely visible, squashed up and overlapping as the papers were. She noted intriguing hints of the day's news, rendered with some unfamiliar spelling choices: MASSIV REDUXION IN ARMY RECRUTMENT; DEATH-PILL BAN SPARKS RIOTS; FREE COLLEXION OF D-FUNCT COMPUTERS; and, half-obscured beneath an advertising supplement, UNDER-30S SHRINK TO – . She tried to read the articles that followed these headlines, but it was impossible to pick up more than snatched phrases from the overlapping mess of pages stuffed untidily into the racks. Scanning down to the local paper, which she guessed would be the least interesting, she noted the uninspiring headline, VANDALIZD STATU TO B D-MOLISHD.

Caryn could make nothing of these snatches of news; they seemed no different from the media obsessions and scaremongering of her own time. She was desperate to read more, but had no idea how to do so. She was about to move away from the rack in search of other possibilities when a man appeared in front of her, having passed, unknowing, through her left arm, and took up the copy of the local paper. His drab raincoat glistened with specks of moisture and his felt hat was darkened with damp. Oddly, he was wearing sunglasses, despite the library's dim lighting. He sat at an empty table and spread the paper in front of him. Looking round furtively, he removed his hat and placed it beside him. Like everyone else, he seemed to be in early middle age, though his posture and expression suggested someone much older. Without removing his sunglasses, he began studying the lead article, about the vandalised statue.

Caryn moved to his side; at least this was an opportunity to pick up some details of what was going on locally and, perhaps, in the wider world. Uninterested in the main story, she noted that enclosed within it was a smaller piece with the sub-heading, 70th aniversary of scientists disaperance. At first she couldn't think of any local scientists from her own time – except Justin. Then, with a heart-shaking realisation, she knew it was about her. Instinctively "correcting" the superficial oddities of spelling and punctuation, she read the following:

210

It is exactly 70 years since prizewinning physicist Dr Caryn Bradley, ex-wife of disgraced scientist Prof. Justin Bradley, vanished from her secluded lab, where she had been working on a practical application for her time travel theories. The machine she had been developing was also missing, leading to much speculation that she had journeyed in it to some other period of time, past or future, in which she had been prevented from returning. Her former husband discovered her absence on the very day she disappeared, when he made a rare visit to share his recent research successes with her. There has since been speculation that he murdered her and, in a fit of jealousy, destroyed her work and faked explanatory emails from her to friends and colleagues, supposedly sent automatically when she didn't return. No evidence has ever been found to support these allegations, which arose only after the disastrous side-effects of Prof. Bradley's *GerontOppose* serum had become apparent. The Bradleys' young children, a twin boy and girl, had been killed in a household accident five years previously, while staying with their father; a terrible irony in view of his subsequent, unwitting destruction of all future children thanks to his initially much-lauded medical breakthrough.

Since her disappearance, Dr Bradley's lab has remained locked up and inaccessible to all but her ex-husband, who decided to leave it exactly as it was when she vanished. He had always retained ownership of the property, despite the acrimony of their marriage break-up. Interviewed at the time, Prof. Bradley argued that if his former partner were ever to return from her supposed time-travelling, it was important that her lab was still in existence. Prof. Bradley himself has not been seen for some years. It is thought he went into hiding after receiving numerous death-threats (see above).

There was far too much in this article for Caryn to absorb in one reading. Her mind struggled for comprehension between the accounts of her own disappearance and of Justin's fall from grace. Quickly, she turned her attention to the main article, about the imminent demolition of the vandalised statue, from which she caught merely a flavour of the shocking effects produced by the mad rush for Justin's anti-ageing drug: the sense of loss and depression that struck those whose bodies remained fixed in early middle age while their minds plunged into the mental abysses of advancing years; the epidemic of impotence that had left the world increasingly childless; and the unbearable weight of responsibility that hung on those fewer and fewer children who, for a while, continued to be born. Surely none of this was possible; it was appalling, unthinkable; yet Caryn could not help relishing the glimmer of *schadenfreude* that haloed Justin's inevitable, deserved humiliation. She felt no guilt about this because she knew, in an instant of utter clarity, that this was only a possible future. Neither her disappearance nor Justin's apocalyptic discovery needed to happen. She would go back to the lab, reset the machine's controls, return to the day on which she had existed just two short hours ago, and change everything.

As she turned to leave, the man sitting beside her removed his sunglasses. His face, though not old, was drawn and pale but, as he looked up from the column about her disappearance, his mouth stretched into that unmistakable, condescending sneer. It was Justin, of course. He must be over a hundred years old but, like everyone else in this world, looked no more than forty. He turned in her direction, as if he were aware of her, standing tense and rigid just metres away. In his dull eyes a spark of triumph flared briefly in the library's dim greyness.

Caryn ran. As she hurtled through furniture, through shelves, through walls, she cursed Justin and cursed herself for still letting him get to her – after seventy years, for God's sake! She burst into the vaporous air of the dripping street, oblivious of her frantic feet sinking into the road surface as she failed to navigate successfully her interlocking relationship with her

212

surroundings. She knew she was heading more or less in the right direction but was surprised to find she had crossed the road to where the imposing new building had usurped the old car park. Above the door, carved impressively into the stonework, was the legend: THE JUSTIN BRADLEY INSTITUTE. She stopped, worryingly out of breath, and scanned the edifice that rose two storeys into the swirling rain and purple sky. Now she was closer to it, she saw that its glass entrance lobby was padlocked and its windows boarded up, with notices threatening the prosecution of unauthorised intruders fixed at random intervals. In front of the Institute she saw now that Justin's statue was brightly coloured only because it was splashed with stars and streaks of blue, red and yellow paint. Its left hand was raised proudly, holding a translucent phial between thumb and forefinger, but the right arm was missing, leaving a ragged tear of metal and fibre-glass at the shoulder. The inscription under the statue was virtually unreadable, having been gouged in criss-crossed patterns by some sharp implement. Caryn thought she could make out Justin's name, and the phrase "immortal benefactor", but the desecrator had otherwise done a pretty good job. Caryn could not prevent herself from smiling, just as a bedraggled jackdaw flapped silently through her chest and perched on the statue's smashed head.

The bird's passage through the immaterial substance of her body shocked her back into urgency. She lifted her feet slowly and carefully from the pavement's surface and moved off, no longer running, in the direction of her lab, her machine and a return to sanity. She needed to remain resolutely calm if she was going to save the world from lingering extinction.

Caryn leaned back in the seat of what she had persistently tried to avoid calling her "time machine", a phrase more redolent of sci-fi than science. She snatched back her thoughts to the matter in hand and determined not to act in a hurry. At first it had seemed obvious: she would return to the exact moment she had left her own time, abandon her work, and plan with care how she could prevent Justin from unleashing his life-changing anti-ageing serum before it could begin its insidious work of human and social destruction. The interview she'd read with him in the morning's paper of seventy years ago did not make it clear how far his work had progressed, but he'd seemed confident that the transition from laboratory testing to practical trials of what he was then calling *AgeBlock* was imminent. Her ideas for curtailing his progress were wild and unfocused. She could make him listen to the story of her trip into the future, or she could, somehow, blow him and all his works to kingdom come. The first plan was unlikely to succeed, at least not without her giving him a personal demonstration of the time machine. The second, tempting as it seemed, was an unlikely project for her to undertake. It would equate her with those urban terrorists who committed increasingly lunatic atrocities against any scientist who failed to espouse the prevailing ideologies: of religion, environmental concerns, or the sentimental anthropomorphism that regarded animals as pseudo-humans on which it was immoral to experiment, even for the benefit of humankind. Caryn pressed the pause-button on her wandering thoughts; there was no point in succumbing to the familiar welling up of anger at the stupidity of the anti-science brigade – especially as she would have to join their ranks to prevent the unimaginable apocalypse about to be wreaked by scientific progress.

Making a sudden decision, she leaned forward and reset the date and time on the control panel, not for the exact moment she had instigated her trip into the future but for three hours later, partly to cover the length of her absence but mainly to avoid running the risk of colliding with herself at her departure-point. Taking a deep breath, she directed her finger towards the START button. The red light turned green, then back to red. The buzzer crooned – the first sound she had heard since her previous time-flip.

At first she didn't dare focus her vision beyond the machine's translucent screens. What if time travel were only possible in one direction, and the past was an impossible, unavailable destination? She peered about her, screwing up her eyes in an attempt to see beyond the misty opacity of the perspex panels. The dim shapes of the lab were familiar, but they'd been so when she'd arrived in the future. Only by leaving the machine's safe enclosure could she ascertain if the patina of grease and dust, the depredations of decades of abandonment, had been lifted, and the lab restored to the condition in which she'd left it that morning.

She stood up and found she was shaking uncontrollably, her heart thumping, her mind frantic with apprehension. She took a step forward and the door slid open. She gazed, blinking, into the dim shades of the lab until her eyes adjusted to the gloom. As the sturdy oak table with its untidy array of disparate paraphernalia gradually came into focus, she gasped with relief: the grease, the dust, the spidery drapes and insect corpses had cleared away as if by magic. She was back. The desk-clock's electric-blue display told her that it was 14.32, exactly three hours and two minutes after she had begun her venture into the future. She felt she'd been absent for weeks, and decided that before she did anything else she would have a shower and change into fresh clothes. She noticed she was hungry and decided to make herself a stack of sandwiches; there was fresh bread in the larder and an unopened pack of ham in the fridge. When she'd eaten, she could sit down and give proper thought to what she should do next.

She had barely taken a step out of the machine when the door opposite the fire exit opened silently. Anya, the cleaner, came in and looked across at her, her face crinkling in surprise. Caryn smiled awkwardly and was about to speak when Anya turned towards a dark figure who followed her into the room. It was Justin, looking much the same as he had in the library, seventy years in the future. The two of them stood there, engaged in animated conversation, ignoring Caryn completely. Caryn realised she couldn't hear what they were saying. She began to panic, caught her breath with difficulty, and shouted out, "Anya? Justin?", but her words were merely a series of vibrations in her mouth and jaw. Anya gestured towards her and the machine, and Justin moved forward. Caryn stepped aside to avoid him, but he ignored her and kept walking, passing through the machine where it stood shimmering in the light from its internal controls, utterly oblivious of its existence.

Caryn's thoughts whirled in turmoil. Gasping for breath, she called out again, "Justin! Look at me, for God's sake! Talk to me!", but her voice was an absence and the air remained undisturbed by any sonic vibration. Justin said something to Anya, who replied briefly. Caryn ached for her husband, longed for him to take her into his arms, to say he was sorry, to say anything. She lurched towards him, her feet sinking slightly into the floor's vinyl surface, which shone in the light from the opened door. She reached out for him, desperate for the love

216

and reassurance he had once been able to grant her before everything slid from their grasp; before the children. He cast a final glance around the lab, looking back at where he knew the time machine had once rested, his expression one of intense thought. Then his face creased into the patronising sneer that she knew so well. He took a step forward and for a brief instant they were locked together in an impossible coinciding of separated existences as she gave vent to her feelings in a long, silent scream of terror and despair.

Jesse

Whatever it was I wanted of him, it certainly wasn't this. From the moment I met him, I knew something was different; something in me. He was immediately friendly, despite the thirty years between us. He had the easy manner of one indifferent to social nuance – an openness and generosity of spirit that he allowed to take him wherever it led. Neither of us could have imagined that it would lead us here. *This white dimness; the hum and throb of peripheral machinery; the antiseptic scent of deferred death.*

Most of it is clear in my mind, even now. We met at the summer season launch party of the Acorn Theatre Company, for which I am – was, perhaps – an occasional director. It was the end of April, and the wind was gusting knots of dense rain across the lake from the west. The late afternoon sun flexed its squinting glare through clumps of thickening cloud. Already, the assembled company of directors and actors, theatre executives and local dignitaries were abandoning the waterside terrace for the shelter of the conservatory bar. They clutched awkwardly at their glasses of cheap wine and the wind-warped paper plates from which loosely piled crisps were sent scudding across rain-flecked paving stones to rest briefly on the lake's troubled surface. Jesse and I were soon the only ones left outside, each absorbed independently in gazing across the turbulent water at the darkening hills. The sun's downward drift briefly edged each passing cloud with a dazzle of gold.

I knew who he was, though we hadn't actually met. Fresh from drama school, he'd been cast in the first two productions of the season. I could see at a glance that he would make a striking Konstantin in *The Seagull*. He wasn't conventionally good-looking, but his slightly lopsided face, with its permanently quizzical expression, was offset by long, thick hair and a dark beard that lent him something of a Byronic air. He became aware of my furtive scrutiny and turned to face me.

"Jesse, isn't it?" I said, feeling the heat rising to my cheeks as I realised how closely I'd been studying him.

"Yes," he replied with a friendly smile. "And you're –"

"Martin Torrance."

"Of course. Good to meet you."

He offered me his hand, which I took with an embarrassed awareness of my limp grasp; every time, I made a conscious effort to strengthen my response, but the moment always passed before I could activate the right muscles. Jesse's grip was firm but not prolonged: the ideal handshake, I thought.

"When do you start rehearsing?" I asked. He must have known I knew the answer, but with his instinctive consideration he indulged me. I felt somehow wrong-footed, and blinked away a flash of brightness from the falling sun.

"Tomorrow for the Chekhov," he said. "Then I think we start *Hay Fever* in about three weeks."

He'd been cast as Simon Bliss in Noël Coward's consummate comedy of manners. Idly, I wondered if he'd be allowed to keep his beard for the two roles; it would be a pity if he had to get rid of it. Already, I was sizing him up, weighing up a part for him in my own production of *Cymbeline*,

219

Shakespeare's improbable romance, later in the season. Was I conscious then that I found him attractive? Was he? As far as I was concerned, my sporadic feelings for young men had ended when I stopped being a young man myself and launched into the first of my disastrous marriages. In any case, I'd always gone for more boyish, feminine types, and though Jesse was little more than a boy himself, he radiated masculinity. It wasn't just the beard; under the actor's fashionable loose grey shirt and faded jeans I sensed a robust physique, and a thatch of dark hair was visible at his doubly unbuttoned collar. I found it disturbing that I'd even noticed.

"Looking forward to it?" I asked lamely.

"Yes; I can't believe how lucky I am. Most of the people in my year are still struggling to get agents."

His voice, like his face, was appealingly odd. He spoke with a strangely unnatural emphasis which, paradoxically, conveyed both sincerity and enthusiasm.

"You're directing *Cymbeline* aren't you?" he went on. "I'd love to be in it. I really liked your production of *Winter's Tale* last year."

He wasn't being pushy – he meant it. I found his openness refreshing and hoped it wouldn't be twisted too soon into the brittle insincerity of theatrical intercourse. I wanted to say, Yes, of course you can be in it; but I knew it would be inappropriate. First, he'd have to show his mettle in the two opening productions; then, the casting for my show would need to be agreed with the director of the season's final production, Gogol's *The Government Inspector*, as well as the assistant directors who were planning the studio repertoire.

"Well, I'll keep you in mind," I said non-commitally. "Let's see how things work out."

I held his gaze for a moment too long, then turned away as a flight of squawking geese, red-backed in the momentary glow of the setting sun, cleaved an upward path across the streaked sky. When I glanced back at him he was checking his texts with that intent concentration of the young, shut tight into their contractual bond with technology. I felt a surge of disappointment, desperate to continue our awkward conversation, to see where it might go. I turned away in embarrassment, pointlessly irritated at being shut out from personal engagement by the spurious urgency of a virtual other-world. A twinge of pain in my lower back creased a frown into my brow.

The rising wind was shaking the branches of the ancient oaks that stretched along the lake-shore from the end of the terrace. Stupidly, I realised for the first time why the theatre was called the Acorn. The great avenue of trees receded into darkness, their fresh spring leaves obscured now in drifts of grey drizzle, the road no longer visible in the thickening red light. I couldn't see how far they went, or where they ended; could hear only the faint, squalling cackle of the geese as they vanished into crimson and indigo.

I can't say I thought much about Jesse after that. I had other projects on the go that took me away from the Acorn, though I came back for the opening nights of both *The Seagull* and *Hay Fever*. I was slightly disappointed in Jesse's performances; he lacked the maturity and finesse to play characters so brittle and damaged, in their different ways, as Konstantin and Simon Bliss. He had cut his hair and shaved off his beard for the roles, which I thought was a mistake, emphasising as it did his quirkily asymmetrical features. Even so, I couldn't take my eyes off him when he was on stage, and I enjoyed his assured

221

comic timing in the Coward play, achieved partly by the louche arrogance of his body language. Until he had more experience, though, I felt he needed roles that exploited his natural warmth and sincerity. Fortunately, *Cymbeline* had two such roles: the young princes, stolen away as children and brought up in the Welsh mountains ignorant of their true identity.

At the first-night party for *Hay Fever*, I took Jesse aside and arranged an interview with him for the following afternoon. Already flushed with the free-flowing wine and the show's warm reception, he could barely suppress his enthusiasm. The summer air was hot and thick, the bar crowded and noisy. My stomach felt tight and uncomfortable and my head was buzzing with an incipient migraine. Jesse's face was sheened in moisture, and I felt a sudden desire to smooth his cheek with the back of my fingers. I had to talk him down, stress that nothing was finalised, that this would just be a preliminary chat. *Cymbeline* rehearsals were nearly a month away, and so far only the central roles of Imogen, Posthumus and Iachimo had been cast, from outside the current ensemble. I knew Jesse was thinking partly of his future; if I didn't cast him, his contract was likely to end when *The Seagull* and *Hay Fever* reached their final scheduled performances, and he would be plunged into the professional actor's default condition of "resting". It wasn't just that, though. I got the impression that he liked me and genuinely wanted to work with me. We talked a lot, interrupted only once by the inevitable call on his mobile which, of course, he had to take. He told me a bit about his parents, about their radical Christian views and their unrealistic ambitions for him. Reluctantly, he had made a deal with them that if his acting career didn't take off after three years he would go back to university to do a master's degree, with a long-term

222

view towards some high-powered academic post. They'd named him after the Biblical patriarch, but he said he identified more with Jesse James, the Wild West outlaw. He spun me an entertaining fantasy of moving to Los Angeles and heading a resurgence of the Hollywood western, riding the range with a rugged expression and a six-shooter at his side. I think he was only partly joking. By the end of the evening, his energy and high spirits had won me over; I knew he was going to be one of the princes, and I knew that I was in love.

I drove home in a state of heightened awareness, feeling both elated and apprehensive. Despite the warning flashes, and the diamond patterns that had been disrupting my field of vision, the migraine had fizzled out, and I enjoyed the warm summer breeze rushing through the opened car window, brushing my face with the freshness and fragrance of night. At the end of the avenue of oaks that passed through my headlights like ghosts on parade, I turned on to the main road and pushed my speed well beyond the legal limit. I must have known I'd drunk too much, but the thought of being stopped didn't even cross my mind. All I could think of was Jesse. My feelings about him seemed perfectly natural, as if something, some previously malfunctioning component of my emotional nature, had finally slotted into its proper place. I knew that I'd never felt this way about anyone else, certainly not about either of my ex-wives. Angrily, I slammed my foot down on the throttle.

When I reached home I remembered nothing of the thirty-mile journey, not even the intervening village with its intricate one-way system. The buzz of intense exhilaration vanished in an instant as I tried to remember whether I'd noticed the flash of a speed camera; there were a number of them along the route. My stomach was aching again and I suddenly felt cold and anxious. I was aware of the wine I'd drunk beginning to throb in my head, and hoped the migraine was not making a return visit. I went heavily upstairs, started to undress but had to lie on my bed to still the room's unsteady movement. I thought about Jesse, and realised with a jolt that it could go no further. I was old enough to be his father, for God's sake. I had no idea of his sexual preferences, but I felt pretty sure they wouldn't run to a flabby, balding guy in his mid-fifties with digestive problems and a dodgy back.

The room seemed to have settled down. I stumbled to the bathroom, aware of the usual dull ache at the base of my spine, then finished undressing and got into bed, wincing slightly at the duvet's cool touch. I lay still, but couldn't empty my mind sufficiently to allow sleep to creep in. I thought myself back to Jesse's age, to how I would have felt if I'd been propositioned by some disgusting old pervert abusing his position of power and influence. What I felt for him was an illusion, a chimera spliced together out of frustration and loneliness. With images of his quirky, open face and echoes of his eager, emphatic voice fragmenting in my mind, I gave myself up to unsatisfactory masturbation and fell into a fitful, uneasy sleep.

Next morning, I felt chastened and embarrassed. Thankfully, I had taken advantage of the previous night's party to arrange a number of other interviews for today, so any sense that my meeting with Jesse might seem like an assignation was easily dispelled. Even so, as I drove along the lakeside under the rich blue of a perfect July day, I couldn't keep anxiety entirely at bay. Though my stomach had settled down, my back was still aching, and the last thing I wanted was to spend the day limping around like an old man. I turned off the main road and the long oak avenue opened up ahead of me. The trees were in full leaf, bright green in the noonday brilliance, yet I felt I was plunging into a dark tunnel that would lead me inexorably to some unknown destination. *But not to here, this dim, white void.* Despite everything, despite my resolutions and determination, I couldn't wait to see Jesse again.

The interview took place in a cramped, hot room on the top floor of the theatre. It had one small window that commanded an uninspiring view of the car park. Jesse was as positive and enthusiastic as ever, and I managed to focus my mind, mostly, on the question of casting him in *Cymbeline*. The only real issue was which of the princes he should play. It was partly a matter of physicality. In their first scene, the two young men are preparing to set out from their cave for a morning's hunting with their foster-father Belarius, the unfairly banished lord who kidnapped them as children. Shakespeare draws a keen distinction between the elder, Guiderius, the more aggressive and impetuously masculine of the two, and Arviragus, his gentler, more poetic younger brother. My idea was that on their first appearance they should be stripped to the waist, washing in the stream before setting off for the hunt. It was really important, I thought, that Guiderius should have the stronger, more muscular physique, with Arviragus slighter, smoother and more adolescent in build. I explained all this, or most of it, to Jesse, with rather more awkwardness than I would normally have felt, and he agreed to come back the next morning with the three other young actors I was considering for the roles, Callum, Jared and Louis.

"I'll have a look at the scene," he said. "What time d'you want me?"

"Will 10.30 be OK? I'll have to check with the others, so I'll text you first thing to confirm."

"Great – that should be all right. There's a *Seagull* matinee tomorrow, but I guess we'll be finished in good time for that."

As he got up to leave, our eyes met for a moment and I felt my cheeks burning. I stood too, and a spasm of pain lanced into my spine. I flinched.

"Are you OK?" he asked, his eyes fixed on mine in genuine concern. For a moment I felt he was reading my mind, such was the intensity of his gaze. I turned away in embarrassment, muttered something incoherent about my troublesome back, and he made some sympathetic response.

"See you tomorrow," he said as he left. "Hope you feel better soon."

As the door closed behind him, I breathed a sigh of relief and sat back down to the accompaniment of another twinge of pain. I was emotionally exhausted. If this was how I felt after half an hour's interview with Jesse, how could I possibly direct him in a show? I knew it would be better, more sensible, to remove him from the equation altogether, to cast the roles of the princes from the other three. But how could I deny myself the opportunity of being close to him, of testing what I really felt about him – and he about me? I reconsidered the moment our eyes had met and held; convinced myself that there had been something more in his gaze than mere polite sympathy. A sudden flash of light from the window made me blink – the sun reflecting off an opened car door, I guessed.

As I sat there, unwilling to expend the effort of getting up to leave, I was surprised to find that my eyes were moist with tears. This was ridiculous. For a brief moment I thought, crazily, of calling the production off, pleading ill health, booking myself a long holiday on some glittering, palm-fringed beach. How could I possibly go on with the show without revealing my embarrassing, adolescent infatuation? But I had no choice. I was contractually as well as emotionally committed to it. If I backed out now, my reputation would be shot to pieces. More than that, I would hold myself in contempt; despise my weakness, my lack of self-control and professionalism. Picking up the phone, I called Annabel, my assistant director, and Hugo, the stage manager, and asked them to be present at tomorrow's audition; checked that Callum, Jared and Louis were available; and recruited Roland Mills, one of the company's senior actors, to read in the part of Belarius. Surely, in the presence of all those people, it would be impossible for me to give anything away. *The dim brightness; the insistent, insidious humming; the smell of antiseptic and death. Why doesn't anybody come?*

It was lunchtime when I finally made it down to the theatre café. Thinking of my stomach, I ordered the blandest item I could find, an egg and cress sandwich. I took it out on to the terrace, where I sat gazing across the lake. A pair of geese sliced like guided missiles into the bright waters in a crashing spurt of white spray. As the startled reflections calmed and settled around them, I felt relaxed enough to take out my copy of *Cymbeline* and begin to sketch out some ideas for tomorrow's audition. As well as the scene I'd suggested, it would make sense, I thought, to look at the section where Guiderius, having killed the villain Cloten, takes back his severed head to his father and brother. This was a testing scene, and would help me to see if Jesse – or one of the others, perhaps – could bring the appropriate macho swagger to the role without losing its essential guileless innocence. By the time I'd made three or four pages of notes on the scenes and characters, I felt confident enough to face the following morning's audition with complete equanimity.

My dreams that night were filled with fleeting images that I couldn't quite pin down, though I knew they were vaguely suggestive of the princes' scenes in *Cymbeline* and that Jesse, or some insubstantial dream version of him, was a constant presence at the periphery of the confused narrative. As I sat in my kitchen over my usual scant breakfast of toast and tea, my mind, unprompted, jumped ahead to the moment in the audition when Jesse would take off his shirt for the business of washing in the stream. Why should this make me go hot and speed up the beating of my heart? Why should I feel the stirrings of an erection at the thought of something so natural, so utterly free of sexual undertones? I had never felt like this before. I'd directed completely naked actors, for God's sake, in *Equus* and *Paradise Lost*, without ever feeling uncomfortable, let alone aroused. Yet the image of this young man with his shirt off was making me, quite literally, weak at the knees. For a moment, I couldn't trust myself to stand up. I knew that if I did, a wave of hot panic would well up from the soles of my feet, rising through my stomach and into my chest, where my heart was already working overtime. If it reached my head I knew I would black out, and I didn't dare close my eyes in case that simply encouraged the darkness to overwhelm me. A bright streak of light shot through my brain, my back throbbed and I sensed the beginning of one of my bad stomachs. With a supreme effort I forced myself to drink the rest of my hot tea, but I couldn't face any more of the pale, unappetising toast. I was startled by my phone signalling the arrival of a text message. It was from Jesse. Thanks for yesterday, it read; looking forward 2 this morning. CU xx.

And now there's someone there in the brightness, dim in the bright white mist, among the wires and tubes, the throbbing hum, the sharp, sweet scent of despair.

A brisk, hot shower restored my equilibrium, but before I left home I booked a long overdue appointment with my GP for the following week. As I drove carefully through the luminous countryside I reflected wryly that it was just as well my overwhelming physical response to the thought of a shirtless Jesse had occurred before I was faced with the real thing. It was an aberration, I decided, brought on, like my health problems, by overwork and the stress of dashing from one end of the country to the other to keep an eye on all my current productions which, thankfully, now seemed to be running smoothly. I had nothing major scheduled after *Cymbeline* until the New Year, so it would make sense to have a proper, relaxing break. I felt sure the doctor would agree that that was all I needed.

I hadn't paid much attention to Jesse's text message when it arrived, but as I turned into the great avenue of trees stretching towards the theatre it came back to me unexpectedly. xx. Two kisses. What did it mean? I had no idea what young people's signing-off protocols were for texts and emails, but I assumed that the various available choices embodied subtle signifiers in the etiquette of intimacy. They could also, I guessed, veer without warning from sincerity to irony. In this case, I concluded, it meant nothing; it was probably casual, automatic, habitual, innocent. xx.

The audition was an unexpected success. The presence of so many people, including Tanya Lawless, the director of *The Government Inspector*, whose show would eventually be running in tandem with mine, helped me to maintain an entirely objective and professional attitude. Roland, as Belarius, was a revelation. Although I'd been planning to cast the role from outside the company, I offered it to him there and then. I tried all four young men in various combinations as the two princes, even though I knew pretty quickly the choices I was going to make. All but Callum turned up in shorts, and they removed their T-shirts without awkwardness or embarrassment to mime the washing in the stream. There was no reason, of course, why they should have felt awkward or embarrassed; I was simply transposing my own feelings on to the proceedings. Jesse had learned both princes' lines in the scene and delivered them, as I'd known he would, with complete conviction. I didn't have to subject him to close scrutiny to know that physically he was best-suited to the elder brother, Guiderius. He was strong and well-built, with chest hair that spread sparingly down to his flat stomach, and firmly-muscled legs that were also softly downed with dark hair. Louis was smoother, with an almost adolescent build and a lighter, more lyrical voice, making him more suitable for the gentler Arviragus. The other two I eliminated pretty quickly; neither of them could make much sense of the elliptical quality of late-Shakespearean verse. For fairness' sake, however, I kept them on to try the severed head scene, which Jesse pulled off with enormously attractive self-assurance. To hear him deliver the lines with casual, innocent brutality was a revelation.

> With his own sword,
> Which he did wave against my throat, I have ta'en
> His head from him. I'll throw it into the creek
> Behind our rock, and let it to the sea
> And tell the fishes he's the Queen's son, Cloten.
> That's all I reck.

It occurred to me that there were depths in Jesse that I'd been unaware of and, cliché or not, a shiver passed with a sharp tingle from my neck to the base of my spine.

Having dismissed the actors, I talked through the possibilities with Tanya and Annabel as I would any other question of casting. They deferred to my choices, and agreed that Callum and Jared should understudy the princes and play a handful of minor roles each. Relieved to have got through the whole business with such professionalism and restraint, I joined Tanya and Roland for lunch in the café. Tanya had to dash off for a meeting with her designer, but Roland had a good hour until his call for the matinee of *The Seagull*, in which he was playing Sorin.

"Another drink?" he asked, finishing his poached salmon salad and pushing the plate aside.

"No thanks. I need a clear head while I get stuck into the rest of the casting." I didn't tell him of my anxiety that I was going to be done for speeding, or even dangerous driving, after my mad journey home two nights previously.

"Good result this morning?" he said. There was some intangible suggestion in his questioning tone and the half-smile that played in his eyes.

"Yes, I think so. I'm really sorry, Roland – I don't know why I didn't have you marked down for Belarius from the start. You had such warmth in those scenes, and sadness too: the proud father who knows these aren't really his sons. And I think you're going to have a fantastic rapport with Louis and Jesse."

His smile creased into a slight frown.

"That's not what I meant, Martin." He paused, as if not quite sure how to proceed. "You got the one you wanted, then?"

"I'm sorry?"

"Jesse. It was a bit fucking obvious, you know. Anyone could see it." He stopped again. "You were trying too hard."

I didn't know what to say. I felt hot and cold at the same time and hoped desperately that the panic wouldn't start to rise again. My face was burning, but I vainly tried to brazen it out.

"I'm not with you," I muttered, trying to compose my features into a semblance of honest puzzlement.

"Never mind," he said, and stood up to go. "Just be careful, that's all. I've been working with him for three months. He's not what you think."

I was so shocked, I couldn't move. I was breathing quickly, conscious of my heart pounding with disturbing rapidity. I watched Roland until he disappeared through the glass door and along the terrace towards the lake, for a pre-performance smoke, I guessed. I was shocked because I knew he was right. I'd been fooling myself. Thinking of Jesse now, stripped to his shorts, I imagined touching him, running my fingers down his spine and into the hollow of his back. The feel of him; the smoothness of his skin, the soft mat of hair on his firm chest. I knew that during the audition I had been suppressing what I really felt. I'd wanted him to go all the way; wanted him utterly, beautifully naked; longed to see his sexual arousal, proud and unselfconscious. I ached for him. *He's not what you think. xx.*

I had to get out of there, but couldn't rely on my legs to support me, not yet. I felt my own erection pressing urgently against the restriction of my clothes, felt exposed to the knowing scrutiny of the scattered lunchtime diners, who seemed to have fallen silent, observing me covertly as they played with the tasteless pap of their chilled sandwiches and lukewarm pasta. Finally I stood up, too fast, wincing as a twinge of pain shot into my back. I took a moment to recover my balance and then walked slowly to the door with a studied, artificial calmness. Outside a summer storm was brewing and a flash of light cut through my brain like a polished scimitar. A thunderous cacophony filled my head and the clouds dropped their stored waters in a vertical torrent of silver splinters.

Somewhere he's there, in the silvery whiteness, the humming and thrum of machinery and oblivion.

For the next few weeks, I coped by pretending that nothing had happened, that Roland hadn't spoken. When the inevitable letter arrived outlining my speeding offence, I booked myself on to the police speed awareness course without demur. I was lucky; I'd been clocked doing 45 in a 40 mph zone, probably the only part of that notorious drive where I'd been less than 10 miles an hour over the limit. I saw my doctor, who didn't seem too worried about my recurrent health problems, but referred me for tests, which I asked him to delay until *Cymbeline* was up and running. With an enormous effort of my conscious will, I pushed down all my inappropriate feelings for Jesse and got on as best I could with directing the play.

Usually, this was the period I found most rewarding, working intensively with the actors on text and character, building the play from its bare bones before the technical complications of mounting a show began to exert their urgent demands. This time, though, I felt disengaged from the process in a way that must have been obvious to the company, at least to those who'd worked with me before. I largely palmed off the direction of the princes' scenes to Annabel, with the excuse that she deserved to be given more responsibility, but I couldn't withdraw from them altogether. Apart from anything else, Belarius and the princes become increasingly enmeshed in the working out of the play's intricate and complex denouement, in a scene so difficult to stage that I would need to direct it like a military operation. Stupidly, I put it off for as long as possible. I was dimly aware of Jesse and Louis striking up a close friendship, perhaps more than that. If I felt any pangs of jealousy, I managed to conceal them even from myself. In a perverse way it gave me hope; at least it showed Jesse was attracted to men.

I did have one idea I was pleased with. My daily drive along the lake-shore had inspired me with a vision for the setting of Belarius' cave, which would be framed by dark-foliaged oaks, silhouetted against a series of ever-changing cloudscapes. Erik Stanfield, the designer, was enthusiastic and I found myself eagerly looking forward to his scenic realisation of my vision. The trees became something of an obsession, occupying my thoughts well beyond their intrinsic interest and beauty. In some ways they were my salvation.

As for Jesse, I avoided him as far as I could, confining my contact with him to brief notes and occasional words of encouragement. Even then, I would find the heat rising to my cheeks and my heart-rate speeding up, but gradually I found ways of controlling these unnerving symptoms. When his presence became too overpowering, I switched my mind to something else, something complex but emotionally neutral, such as the rich depths of mottled green exploding in the great oak canopies that shaded the lakeside avenue, or the intricate patterning of veins on a leaf, or the magical chemistry of photosynthesis, or the seasonal alchemy that turns green to short-lived gold. Sometimes, if he caught my eye, I was aware of our mutual gaze lasting just beyond its natural span, confirming the impression I had gained weeks before that he felt something for me that went beyond mere respect. Whenever this happened, I noticed an enigmatic smile that played on his lips for just a moment – so brief that I convinced myself I'd imagined it. Still, he must have found me distant and unfriendly and wondered what he had done wrong. But he had done nothing wrong; everything he did was right, was perfect. *Everything he did.*

Never had I enjoyed directing a show less, and I couldn't wait for opening night to arrive, so that I could hand the whole thing over to Annabel and Hugo and leave the company to get on with it. Then I could sort out my health, have a proper break, and start to plan for next year, when I had a good chance, I thought, of being invited to do a production for the RSC in Stratford.

There was one awkward conversation with Jesse on the morning of the first preview. He made a point of seeking me out during a break in the technical rehearsal. I was standing on the terrace where we'd first spoken, studying the oaks that stretched along the edge of the troubled lake. It was mid-September and already the leaves had begun to darken towards autumn. Banks of grey cloud scudded and tumbled across the sky and the water seemed agitated, as if expectant of some imminent change. As so often these days, I had a glass of red wine in one hand and a cigarette in the other. Jesse's voice startled me.

"Martin, have you got a minute?"

"Yeh, sure," I answered ungraciously, but when I turned to face him, all my ill-feeling disappeared. He was in his costume, Erik's conception of an Ancient British hunter, consisting of a loincloth and sleeveless jacket crafted out of fake animal skins roughly sewn together and completed with ankle-length boots of artificial leather. His hair was longer and he'd regrown his beard, with the permission of the director of *Hay Fever*, which was still in the repertoire. He looked stunningly handsome, even more so than when I'd first met him. My resolution and control evaporated in the immediacy of his physical presence. I tried desperately to focus my mind on the slow metamorphosis of the oaks in the shortening days; the darkening of their fretted leaves; the imperceptible spread of brown scabs and lichenous growths; the green swell of the acorns in their rough cups; the inevitable fall into winter's stark emptiness. But I had been taken off guard, my emotional safety-net snatched away. My brain flared with a momentary burning of anger.

He came straight to the point. "Are you happy with what I'm doing?" he demanded.

"Yes – of course. Why?" I knew very well why; in the past couple of weeks I'd virtually ignored him, given him no notes at all.

"Well, you haven't said anything about my performance for ages," he answered in his emphatic, ingenuous tone. "I just wondered if you think it's going OK."

I felt guilty. After all, he was little more than a kid, desperate like all kids, like all actors, for constant reassurance.

"Look Jess," I said, "I think you're doing really well, and I love the way you're working with Louis and Roland." (Too well with Louis, perhaps, I reflected.) "But – well – Guiderius isn't exactly the leading role, and you may have noticed I've got some problems to sort out elsewhere." This was true; Posthumus was going through a crisis of confidence and his uncertainties were beginning to affect his on- and off-stage relationship with Imogen. Even so, I regretted the irritable tone in which I'd spoken. With great difficulty, I looked Jesse directly in the eyes and held his gaze for as long as I comfortably could. "You're really, really good. Just keep building on what you're doing and I'll be more than happy."

He looked genuinely grateful. "Thanks," he said, smiling; and again, "Thanks."

Foolishly, forgetting everything, I added, "And you look fantastic."

Instantly I panicked and tried unsuccessfully to summon up the rescuing image of a spreading oak tree. It was just as well Hugo called the end of the break at that point, his voice distorted by the crackle of the tannoy. Otherwise, who knows what I might have said next?

He's there still. A dim shape lost in the white haze, listening to the machines' beep and click, breathing in the thick, sweet scent of dying.

Cymbeline opened to enthusiastic audiences delighted to discover that Shakespeare's rarely-performed fairy-tale was funny, dramatic, enchanting and moving. I can't claim much credit for the show's success, most of which was down to Annabel, and the creative team who provided such a rich visual and musical experience. The special effects were wonderful, with a spectacular appearance by the King of the Gods which, as I was determined it should, fully lived up to Shakespeare's astonishing stage direction: *Jupiter descends in thunder and lightning, sitting upon an eagle. He throws a thunderbolt. The ghosts fall on their knee*s. If anything, the effects were rather too powerful; on press night, the lightning was still flashing in my head at the end of the play.

Much of the acting, though, was oddly lacklustre, and that was entirely my fault. I had cast a company of talented actors in wonderful, challenging roles and then failed to inspire them. Belarius and the princes picked up considerable praise, and I was pleased for them – but I knew they could have been even better. I hadn't spoken to Roland outside the rehearsal room since our unfortunate conversation after the audition, and in largely ignoring Jesse I had also neglected Louis. His touching and beautifully-spoken performance as Arviragus owed very little to my direction, having been created by his own instincts and some nice touches suggested by Annabel. As for Jesse, I could scarcely watch his performance for fear I should give myself away. When he was on stage I thought of leaves and branches, of rough scales of thick bark, of skies broken into an impossible jigsaw by the criss-cross patterns of twigs and foliage. Erik's interpretation of my design idea was a stunning success. Its most brilliant touch was the thick covering of real acorns, gathered daily from the great oak avenue that stretched along the lake, scattered across the artificial grass of the forest floor. Crunched under the leather-booted feet of Britons and Romans alike, they became part of the play's elaborate, evocative soundscape. I focused all my attention on these scenic elements, but what I really wanted was to look at Jesse, to fix my gaze on his rough beauty. I simply didn't dare. Perhaps I should have done; then, maybe…

My intention was to see the show through its first week of performances, after which most of the company, including Jesse, would start rehearsals for *The Government Inspector*. Then I intended to have a complete break, do my duty on the speed awareness course, endure all the health checks the hospital could throw at me and finally take that long holiday somewhere remote and relaxing, with blue skies, crisp seas and bronzed, bikini-clad women. After all that, perhaps I'd be ready to take on my next project.

The company knew I was leaving on the Sunday, and though there was to be no party after Saturday's performance I was expected to do the rounds and offer some parting nuggets of wisdom. I had decided to avoid protracted farewells and to slip away if possible without seeing Jesse. When it came to it, I thought that would be mean and small-minded, and would probably turn into a talking-point in itself. He was sharing a dressing-room with Roland and Louis, so at least I'd be spared an awkward one-to-one conversation. Even so, I left them till last in the hope that they'd already have gone, and I could make my disappointment at missing them clear to anyone who was still around.

The moment had come. I stood outside the door of dressing-room 5, forced back the thickening panic that threatened to rise and overwhelm me, and knocked. Jesse's voice answered, "Come in." I opened the door and stepped in, affecting a cheery smile, which immediately turned to an expression of bewilderment and dismay. Jesse was alone in the room, standing in front of his mirror with his back to me, framed by its glaring lightbulbs. He was completely naked. My breath started to come quickly, the panic shooting like a rocket up through my stomach, clutching at my heart and sticking in a choking mass at my throat. I wanted to speak, but no words would come. I tried to retreat from the room but I had lost all power of movement. A thick, bright haze was swimming in front of my eyes. Slowly, Jesse turned to face me, a broad smile on his face, his prick rising proudly for me just as I had always imagined and longed for.

"What's the matter?" he asked. "Why don't you come in and shut the door? Roland suggested you might appreciate a proper goodbye."

I couldn't grasp what was happening, didn't know if he was genuinely offering himself to me or whether it was just some spiteful joke, some malicious trick at the expense of what I now saw was my far from secret obsession. Whatever it was, I didn't care. I began clumsily stripping off my clothes, dimly aware of the contrast between my pale, flabby paunch and his firm, tanned torso, sketched with a light mat of smooth hair that ran provocatively down to his flat, taut stomach and strong, upright prick inviting me to take what I had always wanted from him. Then I became aware that he was not alone. I heard the door click shut behind me and Louis appeared from nowhere, smoothly, boyishly naked and also fully aroused. He moved across to Jesse and they embraced, front to front. I stood transfixed, choking and gasping for breath. A quick flash of intolerable brightness lit up the periphery of my visual field. They kissed, with slow and deliberate intention. When they drew apart I couldn't look at their glistening moistness.

"We thought you might like to watch," Jesse said, in that familiar, sincere, emphatic tone. "That's what you do, isn't it?"

I think I ran, my clothes flapping loosely, out of the stage door into the booming autumn wind. Under the brooding canopy of the trees the acorns splintered to damp slivers under my feet. Flashes of wildfire split the darkness and the rain scored tears of shame and self-disgust down my blazing cheeks. Perhaps. Perhaps, please God, none of it happened...

So far, I haven't found out the truth. Mere seconds passed, it seems, till I found myself waking up in a hospital bed, prone, immobile; connected up to incomprehensible equipment which, I dimly understand, keeps me stable. I knew immediately that I'd had a stroke, but when? Did any of it happen? Or did my suppressed obsession finally burst like an inflamed abscess, exploding its filth and fantasy through my receptive brain? I can't speak, can't ask anyone. Even if I could, I wouldn't. Not yet. I see only dimly through the thick, white vapours. I can think clearly enough, though; can tell my story to myself, piece it together, try to work out what's true and what isn't. So far, I've only told it in my head, but one day I'll write the whole thing down. Meanwhile, I have a visitor. He sits just a few feet away, in the fog, but says nothing. Perhaps he thinks I can't hear, can't understand. I want to ask him things, but I have no voice. I'm not even sure who he is. *I think it's Jesse. I hope it is. I hope so.*

Prototypes

She'd loved him for as long as she could remember. When the world, effectively, came to an end, they carried on living in their tiny cottage, perched on a rocky headland looking out across the grey wastes of the North Sea. In the grim days of that final war, they'd watched great ships from all sides pass by, uninterested in the useless scrap of coast where they lived. Once there had been a sea battle, a face-off between two enemy fleets that had ended in flame and smoke and spouts of dark water hurtling into the sky. As far as they could tell, none of the vessels involved had survived, and the distant turmoil of conflict and destruction had faded away into the ocean's endless throb. They were too far away to hear the cries and screams of drowning men.

Now, no ships passed. The world was silent.

In the early days, when there was still petrol in the car, he'd made a number of trips into the nearest village, ten miles away. She felt safer staying at home, even with no working radio or television, no computer or mobile phone to keep her in contact with whatever, if anything, was happening elsewhere. Even then she knew it was all over. At least they had no children to worry about, and their own parents were long dead, spared the drawn-out anxiety of civilization's final collapse. For decades it had been inevitable; the only question was when it would actually happen. They had each other; loved each other. They would go on for as long as they could, and when they couldn't – they'd give up gracefully and gratefully, contriving to die quietly in each other's arms.

He didn't say much when he got back from that first trip to the village, and she knew at once he was holding something back. "Everyone's dead," was all he was prepared to tell her. In truth, it didn't much matter, though she sometimes wondered what had killed them, and how they themselves had survived if something toxic had spread through the air or the water supply. He had packed the car with as much as he could that would help them to go on living. They stashed it away in the limited space they had available: tinned and dried foods and bottled water; drugs and medical equipment; practical necessities such as wood for the stove, paper and matches, candles, torches and batteries. They spent a long time making lists so that on his subsequent trips he could bring back everything they would need to survive for – how long? A year? Two years? Ten? They found a perverse pleasure in working so closely together in these grim circumstances. It brought back memories of when they had found the cottage, fallen in love with it, scraped and saved to be able to afford it, worked till all hours to turn it into their home, somewhere they could be together, cut off from the world's increasing insanity, for as long as they had. In some ways nothing had changed.

She often thought back to their early days together. It seemed a lifetime ago, and it was surprising to realise it was just fifteen years since they'd met. She was working as a learning support mentor in a big comprehensive school on the outskirts of Newcastle when he got a job there as a science teacher. They hit it off straight away. There was a girl in his Year 9 class,

Asma, who had real potential in the practical side of Physics and Chemistry, but was held back by her difficulties with reading and writing. They worked hard together to offer her all the support they could, and encouraged her to opt for sciences at GCSE. Her parents were devout Muslims, and spoke little English at home. Half way through Year 10, Asma disappeared into the turmoil of the Middle Eastern Caliphate, having come under the influence of a fundamentalist preacher at the mosque where they worshipped.

They talked a great deal about this; both of them saw it as a personal failure. They should have noticed the signs, been aware of how vulnerable this fifteen year old girl was. Perhaps they'd become too bound up in each other to see beyond their own developing relationship. For within a year of meeting they were deeply, inextricably in love.

They had a lot in common. Both had lost their parents in childhood, and neither had any siblings. Both preferred not to talk about their past, being focused very much on the here and now of their lives, though he did let slip that he had come into teaching after working in the metabiotics division of SI Industries. When he discovered that synthetic intelligence was being increasingly deployed to ensure the winnability of the long-expected war, he walked out on his job in disgust. He couldn't have known then the extent to which diplomatic and tactical decisions were already being made by machines rather than human beings as geopolitical conflicts escalated across the world. They decided they wouldn't get married, instead showing their deep commitment to each other by moving to this wild, remote and isolated spot on the edge of their known world – a world they increasingly distrusted and despised. This was where they had watched in horror, on their antique, flat-screen

TV, when the forces of the Caliphate had swept across the Mediterranean and taken a grip on Europe's southern coastline, imposing their will in a remorseless campaign of intimidation and butchery. They thought of Asma, wondered what had become of her. The Western allies did nothing for nearly a week, while Rome fell and the Islamic troops marched inexorably towards Madrid and Paris. Finally, the allies released their secret weapon: metahuman armies whose existence had never been suspected, transported to the front lines by remotely-controlled armoured vehicles and self-operated carrier-drones, armed with the latest in weapons technology. Within days, the conflict was worldwide. No-one was quite sure how many sides there were, let alone whose side anyone was on. Weaponry was unleashed that had long been banned under international law and supposedly decommissioned decades ago. States without SI technology or metahuman forces sent thousands of hastily conscripted citizens boldly into battle, ill-trained and totally unprepared for the terrifying scenarios of conflict that were being drawn up to oppose them. Nuclear missiles, poison gas, biological agents – nothing was off limits.

They switched off their TV long before the power failed, unable to take in any more details of the world's swiftly unfolding demise. Now here they were, a year on, living on borrowed time. When the car was nearly out of petrol, they made a conscious decision not to go in search of more. What was the point? They both knew that, even with each other, there would come a time when they felt it was right to draw things to a close. They could plan for it, choose their own time of going; and they had the drugs to make sure their decisions could be successfully implemented. What she couldn't have anticipated was the day he began to lose his humanity.

It sounds odd, but she could think of no other words to explain it. A year had passed since the end of the war and as far as they knew they were the only living people left on the planet. The dog and both the cats had disappeared long ago, but there were still birds and small animals around. It was the middle of June, and they had spent a perfect day, as they often did, sitting on the cliff edge watching the constant, repetitive, purposeful activities of the gull colony that had plastered the rocks with white. The steel-grey sea was as calm as it ever got, breathing and heaving in a state of restless anxiety that would never be assuaged. Every few days it deposited human remnants on the pebbled beach that pressed tight between two rocky headlands. At first they had dutifully retrieved and buried the remains, but as neither of them harboured any vestige of religious belief, they had long ago decided to leave these scraps of wasted humanity to be absorbed into the ongoing processes of the natural world.

They spoke surprisingly little. It wasn't necessary; each knew how the other felt, and they had developed a system of unspoken communication that covered most of their everyday needs. They only had to look into each other's eyes to know the depth of the love that existed between them, a love that was often manifested physically, but not sexually. That had ended long ago, unmissed and unmourned.

As the sun's disc began to show signs of its seaward fall into the horizon's green haze, they shared an instinctive glance that said it was time to return home. She smiled at him, took his hand and kissed it; unusually, there was no responding pressure from him. They collected up the things they had used for their earlier picnic and strolled gently towards the cottage. As they approached the gate into their overgrown walled garden, he stumbled.

"Sorry," he said automatically; "my knee went." Then he repeated, "My knee, my knee."

She looked at him, frowning slightly, wondering how to respond. After much thought, she simply said, "Cup of tea," and smiled. He didn't smile back.

Over the next few days, she began to worry. They needed to talk about things, but they'd lost the habit. In any case, what could she say? That he seemed to be getting increasingly frail, even though he was still only forty? That he often failed to understand her, even when she took the trouble to explain something in words? That when he spoke, he repeated himself, churning out the same word three or four times without seeming to be aware that anything was amiss?

A week after their clifftop picnic there was a violent storm. Since the war, tempestuous episodes of more than usual ferocity had become increasingly frequent, which was partly what made them eager to take advantage of the few calm summer days that still occurred. They locked themselves inside the cottage, bolting the doors and fastening the windows to prevent them being blown open by the gale's intensity of violence. The wind roared and screamed like a wild beast set free after years of captivity and ill-treatment, battering at the shutters and whistling dementedly through every gap and crevice it could find. They had lit a log fire but it was fighting a losing battle against the wet gusts that invaded the chimney, hissing and spitting in outraged dignity. Every so often the wind flung cataracts of rain horizontally across the headland, engulfing the cottage in a drenching drive of salt spray solidified by velocity into racketing pellets of noise and destruction.

He sat in his usual armchair, staring blankly into the sputtering fire. Even from the kitchen, where she was cleaning up the supper things, she was aware of his absence. He'd been like this all day, as if his mind had drifted somewhere remote and shut off. She couldn't tell whether he was aware of the storm or not. It was time she said something.

But he spoke first. "Here," he said in a sudden, sharp voice. "Here; here, here."

Not for the first time in recent days, a chill passed across her back and her heart jumped.

"What?" she said, moving into the living-room to him. A mass of rain slammed across the window and the wind called eerily in the chimney.

"Here," he repeated. "In here."

He pounded his fist unexpectedly on his chest and began to cough roughly. She touched his shoulder and tried to think of something to say. He looked just the same as he always had; as far as she was concerned, he hadn't altered in all the years she'd known him. She liked to think the same was true of her, but she was probably kidding herself; fifteen years was a long time. She felt a great weight of sadness pressing down on her. Something serious was obviously wrong with him, but she couldn't explain what it was. She had often thought of how their final days would be, but she hadn't imagined anything like this.

"Please tell me what it is," she begged, her voice raised in competition with the raging wind. "I can't help you if you don't tell me."

He turned his head and slowly looked up at her.

"Prototype," he said, struggling to get the word out. She expected him to repeat it, but instead he simply added, "MHP seven-three-zero-double-two-four-nine-five," before dropping his head forward in apparent exhaustion.

This was Alzheimer's, she thought; early onset. His mind had evidently reverted to a time long ago, to his work as an SI engineer. There was no way she could follow him there; no way she could attempt to understand a time in his life that she'd never been part of. But she had to try.

"Tell me about it," she said, but it was no use. He seemed to have closed in on himself, shut down for the evening. Perhaps it was the storm; perhaps he'd be better when it had passed.

The following day was calmer, the sky torn into ragged strips of grey and green – an unearthly combination of shades that had become increasingly common since the war. The winds were less fraught but still gusting, and an occasional shaft of metallic sunlight brightened the cottage's dim interior. She had managed to get him to bed the previous evening, and he seemed to have slept soundly. She, however, had remained restlessly wakeful, unable to block out either the sounds of the dying storm or the insistent anxiety that was wrenching her emotional stability to shreds. He refused breakfast with a brusque gesture, but managed to get himself up and dressed in time for lunch, a familiar combination of tinned ham with baked beans heated in the coals of a re-energised fire. He ate it, slouched silently in his chair, but seemed to have trouble swallowing.

He stayed in his chair all afternoon, staring into the exhausted fire. Occasionally he would utter some repetitive mantra, speaking his own name over and over again, or half remembering his reiterated sequence of letters and numbers: MHP seven-three-zero-double-two… At first she sat with him, but she didn't know what to say or do. Her heart jumped every time the fading wind roared in the chimney or a gull screeched outside in the buffeting air. She retreated to the kitchen where she stood uneasily at the window, looking out across the headland to the sea's hard glitter. For the first time she felt isolated and alone.

When she went back in to him, crafting a bright smile to suggest it was time for a cup of tea, he was holding up his hands in front of his face, staring at them with a look of horrified recognition. "Prototype," he said again. "Metahuman prototype." His voice had a grating harshness, like the scraping of nails on hard plastic.

"What is it?" she cried, a surge of panic tightening her throat. She took his hands in hers and stared in baffled horror at the thick, dark oil that oozed from his fingernails. She became aware of a mechanical clicking and whirring emanating from inside him as he tried to speak again. His voice emerged only as an unnerving, artificial croak, a final, apologetic realisation.

"All a lie," he said, his voice fading into the renewed keening of the wind and the shrill clamour of the gulls. "Not human. Sorry. Neither of us…"

Then he just stopped. His hands remained raised before his still-open eyes, which also streamed now with the thick, dark oil.

Somehow she managed to bury him, at the foot of the garden under the drystone wall that marked the edge of their overgrown vegetable plot. For the next two days she coped by switching off her thoughts beyond the everyday business of immediate survival, and by keeping herself busy. She changed the sheets on their bed and burned the old ones – she couldn't explain why. She cleaned the cottage from top to bottom, as if this were somehow what he would have wanted. She tidied up and reorganised the contents of all their shelves and cupboards. She took advantage of the return of still, warm weather to weed and dig the flower-beds, which were bright with fragrant roses, foxgloves and delphiniums. Eventually, there was nothing left to do.

Three days after he had died – after he had stopped – she took herself to their clifftop picnic spot and sat quietly, squinting into the barely-risen sun, stretching her eyes as far as she could across the still, grey waters. She wondered pointlessly if there was anybody out there; perhaps they should have made more of an effort to find out if anything of the world had survived. For the first time she allowed herself to think back to his last words, those fragmentary, impossible assertions; that puzzling, uncompleted sentence.

"All a lie. Not human. Sorry. Neither of us…"

Neither of us is to blame, she tried; then, Neither of us could have known.

She gave it up and watched the wheeling glide of the gulls and the purposeful flight of a cormorant, powering straight and low across the waters' shifting glitter. A flock of oystercatchers, rising from the rocks in an outbreak of black, white and orange, disappeared in rough formation round the headland, their shrill calls piercing the fabric of the shuddering air.

Did it make any difference? Did his ending invalidate the long years of their love? Probably not, she thought. It wasn't as if she'd suddenly found out he was a war criminal, or a serial killer. He was still the person she had loved; even if he wasn't human, his deep humanity had been palpable. Their lives together had depended on it.

Had he known the truth, known what he really was? If he did, then he'd deceived her, she supposed. She couldn't believe he would do that. Admittedly, he'd never told her much about his past, before the job at SI Industries, but there had been occasional revelations, odd stories about his family, about his parents' deaths. All these must have been fictions, programmed to lend credence to his place in the world. What kind of prototype had he been? An experiment, perhaps, long ago forgotten about when the urgency of the company's war-work became all-consuming. She tried to convince herself that she still loved him, would always love him.

She was aware that it had begun to rain but stayed where she was, not wanting to return to the cottage. She was alone now. She'd always thought they'd pass from the world together, that neither of them would have to survive the loss of the other. She wasn't sure how long she could go on without him, living alone with an absence. Perhaps he had always been an absence, nothing but a complication of cleverly programmed circuits. She began to wonder how his artificially constructed body had imitated human physiology for so long: how his hair and nails had grown; how he had digested food and evacuated his bowels; how his system had manufactured the physical symptoms of love on those rare, distant occasions when they had felt the need for something more than just emotional intimacy. She thought of her own parents; how strange it was that they, too, had died young, so long ago now that she barely remembered them. For the first time in months she thought of Asma, the surrogate daughter they had failed to save from a despicable ideology of hatred and savagery.

What would she do now? She could end her life today, in a variety of ways. She couldn't have long left in any case, but she dreaded falling into a state of illness and pain, of mental and physical deterioration in which she would no longer be able to take control of the circumstances of her inevitable demise. Still, she ought to think, first. Perhaps she had a duty to survive longer. Perhaps she should go out into the world, find out exactly what the situation was. What would he have done, she wondered, in her situation? What had he been programmed to do?

When they'd stopped using the car, he'd kept a couple of cans of petrol, just in case; in case of what, he never quite explained. She doubted now that the vehicle would still function, but it was worth trying, perhaps. She had an odd desire to see the village again, disturbing as the prospect was. She poured the petrol from the cans into the tank through a metal funnel she found at the back of the shed. To her amazement, the car started first time, though it choked and spluttered and spewed out thick, dark exhaust fumes that caught at her throat and made her cough. She couldn't remember how long it had been since his last journey. She loaded the car with a selection of useful equipment and enough tinned food to last her about a week. She began to feel unwell, and put it down to the fumes. She was constantly clearing her throat, and found it increasingly uncomfortable to swallow. Perhaps she shouldn't go.

It took her nearly an hour to get to the village. The road was potholed and overgrown, and she had to clear away branches at a number of points along the way. She was pretty sure there would be enough petrol to get her back to the cottage if that's what she decided to do. At first glance, the village looked as it always had. The church tower rose proudly through the surrounding trees. The duckpond lay still and dark under the grey sky, but she saw no ducks. The village green had turned into a meadow, thick with dandelions and buttercups. The row of slate cottages leading to the pub seemed generally intact, apart from a few fallen tiles and the odd broken window. The small front gardens were a tangled riot of colourful blooms and creeping trailers of foliage. The petrol station at the far end of the main street had a disturbing air of abandonment and dilapidation. The canopy had caved in, the pumps were rusted, the hoses perished, the concrete forecourt cracked and bursting with enormous weeds.

She wondered why she had come; there was nothing for her here. She might just as well go back to the cottage and plan her own death. Oppressed by the silence, she felt the need to speak aloud, to break the stillness of the wavering air. She had no words, though; could summon only his pointless repetitions. "Prototype," she said quietly. "All a lie." Her voice sounded strange in the unechoing absence. She cleared her throat and swallowed painfully. "MHP seven-three-zero-seven-double-six-two-four." Was that the serial number? It sounded familiar, despite the mechanical croaking of her voice.

She decided that before she returned home she would go over to the church. Neither of them had been religious in the doctrinal sense, though they had often talked of human spirituality, of the tremors and resonances that transcended the minutiae of daily life. She had loved him for his thoughtful cleverness, his humane urge to grapple with the ineffable mysteries of existence. It was organised religion, they decided, that had brought the world to the cataclysmic whimper of its extinction.

Leaving the car in the weed-strewn rubble by the petrol station, she walked slowly across the yellow-splashed tangle of the village green towards the churchyard. The dark stones of the crumbling church rose ominously above her. She raised the latch and pushed tentatively at the rotting wood of the door. To her surprise, it opened easily, exhaling a silent gasp of cold air. The inner doors were ajar, and she stepped straight through into the nave. As her eyes grew accustomed to the gloom, she became aware of incomprehensible dark shapes humped randomly around. Patches of faint, kaleidoscopic colour revealed themselves to her clouded vision, projected from the cracked jigsaws of stained glass. There was a complex scent of oil, and rust, and something rich and sweet. She felt a deep sense of awe, and imagined that he was with her, but the reassuring clasp of his comforting hand dissolved into nothingness.

In a moment of epiphany, she realised that the humped shapes were people, hunched and slumped in the pews, tumbled across the stone flags, sitting propped against walls and pillars. There must have been a hundred or more, gathered here for some unfathomable reason; gathered here to die together, perhaps, knowing the end was imminent. She would die alone.

She knew she should have felt shocked, or sad; should have been overcome with the compassionate, tragic empathy of pity and terror. But she felt nothing, just curiosity. What had happened to draw these people together, these ordinary people from this ordinary, isolated village?

She moved closer to the nearest of them, a dull shape leaning awkwardly back in its pew, face open-mouthed in homage to the impossible colours of the Ascension that glowed in the cracked window above. The face, she saw, was neither rotted nor mummified, yet it seemed to have collapsed in on itself. One eye, a shining white marble extruded from its socket,

255

hung limply on the cheek from what looked like plastic wires. The right hand was raised, as if about to touch the face, which was stained and smeared with the smudged remnants of thick, dark oil. No longer was she unmoved. She stepped back, gasped involuntarily, painfully swallowed down a convulsive sob. She turned quickly and stumbled out of the church, unable to compute what she had seen, though she knew in her heart what it meant.

Two hours later she was back at the cottage, feeling his absence as a thick sense of loss and bereavement. She walked to the clifftop, conscious of an unfamiliar stiffness in her knees and an increased tightness at the back of her throat. When she reached their picnic-spot, she sat down in the sheltered hollow of rough grass and gazed intently at the distant horizon and the puzzling immensities that lay beyond. For the first time since his ending, she felt tears welling in her eyes. Wiping them away with her cold hand, she noticed the oily smears on her skin and the slow oozing from her fingernails. She thought of him sitting beside her in the grassy hollow, spooning cold baked beans from a plastic bowl. She had always loved him, and now she loved him even more. "Neither of us…" The gulls wheeled and screamed, scooping great curves out of the still air. The sea crashed and whispered, far below. Slowly, deliberately, she stood up and walked calmly back towards his quiet grave.